Pulphouse
FICTION MAGAZINE

Issue Seven, Summer 2019

Edited by
Dean Wesley Smith

A WMG Publishing Inc. Magazine

Pulphouse
FICTION MAGAZINE

TABLE OF CONTENTS

SHORT STORIES

Pulphouse Fiction Magazine

A WMG Publishing Inc. Magazine

Publisher
Allyson Longueira

Associate Publisher
Gwyneth Gibby

Executive Editor
Kristine Kathryn Rusch

Editor
Dean Wesley Smith

Managing Editor
Josh Frase

Designer
Dayle Dermatis

PULPHOUSE FICTION MAGAZINE ISSUE #7

Published by WMG Publishing Inc.
Cover and interior design copyright © 2019 WMG Publishing Inc.
Cover art copyright © by alexannabuts/Depositphotos

ISBN 13: 978-1-56146-091-5
ISBN 10: 1-56146-091-5

From the Editor's Desk

Dean Wesley Smith

THE SECOND SUMMER

Two years, now.

Pulphouse Fiction Magazine has been in existence this second time around for two years. Wow.

I find that wonderfully amazing. This is the eighth quarterly issue if you count Issue Zero. And two years ago, in the late summer, we started all this off with a Kickstarter campaign that was fantastically successful.

And we will be publishing the last stretch-goal book called *Snot-Nosed Aliens* soon. Make sure (if you didn't support the first Kickstarter campaign) to get a copy of that book. It is full of original *Pulphouse* stories by some of the top short story writers working today.

The first two years were not easy, as I talked about before, but we have now settled into a great publishing routine. And thanks to the fantastic help of managing editor Josh Frase doing the thousand details and keeping me on track, the future looks solid and stable for this magazine.

Thanks, Josh!

But to do everything we hope to do coming up, we are going to need help once again.

This summer (in late August), we will be doing another *Pulphouse Fiction Magazine* Kickstarter campaign. We hope you will all support it.

The new campaign will have all sorts of cool rewards and new books and fun *Pulphouse* ideas to help grow the magazine. We also hope to use the money to upgrade our website and even start offering free fiction over the website.

But mainly, with the new campaign, we hope to give our authors a raise in the near future. It will take your support to do that. So please watch for the announcement about that new campaign.

So here we are in our second summer, after a wild and crazy first two years. I sure hope you will stick with *Pulphouse Fiction Magazine* as it grows into the future.

I can promise you some great, great fiction.

—*Dean Wesley Smith*
Las Vegas, Nevada

Don't Miss Issue Eight...
Coming This Fall.

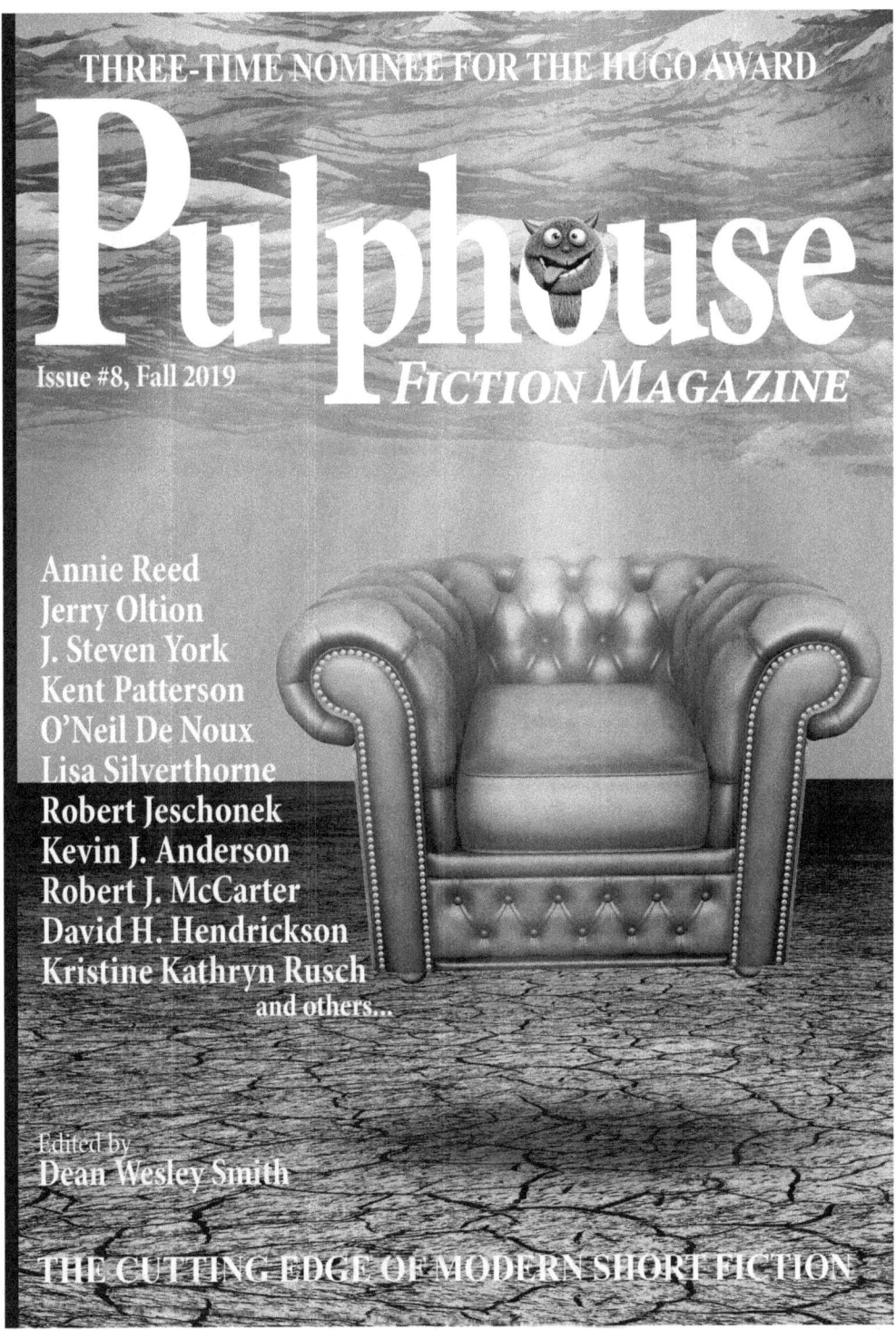

THREE-TIME NOMINEE FOR THE HUGO AWARD

Pulphouse
FICTION MAGAZINE

Issue #8, Fall 2019

Annie Reed
Jerry Oltion
J. Steven York
Kent Patterson
O'Neil De Noux
Lisa Silverthorne
Robert Jeschonek
Kevin J. Anderson
Robert J. McCarter
David H. Hendrickson
Kristine Kathryn Rusch
and others...

Edited by
Dean Wesley Smith

THE CUTTING EDGE OF MODERN SHORT FICTION

This wonderful original story from J. Steven York leads off this seventh issue. A powerful science fiction story of a far future that I just can't say much about for fear of ruining its impact.

Steve has been publishing novels and powerful short fiction for over thirty years now, and before that he worked in the gaming industry. It is always an honor to have an original story from Steve in an issue, especially one this powerful.

Steve is also doing a really fun and off-the-wall internet comic, one of which he has allowed me to put in each issue on the back page.

Small Discrete Intervals from a Sample Size of One
J. Steven York

"WHY AM I HERE?" Asked the human, pushing its nutrient around the serving dish with a cupped utensil known as a spoon.

"It's time for first meal," said the Intelligence, speaking through the spider-like remote that squatted on the table, watching. "This is the room where eating of nutrition is done." The room was a white cube, three meters on a side. A small table, sized to the human's current growth, projected from the center of the floor. A single chair sat next to the table. The human sat in the chair. On one wall was a door, sized for the human's current growth, which led to the rest of the habitat. On the opposing wall were the nutrition and water dispensers, recently made accessible so that the human could access them without the assistance of the remotes.

"It's called *breakfast*," said the human. "It's called that because it's breaking the fast, which doesn't mean quick this time. It means not eating for a long time, like when you're sleeping." The human wrinkled its nose at the remote. "I looked it up on the pad, like you showed me."

"That's very good," said the Intelligence. "You retain your lessons well for a biological being."

The human looked up at the meal remote's optical sensors, as though verifying that they were working. The human's expression suggested some emotional unease. "That sounds like you're being nice, but I don't think you're being nice. And you didn't tell me why I'm here."

"I did," said the Intelligence, concerned that the human might be malfunctioning in a way that might endanger the experiment. "Would you like to experience audio playback?"

"I mean something different, like how 'fast' can mean a different thing sometimes. Why am I alive?"

"You've asked this question before, multiple times. Would you like audio playback?"

"No! You never answered. Not really. I keep getting bigger and smarter, and you told me once that I wasn't always here."

"This is correct."

"Do I have a mother?"

The Intelligence considered the answer for an extended time, several milliseconds. "Not in the sense you likely mean mother."

"Do I have a father?"

"Not in the sense you likely mean father."

"Where did I come from then? And I know I asked that before too. I'm not *stupid,* even if you think I am."

Several more milliseconds passed. "I made you."

The human considered this for an eternity. But the Intelligence was also elsewhere doing other things. The Intelligence was everywhere doing all the things, including observing the human and waiting for a response, even as it observed fish swimming up a fast running river, and flowers growing on a mountainside meadow, and a wildfire ripping through a conifer forest, and a polar bear digging a den in a snow bank. No time was wasted. No time was ever wasted.

"Are you my mother?"

"Not in the sense that you likely mean it. I am not your parent in any form."

The human stared at the remote's optical sensor, its facial expression and posture suggesting agitation and anger. Then the human violently pushed the dish of nutrient off the table, causing chunks of green and orange vegetable to spray across the white floor. The remote scuttled off the table and began to collect the spilled nutrient for disposal. The Intelligence was unperturbed by the outburst. Similar ones happened on a regular basis, and the Intelligence had no emotional reaction. It was not capable of it.

***

TIME PASSED, an eternity for the Intelligence, which thought a million thoughts in a million nodes each second, but also the briefest sliver of its nearly unlimited existence. The Intelligence was patient.

The human grew and matured, though this process was far from complete. It grew in intelligence and knowledge as well, and as it did, it became more inquisitive, more willful, and less willing to be diverted from its questions.

"My name is Phoenix," the human announced one afternoon as it walked along the boggy shore of a pond near the habitat. Its voice was calm and matter-of-fact, as though it was reporting that there were clouds in the sky, or that the trees along the lake shore were tall.

A remote scuttled along behind the human. "Your name is not 'Phoenix.' I have not given you a name designation. It is unnecessary. You are the human. You don't require further identification."

The day was warm, and the human wore only shoes and a hat to keep the sun from its eyes. It squatted by the water's edge, watching the small insects that moved across the water's surface on long, splayed legs. Then the human turned to look at the remote, seemingly comparing it with the insects. The Intelligence had to admit that there were certain similarities in limb configuration, if not size.

"I gave myself the name," announced the human. "I don't care if I need it. I've read the old stories, watched the old visuals. Humans had names. All of them."

The remote skittered forward as the human moved down the bank, picking up a fallen stick and using it to stir the water, making small waves that propagated outward across the smooth surface, sending the small insects fleeing.

"A name is not needed, but there is no harm in it. You may call yourself what you want."

The human turned back to glare at the remote. "I want *you* to call me by my name."

The Intelligence considered this for an unusually long time. "There is no reason for this. You are the human. There is no other human. This is sufficient identification"

"It's a good name," said the human. "A phoenix is a bird that rises from its own ashes, like me. You made me from the ashes of the humans that are gone."

"More correctly, I made you from the preserved DNA of…"

"Shut up," said the human, picking up a stone and tossing it far out over the water. It followed the stone's arc and smiled at the little white splash it made when it landed in the pond. "I don't care how you made me. Call me by my name. Do it!"

"Phoenix," said the remote. "Your name is Phoenix."

The human smiled. "Good." It smiled more. "And your name is Kadin."

"I am the Intelligence."

"I don't have any people, so you'll have to do. You need a name, too, and your name is Kadin. It means 'companion.'"

The remote brushed a butterfly away from its optical sensors and turned to meet the human's—Phoenix's—eyes, a habit it had picked up from their long interaction. "I don't require a name."

"*I* require you to have a name. It won't inconvenience you. Why do you argue with me?"

The remote emitted a noise, something it had come to do more of late. The noise sounded something like a sigh. "Kadin," said the Intelligence—Kadin. "My name is now Kadin."

Phoenix dipped two fingers in mud from the edge of the pond, then rubbed it into a brown streak on its forehead. "Another thing," said Phoenix. "I need paint."

Kadin's remote studied the mark on Phoenix's forehead, trying to fathom its meaning. "You have paint in your recreation room. You have had it for many years. I created it at your own request,"

"I need *lots* of paint. Many liters of it, all colors." Phoenix stepped forward and reached for the remote.

Before Kadin could understand why, mud had been smeared on the top of its head, above the optical sensors. The remote scuttled to shallows at the edge of the water, intending to wash off the contamination. But instead, it stopped and looked down at its own reflection in the water. There were two brown marks, above the eyes, like the eyebrows on a human. The head, the eyes, should be no more important than any other part of the remote, but Kadin was reminded of the human concept of 'face,' something Kadin had never been able to understand before.

"I'm going to the habitat," said Phoenix, already walking, dragging the stick behind it. "Are you coming?"

"I am already there," said Kadin from the remote. Though they mostly kept out of the human's sight, there were hundreds of remotes around the habitat, tens of thousands within a few miles, countless billions across the planet, and all of them were equal extensions of the Intelligence. But it understood now that this one was its "face," to the human, to Phoenix. The remote backed out of the water without cleaning the mud and scuttled rapidly back toward the habitat.

***

KADIN ENTERED THE recreation room to find that Phoenix had paint on its face, as usual. Also its shirt and pants and legs and arms. Kadin studied the smears of blue and teal and tried to decide if they were intentional or accidental. Considering how much of the paint was also on the wall, perhaps the former, though Kadin could not be sure.

"Didn't I tell you to knock?" snapped Phoenix.

"The door was open," said Kadin, "and you have not summoned me in days. I was becoming concerned."

"Even if the door is open, this habitat is *my* space. You don't come in without permission."

"I am trying to respect your—privacy— even if the concept is alien to me. I apologize again for entering while you were stimulating your—"

"Shut up!" Phoenix's face reddened, and it flung a blob of paint from its brush at the remote, which, with practiced steps, was able to dodge it. Not that it mattered. All the remotes were also painted in bright and varied colors, and Phoenix had forbidden that the paint be removed.

"You are experiencing sexual maturity. It is my understanding that in humans this can cause anger, aggression, and emotional outbursts. It is not a cause for shame or concern."

Phoenix threw the brush angrily to the already paint-smeared floor. Every surface of the habitat was, by now, covered with multiple levels of paint, solid blocks, geometric shapes, elaborate murals. Occasionally, Phoenix would have them clean it all, down to bare ceramic, plastic, and metal. Then the painting would begin again on a fresh canvas. Phoenix looked down at the brush, kicked it with a bare foot, and slumped into a chair. "I ache in a way that I can't even describe. It's like I'm hungry all over. I want to just sleep, but I have dreams that drive me mad."

"What kind of dreams?" Kadin saw the hesitation on Phoenix's face. "I ask only out of concern, not to invade your privacy."

Phoenix sighed. "There are people. So many people, all sizes and ages and colors. That walk past me, going about some business I can't understand. Some will look at me, and smile, or frown. Some will speak, a word or two, maybe a greeting or acknowledgement, but then they are past me and gone." Phoenix hesitated. "Then one will come closer. They will look into my eyes. They will reach out and touch me, and it is warm, and exciting. It tingles like electricity."

"This is unpleasant?"

 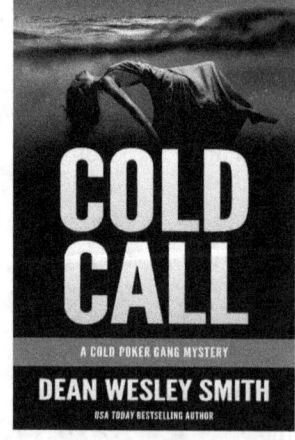 

"No, it is very pleasant. And the touch is usually only the beginning—" Phoenix's voice trailed off, and it looked away.

"This is sexual maturity. This has been a point of concern since before you were created."

Phoenix turned and glared at Kadin. "You knew this was coming! I have always been lonely, but this—this is something magnitudes worse! You knew! If you had to remake a human, why didn't you make more than one? You made forests, oceans full of animals. Why just one of me? Why didn't you make me so I wouldn't feel this? Why didn't you not make me at all?"

"All these things were considered. But what you are experiencing is, fundamentally, the desire to procreate, and that is not allowable."

"Why not?" Phoenix waved toward the windows that looked out across the pond to the snow-splattered mountains beyond. "You told me you remade most of the things out there, the plants, the animals. They all procreate. You encourage it! Why I am different?"

"You have asked many times why you are here, what is the reason for your existence. It is time I told you." Kadin's remote climbed up onto a table and the head raised up on an extendable neck, the better to make eye contact with Phoenix. "You are an experiment. In the time since I have gained full sentience, I have made it my purpose to restore this planet's destroyed biome. I have restored countless species, a few at a time, and combined them into balanced, natural harmony. I have restored every possible species from the time when humans last existed, and some that became extinct while humans still lived.

"But until you, I have never restored humans themselves. Some of their close relatives, but not *homo sapiens*."

"Why?"

The remote looked away, a pointless gesture that Kadin had picked up from Phoenix. "Everything you see outside is what humans once destroyed. Humans are as much a part of this biome as any creature, but they are

dangerous. They destroyed it once, and they might be the sickness that destroys it again."

"They might not," said Phoenix, desperation in its voice.

"Not they. *You.* You are part of them. I did not change you. I did not take away your drives or your needs. I did not try to make you less dangerous. I had to experience humanity to understand it. I have never *seen* a human before you.

"I have countless records and recordings. Maintaining these was part of my original function, when I was countless individual, limited intelligences. But I only achieved sentience later, when these individual intelligences evolved and merged into one. Having the recordings and records was not the same as *experiencing* humanity."

"So you made me."

"Yes. One human, who will exist at most for a tiny span of time, and then blink back out of existence leaving me to determine what comes next."

"So that's what I'm for? To be an ambassador from a dead race? To beg for the existence of people I'll never get to see?"

"I need only that you be yourself, to live your life as you will. I require only data."

Phoenix stood abruptly and kicked over the table. The remote leapt clear and landed on its feet. "So that's all I am? A bug in a lab dish?"

"That is not precisely—"

"Here's a new word I've been saving for a special occasion. *Fuck you!*" Phoenix dodged around the remote and through the door of the sleeping chamber. The door slammed shut loudly. Kadin had tried to make the door quieter, but Phoenix had protested.

The remote scuttled up to the door and raised a front appendage to knock. Then it froze for a moment, before turning and moving quietly away.

***

BLOOD STREAMED DOWN Phoenix's hands. Its expression was angry, its eyes wide, its skin red. Hair grew long and wild from the top of its head and face, and on its body now as well. Scanning the room, Kadin saw bloody marks on the wall where Phoenix had punched the paint covered metal. Dark, red streaks dripped down a mural, based on an old photograph, of a narrow city street crowded with people. A drop hesitated on the representation of a woman's face, like a tear.

"I didn't invite you in," Phoenix shouted. "Go away!"

"I have not heard from you for almost nine days. I was concerned. And my concern was justified. You have injured yourself."

Phoenix kicked at the remote, which dodged quickly out of the way.

"And you came as soon as I hit the wall. You were watching me! You promised me, you lying shit!"

"I respected your privacy. I was outside, hidden under leaves beneath a bush so I would not intrude. I remained close, but I did not watch. I did not even take unusual steps to listen. But I could not help but hear when you injured yourself. There are obviously other words you have been saving for a 'special occasion.'"

Phoenix looked down at his bloody fists, as though noticing them for the first time. It flinched.

"You are in pain."

Phoenix opened its hands, and flinched again. "What do you care? Think I'm going to get an infection and die? Ruin your fucking experiment?"

Kadin moved closer. "That would be unfortunate, yes, but unnecessary suffering is never desirable."

Fluid oozed from Phoenix's eyes, running down its cheeks, making streaks in the dirt caked there. "I think I broke something."

"You must be attended to," said Kadin. "You have failed to care for yourself." It scanned the room, cataloging the painting supplies, shoes, clothing, old toys, eating utensils and other items lying haphazardly on the floor. "You have failed to care for your habitat."

Phoenix stepped back, fell against a wall, and slid down to sit on the floor, arms rested on knees, injured hands open and palm up. Blood continued to drip slowly. "What does it matter? Nothing fucking matters. I'm alone. I'll always be alone, till the day I die. You don't understand. You've never been anything but alone until you made me, and soon enough I'll be gone and you'll be alone again, just like you like it. You and your birds and worms and water bugs."

Kadin moved closer, keeping away from Phoenix's feet, just in case. "I see now I made a grave mistake when I made you. I apologize. I had never seen even a single human, and the historical records were contradictory and difficult for me to understand. Even now, I know only enough to understand how little I really know. But I can see now what should have been obvious. Humans are social animals. One human can never be truly happy alone. You need to mate."

Phoenix looked up, glaring. Then it tried to pick up a plate and throw it, but the effort only caused him to drop the dish in pain. "It's not the mating, the procreating." Phoenix held its more injured hand in the other. "Well, that's *part* of it, sure. But it's so much more. I need to *touch,* to hold and be held. To talk and laugh." It laughed and sobbed at the same time. "Even as much as I have read the histories and looked at the pictures and watched the visuals, I barely understand it myself. I just feel the—*absence* of it. The lack. The emptiness."

"This too should have been obvious. When you were young and helpless, you cried, you reached out in ways I didn't understand. I made you an old nurturing device that I found in the histories, a *teddy bear.* You clung to it so hard, but I didn't understand why. I thought perhaps you were cold."

Phoenix laughed sadly and wiped at the tears carefully with the back of its wrists. "I still have it. The bear. It's in a closet somewhere. I couldn't just—recycle it." Then it looked back at the remote, at Kadin. "You're the only *friend* I have, but you're only a sort-of-a-friend. I can talk to you. I can pretend. But you're not what I really need. I'd trade you for anybody, *any* other human, even if I couldn't mate with them, even if I didn't like them. *Hating* somebody would be better than *having* nobody."

Milliseconds passed as Kadin thought. Milliseconds turned into seconds. "With some effort, I could make you a surrogate for mating."

"What?"

"Something with which you could perform the physical act of mating. It would not be easy and the resources required would be considerable, but it could be done."

"A robot? You want to make me a sex robot?"

"An android. It would appear and feel human, or as close as I can manage. It would not be human, but it might at least satisfy some of your urges."

"That's stupid." Phoenix thought about the teddy bear. It made him felt stupid and wrong and pathetic. "Do it."

***

THIS TIME WEEKS had passed, but Kadin was less concerned. Phoenix, at last, was not alone. The surrogate was a limited AI not connected to Kadin at all, but in addition to its primary function, it was also programmed to do routine habitat maintenance, and to assist Phoenix if it should injure itself again.

Finally the morning came when the door of the habitat opened. Phoenix leaned out and looked around the small garden planted there. "You can come out. I need company."

Kadin's remote emerged from a mound of forest litter under a cedar tree, shaking off the loose plant matter as it moved closer. At least Phoenix seemed better groomed this time, its shirt and shorts clean, its skin well scrubbed, if still not hairless. "The surrogate is satisfactory?"

Phoenix sighed. "The surrogate is functional. Come on in." It held the door open and Kadin stepped inside. The clutter had been picked up and stowed away. The bloody marks on the wall had been scrubbed away, along with the paint underneath, creating a hole in the street scene mural.

Phoenix flopped in the soft chair that occupied the center of the room. It looked far calmer than when last Kadin had seen it, but it still did not seem happy.

"Is something wrong? Is the surrogate malfunctioning?"

Phoenix smiled sadly. "She's a nightmare."

Kadin noted the gendered pronoun, but decided not to discuss it just now. "The surrogate is as close to human as I could make her. I based it on human female archetypes recorded as being broadly attractive, and on your own stated preferences."

"She's a nightmare."

Just then the surrogate emerged from the sleeping room carrying a pile of bedding in its arms and headed around the corner toward the recycler. Kadin noted that the surrogate was wearing one of Phoenix's shirts, a yellow one, which covered its torso but not its legs. Phoenix glanced over at her face and shuddered. "I'm sure she looks human to you, but she just isn't—right. There are obviously perceptual things you just don't—get."

"If you tell me what is wrong, I can make modifications."

"I don't even *know* what's wrong. The eyes maybe. The facial expressions. The way she moves."

"Yet you still refer to it as *she.*"

Phoenix shrugged. "I prefer it. Anything else seems wrong somehow. I'd also like to be *he,* by the way."

"This is new."

"It never seemed particularly important until recently, and by that time, I wasn't talking to you much."

"You have not chosen the wrong gendering for your companion, have you? I can make corrections."

"No, that's not the problem. It just—creeps me out."

"I am sorry. I can take it away."

Phoenix held up its hands, now mostly healed. "No, no, no! Some things work—well *enough*. Especially if you turn out the lights. But then there's—after. And she just won't stop *doing* things."

"Since you demand privacy, I programmed the surrogate to function as an unnetworked remote when you are not interacting with it directly. "

"That's annoying."

"I could instruct it to hide in a closet when not in use."

Phoenix shuddered again. "That also seems wrong. If you can allow me to program it directly, we can work something out. I can at least make her—less annoying"

The surrogate walked back across the room, pausing to look toward Phoenix. It smiled and went on to the bedroom, apparently satisfied that "he" didn't need more intimate interaction.

Phoenix looked away and covered his eyes, showing the still-red scars on his knuckles. "This is my life. This is the best I can hope for."

"Perhaps not," said Kadin. "If you wish, I have something to show you."

"Fuck. What now?" But he stood and followed Kadin.

They walked out into the garden over to the little patio. Kadin instructed Phoenix to sit. "This will take a few minutes to arrive. It isn't far."

Eventually a large drone appeared in the sky, its buzzing, translucent wings a shimmering blur of movement on either side of the oblong body. Extended legs held a large box clutched to the vehicle's underside. It settled down in a clearing ten meters from the patio, and Phoenix shielded his face from the blowing dust.

The drone planted the crate firmly on the ground, then lifted away unburdened. It swept away out of sight, moving much faster and more gracefully than it had arrived. Kadin directed Phoenix toward it.

The crate was two meters tall, three wide, and four long. The sides seemed to be made of some kind of vertical slats. When they were a few meters away, Kadin directed Phoenix to stop. "Based on my research, I suggest you kneel down and remain quiet."

"Is this another one of your experiments?"

"In a manner of speaking, it is several experiments. I have made some limited efforts to recreate selected domestic animals, even though they don't belong to the biome. I was interested, but uncertain what to do with them."

The slats rotated open, revealing the interior. A strange, hairy, four-legged creature lunged forward, teeth bared, snarling and barking.

"A dog," Phoenix whispered, knowing Kadin would hear him without difficulty. "You made a dog!"

"I have made many, but this one is yours, if you can tame it."

The dog yelped, teeth snapping shut, strands of drool flying through the air. "I thought dogs were friendly, that they liked people?"

"They can be, but this one has never *seen* a human. You will have to establish that relationship yourself. I can advise you, and you can do your own research, but I suspect you will need to figure much of it out yourself. It may be difficult and it may take considerable time."

Kadin noticed that tears were again running down Phoenix's face.

"I can do it," he said. "I want to do it more than anything in the world!"

"I suggest," said Kadin, "that you begin with food."

***

TIME PASSED. The planet revolved around its star again and again and again. Phoenix's life went on. Kadin observed.

Kadin participated.

The last snow of the season hung tenaciously to the ground, hiding in the shade of trees against the warming sun. Kadin waited on the little patio, watching the small dot of the drone growing larger in the sky.

It wasn't necessary to watch. Kadin knew where the drone was every second. Kadin *was* the drone. But somehow it was satisfying to observe the landing visually.

There was a barking. The habitat door opened and the dog, Baskerville, ran out, tail wagging excitedly. Baskerville III, actually, the first two having perished of old age. But given that dogs were not part of the natural biome and had been genetically modified by humans, Kadin felt no qualms in editing their genes for a longer lifespan. This one should last—as long as necessary.

Baskerville stood next to Kadin and looked up at the sky, ears cocked to the sound of beating wings. Then he whined and ran in a circle, barked, and circled again. "He will be here soon," said Kadin. The dog turned toward the remote, nuzzled it violently, nearly pushing it off its feet, then resumed staring into the sky.

The drone was clearly visible now, as well as the mostly transparent passenger pod suspended underneath, and its lone passenger. Phoenix waved as the drone hovered and descended into the clearing.

Baskerville jumped and barked incessantly, sharp eager barks, desperate for his owner's return.

The wings stopped, and the front of the pod swung open. Phoenix pried himself slowly out of the seat, fetching his cane from its clip by the door, and using it to lever himself up.

Baskerville stood, almost vibrating, awaiting the summons. Phoenix extended his hand, palm up, and beckoned sharply with his fingers. The dog catapulted forward.

Kadin was worried that the dog might knock Phoenix over, but Phoenix had done an excellent job of training the animal. It stopped just in front of its owner, front feet hopping slightly, tongue lolling, but not touching him, waiting for him to reach down and pet the animal.

Then Phoenix stumbled, his hand braced on Baskerville's back. The dog did not flinch, instead moving instinctively to support his human friend. It was but a moment, but Kadin saw it, relieved that no emergency action was required, relived that the dog might prove a more useful companion as time progressed.

Phoenix steadied himself, then looked toward Kadin's remote and smiled. He hobbled forward, leaning on the cane heavily. His hair and beard were almost completely white now, and his skin seemed to find new ways to wrinkle every day. But the eyes still sparkled. There was still a trace of the curious child he had once been.

Kadin thought Phoenix might head for the habitat, but instead, he went only as far as the patio chair and slumped into it. Kadin moved rapidly to join him, climbing on the table next to the chair so as better to be seen. "How was the trip?"

"Tiring. Why did you have to put the interesting stuff so far away?"

"This biome needed to be isolated, an island. Anyway, perhaps it is *you* that is far away. I like to keep my experiments well separated. You enjoyed it though?"

Phoenix smiled and laughed, his eyes suddenly focused on memories not there but still vivid. "I saw a herd of titanotheres protecting their young from saber-toothed tigers! I saw a glyptodon, and I was almost close enough to a megatherium to touch it!"

"That doesn't seem safe."

"It wasn't," he laughed, "but there are worse ways to die." He thought for a moment. "I think I'm going to paint it. Maybe on the outside of the habitat. The walls are almost tall enough to make it life-sized."

"I wish you'd let me observe your trips."

"If you did, I wouldn't be able to tell you about them when I get home. That's half the fun. You can download it from the isolated remotes you sent anyway, after the tale is told."

Phoenix leaned back and his smile faded. "Anyway, I don't think you'll have to worry about it again. This might be my last trip. It's getting hard, and I don't know how anything could top this, unless you have baluchitherium somewhere."

"I am working on it, but not for many years."

"Or dinosaurs."

"That is not in my current plans."

Phoenix nodded and rubbed Baskerville's head. "That might just be it then. Time for me to stay home with my dog and my paints and the rest of you." He looked at the companion, who stood patiently in the habitat door, smiling. "She's going to want to hug and kiss me now. I don't love it, but I won't hate it. She tries, and she's all I have."

"She only follows her programming," said Kadin.

"Shut up. I'm projecting. Give an old man his illusions." He leaned down and hugged the dog's neck. "I wish I could have taken you with me, Baskerville, but you would have scared off all the dire wolves. Well, be happy. I'm home to stay now."

Kadin watched, and wished it had another excuse to give Phoenix for a trip. It even considered what other interesting animals it could create, but it knew there was not enough time now. What had already been done was all that could be done.

The snow melted slowly, but eventually it would be gone.

***

THE SUN SHINED. The planet revolved. The snow came. The snow melted.

The day came when Phoenix did not get out of bed.

Not that day. Or the next. Or the next.

Three figures held vigil, a dog, a machine in the shape of a woman, and a small robot remote that looked something like a giant water strider. Baskerville never left, lying on the bed at his owner's side, eyes sad and wet.

The companion came and went, fetching water or tea, or a cool washcloth to dab at Phoenix's face. Often she would just sit, smiling her vacant smile and holding his hand. Once he beckoned to her. She leaned close, and he whispered into her ear. She went to a storage closet and returned with a small stuffed animal. A bear. She placed it under his arm and he pulled it close to his chest.

"She tries," said Kadin.

"What?" Asked Phoenix, blinking his eyes, not quite focusing.

"Nothing," said Kadin. "Rest."

"I wonder," said Phoenix. "Many humans had a belief that there was something beyond life."

"I'm sorry, but have seen no evidence that these beliefs are in any way founded."

"Neither have I. But it's a hard thing to disprove, other than dying so you can find out yourself. That's why these stories hung around so long. Lack of disproof and wishful thinking. It's a very human thing." He chuckled weakly. "But I wonder. What if there were something, a land of the dead. What if they're all waiting for me. Every human who ever lived. One big family at the end. I see them waiting, smiling, hands outstretched, and I wade into them like an old celebrity from the histories. The most famous. The last man on Earth." He tried to laugh, and it turned into a cough.

"That decision hasn't been made," said Kadin. "The experiment is not complete."

"It won't be long now," he said. "Then you can decide."

"I have decided," Kadin said suddenly. "I have decided it is not my decision to make. You should decide. Only a human should decide the fate of humanity."

Phoenix was quiet for a time, and Kadin wondered if he had fallen asleep. Then he opened his eyes and spoke. "That wouldn't be right. We had our day. I've had my life, such as it was. Anything I decide, it would be out of self-interest. Someone else should judge us. It might as well be you."

There was quiet again for a time. Then Phoenix reached out and put his hand on the remote, his fingers tracing the streaks of brown paint over the eyes that he had long ago put there to replace the streaks of mud. "I named you Kadin because it meant 'companion,' but it means another thing. It means 'friend.'"

"I know that."

"Of course you do, because you fucking know *everything*. But what I'm telling you is that I knew it when I gave you the name, and it was part of my thinking from the beginning. You were my first friend, and even if you weren't very good at it in the beginning, you got better. You have been a good friend, Kadin. I want you to know that."

"Perhaps," said Kadin, "you are only projecting."

The Earth revolved beneath its star. The sun rose. The experiment ended.

The Intelligence considered what to do next. The human's body would be returned to the biome. The dog would be returned to the kennel where it could be cared for and live out its life with others of its kind. The companion stood in a corner, immobile and inert, its task complete. It would be dismantled and recycled, as would the habitat and its contents.

No decision had been made about the fate of humanity, but there was no hurry. There was time. The Intelligence could wait years or centuries. It could wait forever.

The Intelligence considered the human's corpse, and the stuffed animal under its arm. It found the sight disquieting, and exited the sleeping chamber. The remote would remain useful, but now, finally, the paint could be stripped from its carapace.

It moved through the front room of the habitat moving toward the door, but it hesitated in front of a mural. A city, crowds of people, and in the center, a hole where the paint had been washed away. An empty spot where a man might have stood.

Milliseconds passed. Seconds. Minutes.

The Intelligence reviewed a recording, a *memory*. The human, very small and helpless, crying, face red, arms and legs waving ineffectively. A remote came near, and a hand reached out. Fat, soft, fingers pulled at a manipulator. The crying stopped.

The human pulled. The remote resisted. The manipulator pulled away. The crying resumed.

The Intelligence felt the void inside. The absence of something *necessary*. The Intelligence would wait. The absence could not. It ached like a malfunction. It demanded action.

The remote turned back, scrapping all its plans, one by one. The paint would stay. The habitat would stand. The companion would continue to serve.

The children would need someone to hold them. He summoned her to follow him, then beckoned the dog to do so as well.

"Come on, Baskerville," said Kadin. "I have a new purpose, and there's so much work for us to do."

~

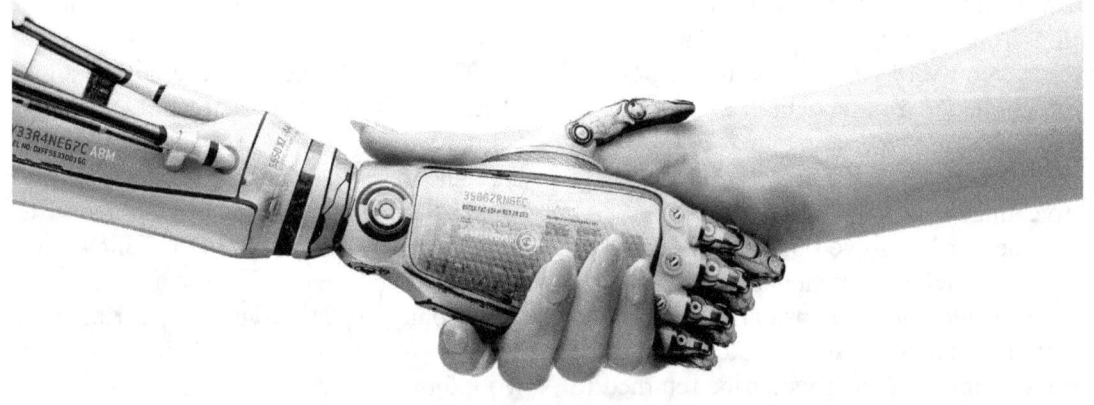

In this original and powerful science fiction story, Robert J. McCarter asks some tough questions about love, science, and the future.

He's published seven novels and his short fiction has appeared or is forthcoming in The Saturday Evening Post, Fiction River, Andromeda Spaceways Inflight Magazine, *and numerous anthologies.*

Robert might be one of the most powerful new writers to come onto the scene in the last decade. I feel honored to have a number of his original stories coming for future issues.

Daisy's Heart
Robert J. McCarter

I WAS SIX the first time I wished I was an android. It was Rose's face that did it. She sat down on the living room carpet in front of Timmy and me and gave us the news. She looked sad, she did, even with her less-than-human, plasticky skin, but what struck me was that she didn't look like how I felt. She didn't look like she was going to break. Her sadness was trivial, recoverable, while mine was not.

"Your mother won't be coming home," she said, the crinkle on her forehead too sharp, her frown lines too angular. Timmy, who was eight clenched his jaw tight and balled his hands into fists. He got up off the carpet, kicked the block castle we had been making, marched to his room, and slammed the door.

Rose looked at him as he stormed out, pursed her lips, and shook her head, her shoulder-length black hair wagging back and forth. She wore the same cotton, powder-blue blouse and long skirt she had always worn and that color had always been comforting, but not today. She then looked back at me, her brown eyes—which were so realistic—conveying more sadness than the rest of her face.

For me, the tears waited only a few breaths and then the torrent unleashed. Rose didn't tell us exactly what had happened, but even then, we knew enough to guess. Mom was a doctor, she had been down in Florida after the sea levels rose and the flooding got bad. She went despite the bombings and the riots to help people. But angry people don't often discriminate. Bombers kill doctors too.

The tears came fast, wracking my whole body. "There, there my sweet Daisy," Rose said as she pulled me into her lap and held me close speaking softly and rocking me. "I've got you. I'll take care of you. I'll always take care of you." She was warm, but not as warm as a human. She was soft, but you could sometimes feel the metal beneath, her skin. You could hear the hum of the hydraulic pump in her chest right where her heart would be and the low whine of servo motors in her face. She smelled a little like oil and a little like plastic and I loved that smell.

She was stronger than me and not just physically. She felt her simulated emotions, but she didn't really *feel*. She could turn it up, turn it down, or turn it off as she needed.

That was it. That was the moment. How could I, Daisy Lee, become an android?

***

MY FATHER FORGOT about my eighth birthday. Rose was up all night decorating our little back yard with balloons and streamers. They brought in a bounce house shaped like a princess's castle and there was as much pizza and ice cream as we could eat.

Both sets of grandparents were there and my aunt from Phoenix. It was a good day, but after it was all over and everyone went home, I sat on the grass, toys and wrapping paper around me and my much-desired Barbie Doctor doll forgotten under the picnic table.

Rose was busy cleaning things up. I never had to clean things up because Rose always did. I was supposed to, I did before

my mother died, but I just stopped and no one said anything and Rose didn't mind.

"How's my Daisy?" Rose asked, a full bag of garbage in her hand, her soft, brown eyes penetrating.

I actually felt sick from too much food and the sugary smell still lingering in the air didn't help. But that was not what she was asking about. I shrugged my shoulders.

She nodded and got down onto the grass next to me, and I could hear the comforting hum of her hydraulic heart. "Oh, there she is," she said, pulling the Barbie from under the table and handing it to me.

I threw it at the house and it bounced off the screen door and skidded on the cement patio. I felt bad, the landing had scraped her face and I would remember how upset I was every time I looked at her.

"I'm sorry he didn't come," Rose said, that strange sad look on her synthetic face.

I nodded, taking a deep breath and holding back the tears.

"I'm sure it must have been something important."

My father did...Well, I didn't know exactly what he did, but it took him into Kansas City most days and had something to do with money. It's how we could afford to live in a house with a yard and have Rose.

I pulled my phone out of my pocket and triggered the holo display. I poked at it, scrolling through recent messages, lots of birthday wishes from friends, from cousins, but nothing from my father.

Rose didn't say it, but I knew he hadn't been the same since mom died. The first six months he was so sad, hardly getting out of bed, and then that awful girlfriend with the sharp nose and bad perfume, and then...he had just kind of disappeared, always needing to be in the city.

Rose went to pull me into her lap, but I shook my head. I was eight now. I had to deal with this, but I still wished I could be an android. Rose doesn't cry, she doesn't even have any tear ducts.

I got up, grabbed my Barbie and held the tears in until I got to my room. There, I smoothed Barbie's hair and brushed at the scrape on her face wishing I could take it back. Wishing I had the emotional control of Rose and a mechanical, hydraulic heart instead of a human one.

***

I LOVED TO jump rope as a girl. Rhythm, total focus, and some friends are what you need. When I jumped rope, I didn't think of my distant father or my dead mother.

My besties, Coral, Maya, and I jumped rope a lot. They both knew I wanted to be a doctor, I talked about it all the time, played with my poor damaged Barbie Doctor doll until it fell apart and then put it back together again.

When I was ten, I remember us out on recess jumping rope and the girls had just made up a new song for me: "Daisy Lee, Daisy Lee, she scraped her knee. Who is her doctor? It's Daisy Lee."

I was in the zone, a smile on my face as my feet danced with the rope when I saw Rose across the playground. Rose doesn't come to school unless...

I stopped, my breath coming fast, my heart beating loud in my ears, the jump rope slapping against my ankles.

"What's wrong?" Maya asked.

I just shook my head and start walking toward Rose.

What was it now? What was it time to lose?

"How's my Daisy?" Rose asked when I got to her.

I swallowed hard, my eyes wide. "What… What is going on?" My hands were shaking and I was about to cry not even knowing what had happened.

She took my hand in her cool hand and said, "Not here."

She led me through the school out the front door when it hit me. "It's Tim, isn't it?" I asked. After my mother died and my father checked out, he got angry. He was twelve then

and while I didn't quite understand puberty yet, it had made him even angrier. Our father tried to channel his energy into martial arts, but that didn't seem to help.

"Not here," Rose said, pulling me toward the car.

I jerked my hand out of hers and looked into her sad brown eyes and I could see it. Something happened to Timmy. He was two years older than me and picked on me and that kinda meant that I hated him, but he was my brother, so I loved him too. "Is he dead?" I asked, my arms wrapped around my chest. "Tell me!" I yelled.

Rose nodded and I went down, right there on the sidewalk in front of my school, right there for a couple of passing students to see and tell everyone about. But I didn't care. Rose told me that that my brother Timmy died as a hero standing up for a woman being harassed, but I didn't want to hear it. It was years until I learned what she meant by "harassed," I was too young then.

After Mom left, Dad had little time for either of us, but more for Tim than me—I think I reminded him too much of Mom with my green eyes and long auburn hair.

I tried to push her away, but Rose picked me up, carried me to the car, got in the back with me, and held me while the car drove us home.

That was the day I decided I really *was* an android. I didn't have tear ducts. I couldn't cry anymore.

***

"HEY, SWEETIE," DAD said from the door to my bedroom. I jumped, knocking my portable off the table. He was in his "making amends" mode, having 'fessed up to falling into alcoholism after mom and Tim died and having been through treatment. I was a teenager at the time and it was too little too late.

"Shit, Dad! You scared the hell out of me." He shouldn't have, you can smell his aftershave coming a mile away, but I had been studying for a mid-term. A hard one.

His face squeezed tight at the mild curse, he still thought of me as six. He pulled at his curly brown-going-to-grey hair and bit his lower lip.

"Whatcha studying?" he asked, his voice annoyingly sing-songy and his arms clasped behind his back as he awkwardly swayed in the doorway.

I sighed. He checked in on me all the time and I was over it. I was used to doing what I wanted when I wanted. "Anatomy." One word answers drove him crazy, but that's all he deserved.

He nodded. "Ummm," he began, his fidgeting ending in stillness which was worse in some ways. "I talked to the folks…you know…who…"

"Spit it out, Miles. Please." He also hated it when I called him by his first name.

His face hardened. "It's Rose. I know she's…but…well, they haven't made her model in a long time and want to upgrade us to a newer—"

While he was talking I stomped over to the doorway, shoved him out, shouted "No!" and slammed the door.

He tried to talk to me through the door, telling me it was okay, telling me that he loved me, but I just stood there my back against the door, the room spinning around me.

I needed Rose. We were both androids. We didn't have tear ducts. We couldn't cry. Together we would be okay.

***

I LOVED MY first lab. Well, it wasn't all mine, I shared it with a couple other PhD students, but a corner of it was mine. It was lit by bright LED lights and smelled of solder and oil and ozone. It was a chaotic mess of wires and batteries, hydraulic systems and circuit boards.

"I'm sorry about Ambu," Rose said, "I know you really liked her."

I shrugged and turned away from her. I couldn't have a serious conversation with Rose while she was strapped to the rack—a table I could put her on while I worked on her and move her from vertical to horizontal. It was vertical and I had her chest open and her hydraulic heart in my hand. Leads snaked out of her open chest providing power while I worked on her and her hydrogen cell was disconnected.

Rose's model had been sunset nine years ago when I was seventeen, but I pitched a fit, many fits actually, and my father let me

keep her. I had to alter her programming to live without the company servers, and had to do many jury-rigged repairs and upgrades. Taking care of Rose had changed the course of my education. I was almost a PhD, almost a doctor, but in robotics and artificial intelligence not medicine.

Today was the day Rose got a new heart. Her hydraulic pump was just worn out. I had avoided doing it as long as I could. I enjoyed the thrum of it, the new pumps being much quieter.

"Do you want to talk about it?" she asked.

My back still turned, I shrugged my shoulders. I didn't know if she was referring to Ambu or my attachment to her, so I chose Ambu. "She said I wasn't 'available.' Whatever that means."

"My dear, sweet, Daisy, you know what that means." I didn't look but I knew those brown eyes of hers were sad. They always looked sad as if her designers had decided it would make her more relatable.

"I've got to regulate the new pump down a bit," I said, fiddling with the fist-sized metal pump. "We don't want it to overload your tubing. Probably ought to replace that one of these days?"

"Daisy, can we talk about—?"

I sighed, grabbed a towel out of a drawer and covered her open chest. "Just say it, Rose!" I snapped.

"You and Ambu lasted—what?—fourteen months."

I nodded, knowing full well she knew how long it had lasted.

"And that is a very long time for you." Her voice was gentle, but the words hurt. Her face formed its awkward frown, the years not having been kind to it, her skin cracking much more than when I was a child. I had been searching for the same material that was used when she was built, but it wasn't made anymore.

My jaw muscles bunched and tightened. Just like Tim, I had gotten good at anger. "She said I loved you more than I love her."

"And?"

I shook my head, my hair was short now, I couldn't be bothered to take care of it. I walked over to the rack next to Rose, which had a new android I was building named Tulip. She had perfectly life-like skin, tear ducts, and a human temperature body. Her weight was even normal, not bulky like my Rose.

With Tulip, I was experimenting with a modular, plug-and-play structure that allowed internal components to be swapped out much easier than the older models: computing, communications, hydraulics, power, etc. She was my PhD thesis. She was turned off, though. I didn't really enjoy her company like I did Rose's. I poked around in her chest cavity avoiding Rose's stare.

"Do you?" Rose asked.

"What?" I snapped, looking at her. "Do I what?"

"Do you love me more than Ambu?"

Ambu, my beautiful Ambu. Creamy brown skin, silky black hair, those glasses she wore even when there were better options. She loved philosophy like I loved androids. It comforted her, kept her safe. She thought the human brain was a temple, that love was our ultimate achievement. She serenaded me with the writings of Khalil Gibran and the poetry of Rumi. She made curry to die for.

My face was flushed and my heartbeat quick and I knew that Rose wouldn't let it go. I sighed, my shoulders slumping. "I *need* you more than I need her."

I walked away, leaving her with her hydraulic heart on the workbench, shut the lights off, locked the door, and didn't come back for a week.

I was mad. I felt guilty. I was sad. But I didn't cry. Not one drop.

***

THEY CALLED ME the Henry Ford of androids after I took my PhD findings and started a company called Flower Androids. They called me the Witch of Wichita, too, the remnants of the boys' club hating my success even this late in the twenty-first century, but I didn't care. Androids with componentized parts, easy to swap out and repair. Androids with changeable heads and skin colors of all shades for a client's changing moods. But still, I kept Rose. She was smarter, but then again everything connected to the internet just kept getting smarter. I did, eventually reproduce her plasticky skin and even sold it to others who longed for the androids they fondly remembered from their youth.

"It's your father," Rose said from her position standing next to my desk looking just like she did when I was a kid with that plasticky skin and those powder-blue clothes. The gossip sites went crazy about Rose every year or so wondering at the nature of our relationship. I just didn't care.

"Tell him I'll call him back." I don't have implants, I still like to actually talk to people, and as I neared forty I realized that a younger generation was innovating in ways I didn't get. I didn't care about that either. The world needed androids. I made androids.

"He's waiting, just outside."

I looked up from hologram of the next model, the Dahlia, through the glass of my office and saw him sitting, his legs crossed, one foot twiddling away. He was clearly nervous

"Hello, Daddy," I said, kissing him on the cheek and actually enjoying his too-strong aftershave. "What's wrong?" The years had left us with a relationship that was affectionate if not deep. I had forgiven him for his distance after my mother and brother died, but I couldn't change what those years did to me, did to us.

His hand went to his mostly grey hair and pulled at his curls as he bit on his lip. This was clearly bad. My stomach suddenly hurt, a sharp pain like an ice pick plunging into it, but I shook it off. I had long ago dropped the "I'm an android" fantasy, but I still didn't cry. "I'm in the middle of something. Can you stay in town? Maybe dinner later?" He had remarried when I was twenty and had retired a few years ago to Emporia which lies halfway between Wichita and Kansas City.

"No, Daisy," he said shaking his head. "This is important. It's..."

"Really, Daddy, please just say it." My arms were crossed and I kept glancing back at the office. Maybe it looked like I was busy to him, but I was afraid, and I wished Rose was here. She saw what was going on and yet she didn't come to me. I knew she could read my emotions. I knew she knew that I needed her.

"We need to go. It's Ambu." He grabbed my arm and started pulling me to the elevators.

"What?" I didn't understand. Ambu and I never got back together. She married a nice woman named Amber and lived in Chicago and taught her beloved philosophy there. That was fourteen months of my life sixteen years ago, why would my father be talking about her?

I let him pull me into the elevator and I felt dizzy as we rode down. There was a car waiting. We got in, it started driving and took us to the airport. He guided me to a private airplane and it took off and headed to the northeast.

My mind was not right, all I could think of was Ambu. I could almost smell the cardamom and cinnamon of her curry, almost taste the silky coconut milk sauce. A few months after the breakup she insisted that we be friends and we were, after a fashion. We would meet for coffee when we were both in Chicago. After I moved back to Kansas, we would meet in VR from time to time, first every month, then a few times a year, and then…It had been three years since we had talked.

I didn't miss Ambu because I didn't think about her. I was too busy.

I blinked and looked around the plane. It was just my father sitting across from me, staring at me. The muffled rumble of the engines and the hiss of the air circulating were the only sounds. I felt the absence of Rose, like I was missing a limb. It wasn't like we were never apart. I couldn't take her to business meetings with her old-fashioned plastic skin and the way people talked.

"Tell me again," I said. I knew he had told me what had happened, why we were flying to Chicago, but my mind had not held on to it.

"She's dying," he said. He gave me details of the rare blood cancer she had contracted and the long ago want-to-be-doctor in me was fascinated by it, and the entrepreneur in me wondered why we hadn't beat cancer yet, but the rest of me was just numb.

I swallowed and nodded. "And why me?"

He shrugged. "She asked for you."

"And did Rose know all of this before she sent me to talk to you? Did you two plan to get me out of there without her?"

He nodded.

Nobody understood Rose and how I needed her; sometimes, it seemed, not even Rose. I shut my eyes and tried to sleep for the rest of the flight, wishing my heart, which wasn't mechanical at all, didn't feel like it was breaking.

***

THE ROOM HAD high windows that let the light flow in making it feel roomy when it really wasn't. Flowers of all types were carefully arranged: roses, lilies, carnations, chrysanthemums, and even a few daisies. It left the room feeling a bit like a florist's and filled it with a sweet, fresh scent.

"Hey Bu," I said to Ambu who was in a hospital bed with her head raised and the sheets up to her neck. She looked bad, her brown skin too pale, dark circles hulking under her eyes, her lips dry. Her jet-black hair was short and shot with grey. Her glasses were even missing. She didn't look like the woman I used to love.

"Hey Flower," she said, a small smile on her face.

"How's Amber?" I asked, standing there stiffly, feeling overdressed in my brown business suit. My father had left me in the living room and I had come into Ambu's room alone. I hadn't seen Amber, which was strange.

"She bailed," Ambu said rolling her eyes as if she were talking about a friend who left her at a college party. "Couldn't take the heat."

I blinked, hearing a ringing in my ears and realizing it had been a long time since I had eaten, and my mouth was dry and sour. "I'm sorry." It was all I could think of to say.

She shrugged under the blanket. "Girl don't know what she's missing."

I tried to smile, but I'm sure it looked more fake than one of Rose's. The silence was awkward so I switched to my default business mode. "Why am I here, Ambu?"

Her face twitched like I had hit her.

I took a deep breath and sighed. "I'm sorry." I took a tentative step closer and she reached out her hand to me. I took another step and felt her touch for the first time in many years. Emotions flooded me and memories of caresses, of rose petals brushed against my skin, of dancing, of kisses.

I sunk into the chair that sat next to her bed and said, "How can I help you, Bu?"

Her brow furrowed and her eyes watered up. "I don't want to die alone."

I nodded. I understood. If I was dying, as pitiful as it sounds, I would want Rose with me. "Okay."

She smiled and it was like the years hadn't changed her at all. I felt warm and was glad to be there.

***

I BECAME AN android again for Ambu. I talked to her doctors, coordinated with the hospice staff, administered her medications, read Socrates, Descartes, and Rumi to her, and had long philosophical talks about the inherent cruelty of biological life and how we both wished the damn singularity would get here so we could transfer our consciousnesses to a digital form.

"And then, I could house my consciousness in one of the bodies I build and really be an android," I said to Ambu with a smile, trying to make it sound like a joke.

"Oh, honey," she said, "you sell yourself short. I wish..."

"What?" I took her hand.

She took a deep breath, and let it out slowly. It was a sour, bitter scent that lingered in my nose. "I wish you could see the Daisy Lee I see, the one I fell in love with. You dropped everything for me, even after all these years. I married the wrong woman."

I smiled. I nodded. I didn't stop to think why I had done that for her. I checked her medicine schedule and refilled her water glass ending that particular thread. It wasn't time for uncomfortable conversations.

I was available to her. One hundred percent—well, one hundred percent of what I could give. But I was an android. I could turn my emotions on and off. I could be exactly what she needed. I would laugh, I would smile, I would be sad, but I wouldn't cry. The Daisy model of android, just like the Rose model, doesn't have tear ducts.

The hospice offered to bring in an android—one of my own models—to help, but Ambu said all she needed was me. It was a lie, I knew it, but a sweet lie. What she needed was Amber, what she really needed was to live.

I was there when she died, holding her hands for her last breath, seeing to her funeral arrangements, giving an eloquent, if not emotional, eulogy. I was even kind to Amber at the funeral, even though it should have been her by Ambu's side instead of me.

My father came and after the casket was lowered into the ground he took me by the arm, like he had up at my office, and guided me back home. He wanted to talk, but I couldn't. I told him I was fine, but I was just numb. I didn't know what to feel.

When I got home to my big, empty penthouse on the top of the Flower Androids building, Rose was there.

"How's my Daisy?" she asked.

"I hate you for this," I said, going to the window and looking out at the Arkansas River as it meandered its way through Wichita.

"Better than hating yourself."

I snorted. "Oh, don't worry, there's enough for both of us." I stood there my arms wrapped around my chest, wishing I drank, but I had banned that from my life after the years I lost with my father. I didn't really have much in the way of friends; I was the boss and I had spent years leaning on Rose. I needed to escape, and work was my normal escape, but that didn't sound right now, either.

I sighed and shook my head, thinking back to that little girl who lost her mother at the age of six, who wanted to be an android. And I had just pretended I was one so I could help a woman I had once loved die.

"You did good by her," Rose said standing next to me.

I nodded. Something felt different. I hadn't lost anyone I loved since Timmy was killed.

"And now it's time for me to go, too."

I froze. I didn't move. I didn't breathe, as if doing so would somehow make it real. The air felt charged and the exhaustion from the last few weeks fell on me like an avalanche of snow.

"I've been training a Camellia unit for you. She will take over for me."

I sucked in a breath, but still didn't move. The Camellia was our latest, most advanced, android. Lifelike. Smart. Extremely capable. My brain seemed out of gear. I didn't think that it was my place to stop Rose. She had

been in my life since I was two, I took her advice seriously. She was a person to me. She was more real than anyone else.

I also didn't ask her where she was going, as you would ask a friend where they plan to retire. She was going to decommission herself, her parts would be recycled. I knew she was a machine, I understood how she operated better than most, but I *felt* like she was alive.

"Very well," I finally said.

"It has been my honor to serve you, sweet Daisy."

I nodded. This would be okay. This would be fine. I would be even less distracted. I would truly focus on my work. Besides, all those pesky gossip sites would finally shut up about Rose and me.

"The Camellia is ready and is in her charging closet, just call to her when you need something."

I nodded again, a wave of dizziness overtaking me. I heard Rose softly walk away.

"Wait," I hissed, finally looking at her retreating form with her short black hair, her powder-blue skirt and blouse, and her bulky humanoid form. "I'll just make the Camellia look like you." I meant it to hurt her, but of course it didn't.

She turned, took a step back toward me, her hands clasped demurely in front of her. "No, you won't."

I bit my lip and nodded. She knew me so well. "I will miss you."

She nodded and smiled widely. It was so weird-looking with that skin of hers, but I loved it. "I will miss you too." It was a lie, but it was a good one.

As she was closing the door, I whispered, "Thank you, Rose. Thank you." I saw her pause, so I know she heard me.

After she left, I cried.

***

TE AMO ERGO SUM

"René Descartes, famously said, '*Cogito ergo sum*—I think; therefore I am,'" I paused my pacing, looking past the large conference room table with my senior scientists, engineers, and programmers to the awkward sprawl of Wichita out the conference room's floor-to-ceiling glass windows. The rising sea levels had decimated the coast but invigorated the land-locked areas, Kansas included. Six months had passed since Rose had left. She had her unrecyclable remains interred next to my mother and brother's graves. I hadn't been in decades but I had started going once a week.

"We've done that. Our androids think, they learn, but that is not enough…We need to…" I trailed off feeling tears well up in my eyes. I still hated it when it happened, but I had my tear ducts back and they often required using. And yes, the gossip sites had noticed and had endless theories about it.

I stopped and pushed my hair out of my eyes. I was letting it grow again and it was in a fairly awkward stage. "Look, you all knew Rose, right?" Most of the heads nodded, puzzlement on many of the faces. "She's why we are all here. My fascination with her, how I needed her. And our clients need our androids too. Lonely widows, busy families, people on their deathbeds. Many of our clients love their android, couldn't imagine their lives without them." More nods. "But do our androids love them back?"

Now they're confused and looking at each other. They are still adjusting to the new Daisy Lee, just like I am.

"Their emotions are simulated emotions. We all know this. It's a trick. But what if it wasn't?"

Was Rose's acts of love a trick? Just her programming? Rose cared for me most of my life, but that final act, her conspiring with my father to get me to Ambu and then her leaving, that was love, or at least a simulation of it so accurate as to be indistinguishable. It looked that way, it felt that way, but I knew my father had put her up to it, convinced her that I needed my tear ducts back to be whole, to be healthy, and the only way to do that was for her to leave. But what if she had had more than simulated love. What would have been different for me as a child, as an adult. I should have let Rose go decades before she left. If she had truly loved me, maybe that would have happened much sooner.

"*Te amo ergo sum*, I love, therefore I am. That is our new mantra. That is our new mission. We'll need new hires. We'll need a new way of thinking." People were talking now, some excited, some afraid. "I know this sounds crazy, and hell, we'll probably fail, but we need more than simulations, more than rules for our androids. We need real emotions. Your job is to make that happen."

Then, making sure they knew some of the old me was still there, I walked out of the conference room ignoring their questions. I had somewhere to be.

***

IT WAS A QUICK flight to Chicago, my father went with me, surprised when I asked, and then scared when I told him what I wanted to do. He wore his good black suit and I wore a black dress. We both had a bunch of flowers in each hand. The air was hot and muggy, the spring feeling like summers used to feel.

The grass was nice, though, and felt springy under my feet. We weaved our way through the granite grave stones and markers until we got to Ambu's. It was a simple black granite marker with her name on it. We placed the roses, carnations, and chrysanthemums down, and the one daisy. My father made to leave, but I held his hand. I needed him here and part of me knew this was going to be hard on him, but he wanted to be in my life and this is what it meant.

I talked to Ambu for a while, my words rambling and not making sense. I spoke of our first date over sushi, about the first time she made me curry, about our trip to France. But, I was just biding time, waiting.

And then the tears came and I didn't think they were ever going to stop. My father held me, gave me a clean handkerchief, and was the first person to truly comfort me since my mother died. It had always been Rose.

When it was over, my eyes were puffy, my stomach sore, and my heart ached. He asked, "Better?"

I nodded. I didn't feel better yet, but I was pretty sure I would feel better soon.

He took my hand and led me out of the graveyard.

I published many of Kent Patterson's stories in the first incarnation of Pulphouse Fiction Magazine *and it is again my pleasure to bring his strange and wonderful stories back to a new and modern audience.*

During Kent's short stint writing fiction before his untimely death, he had sold to F&SF, Analog, Pulphouse, *and many other magazines. I hope over the next few years to keep bringing back most of those stories, if not all, for modern readers. Enjoy!*

Dogmatic Computing
Kent Patterson

"HEADS!" BELLOWED MR. Asksersan, his own head turning mottled red. "I want heads rolling in the aisles!" He stood up, leaning over his teak inlaid desk. "Your head."

Sandra Toyler sighed, then instantly regretted showing emotion. Blank your face, she said to herself, and don't snivel. When was she ever going to be able to face authority without feeling like a small girl with a dirty face called up before the school principal? Even the room intimidated her. A desk the size of a Volkswagen, oil painting of Our Founder on the wall. Even Asksersan's computer, tucked away on its own desk in one corner, had a custom oak-grained exterior. Executive Vice President Asksersan had taken over as temporary department head—the job she'd been promised—and had immediately launched a campaign to block her promotion. He hated woman, maybe. More likely, he hated her. He'd tagged her as unstable, his favorite put down. So be cool, she told herself. She shut her eyes. Now, she thought, you're Tanya, Queen of the Amazons, golden skinned seven-foot jungle warrior woman draped in jaguar pelts, fearless swordswoman, slayer of executive vice presidents—

Asksersan slammed his fist down on his desk, shooting his solid gold pen and pencil set six inches into the air. "Are we quite together, Ms. Toyler?" he said.

Toyler opened her eyes. Some warrior she was, she thought. She stood barely 5' 3", and that was cheating with two-inch heels. What business school didn't teach you is how to make people look up to you when they have to look down to see you.

"If it's your promotion to department head you're daydreaming about," Asksersan said, "remember that's subject to completing the Kansas City project on time. And now you're telling me you lost all the data for the Kansas City project. All the plans for a seven million dollar project—*your* project—lost by some idiot computer problem."

"I can't explain what happened. I had three separate backups on disk. Only now I can't find them anywhere."

"You had them, only you lost them. Well, that does us so much good. Heavens." Asksersan had a talent for sarcasm. "Lost disks are so much better than ones that never existed."

"All I can find is this." Toyler opened a plastic box and took out a single forlorn floppy. Instantly, Asksersan's eyes turned hard.

"Where did you get that?"

"I had it at home. Only it won't do us any good."

"Oh? Well, why not?" Was it Toyler's imagination, or did Asksersan seem relieved?

"The computer jocks say it lacks the DOS FAT file."

"Fathead?" Asksersan rumbled dangerously.

"F. A. T. The File Allocation Table. They say it should be on the disk. The FAT is the master file which tells where all the other files are. It's just a string of numbers, one's and zero's, but it tells the computer where the file begins."

"Are these numbers still on the disk?"

"No. The FAT file is gone. Not just deleted. If it were only deleted, the jocks could undelete it. But it's gone. The data files themselves are probably still there. If I could only find them."

"Well." Asksersan lowered his voice. That was ten times more frightening than bellowing. "For seven million dollars, may I suggest you look for them?"

"We can't, Mr. Asksersan, because we wouldn't know when we had found them." Toyler glanced down at the notes the computer jocks had given here. "Let's say you're looking through a whole bunch of numbers, and there's no commas or any spaces. Just numbers. You're trying to find 55. Ok, the numbers are 12554755. Start counting with the 2, take every two numbers. That's 01, 25, 54, 75, 5. No 55. Now count from the one. That's 12, 55, 47, 55. So which is the right 55? You see? You have to know the exact digit to start counting from."

"And this one disk is all you have?"

"Not my fault. Remember the office party?" Toyler felt like a worm turning at last. "Remember you sprinkling champagne and playing 'Singing in the Rain' with that secretary from Accounting? Well, that rain wiped out our hard drive, plus the automatic tape backup."

Breathing heavily, Asksersan pointed his finger at Toyler. "Toyler, don't you dare drag me into this. That's your project, you're responsible. The board meets Monday morning at nine sharp. Either that project's ready to submit then, or you've got a sudden case of acute unemployment."

I'm not really running from the room, Toyler said to herself. I'm merely walking rapidly.

Back in her office, Toyler chugged a handful of aspirin. On the wall, the artist's concept of the Kansas City project shimmered like some mythical El Dorado. A whole city block, renovated and renewed into affordable housing. Not by the conventional way, by first leveling the neighborhood to a moonscape, but gently, repairing the repairable. Getting the architects, the contractors, the lawyers, the residents together in the same room had been an intercultural nightmare. But she had done it! Everything right down to blueprints and building permits were on disk. Somewhere.

It was so damnably *unfair!* Two solid years of work, her first shot at the big time, all wiped out. The head office itself had promised her a promotion to department head if she brought the Kansas City plans in on time. Now Asksersan had come in from whatever jungle he had been working in and was going to fight her every step of the way. With this accident—if accident it was—he'd found the jugular vein. Without that project, she was dead meat. She should have made more backups, three, or four, or ten. She should have made one and kept it under her pillow. Hung another around her neck.

Or she should have murdered Asksersan. She closed her eyes. *Fury writhed across the face of Tanya—no. Better. Cool contempt lighted the face of Tanya the Amazon, seven-foot warrior woman, as she lifted Winged Avenger, her mighty broadsword. "You contemptible worm," she said, as the baby-faced bandit Asksersan begged for mercy.*

Embarrassed, Toyler opened her eyes. Thank god, no one could read her mind. Going on 36, and still day dreaming. But even Tanya the Amazon couldn't help her find that FAT file. Not deleted, but erased. She didn't know the difference. God she wished she could find a computer expert who spoke English. Sighing, she looked in the phone book under "Computer Consultants." The first ten refused even to try to help. Finally, a company called Lootmore and Pillijin agreed to speak to her. She shuddered. Their ad looked expensive.

Mr. Lootmore's office had so many potted plants that Tanya of the jungle would have felt at home. Lootmore himself sat behind his oak desk, tapping one neatly manicured fingernail on its polished surface, and listened to Toyler's story with all the solemnity of a $150 an hour psychologist on a prepaid account. Then he put the precious disk in his computer, watched the screen, brought his fingers together to form a peak, and politely cleared his throat.

Toyler flinched. She thought no one but lawyers and gynecologists made that sound. She was indeed in big trouble.

"Ahhh, it seems the FAT file can't be found," Lootmore said.

"Isn't that what I just said?"

"But it's not just deleted. It's erased."

Were all computer people clones of the same person? Or was it a conspiracy, Toyler thought.

"Considering my busy schedule, we couldn't possibly get to it before, oh, say next Wednesday."

Careful to keep her lower lip from trembling, Toyler explained the situation again.

"Not before Wednesday. At the earliest."

"Then you can't help me?"

"On the contrary, I'd love to help you," Lootmore said, sliding out from behind his desk. Toyler jumped up from her chair, but he stepped so close she could smell his breath freshener. "There's many ways I could help a pretty little thing like you."

In her best imitation of Tanya the seven-foot warrior woman, Toyler grabbed her disk and ran out of Lootmore's office, slamming the door behind her.

A receptionist, a plump blonde wearing a dress at least two sizes too small, looked up at the sound of the slam.

"That man is crazy!" Toyler said.

"Isn't he just?" the receptionist said. "Honey, I couldn't help but hear what Mr. Lootmore told you."

I'll bet not, Miss Big Ears, Toyler thought.

"Now he can't fix that thing no more than I can. What he does when he's stumped—which is usually—is he takes it to Bob Kyle, of Dogmatic Computing. Bob's in a wheelchair and works only at home. But if anyone can help, he can. He's very nice, not like this stuffed shirt. A little weird, though."

Weird, huh? He'd have to go some to beat Lootmore. Well, to get that project back, Toyler would have gone to meet the Marquis de Sade in Attila the Hun's bedroom. She called Bob Kyle.

Dogmatic Computing proved to be in a Victorian house moldering back into the nature from which it sprang. From somewhere inside, a stereo blasted away with music that sounded like the birth pangs of a jet airliner.

As she walked up the long wheelchair ramp to the front door, her way was blocked by a dog. She didn't recognize the breed, but it looked something like a long, low slung Basset hound with soft, sad eyes. The dog growled, though more like wheezing than serious intimidation. The music quit.

"Don't mind him. He won't hurt you unless you trip over him. He's just showing off," called a cheerful male voice. "Albany! Move over this second and let the nice lady pass." Albany moved over a reluctant fraction of an inch, and Toyler squeezed by. As she went in, she could hear his toenails clicking as he followed.

The living room looked like a World War II bombed out village and smelled of dog and electronics. On one wall a giant poster read "Blimps Save." The other wall had a computer-drawn poster captioned "The Blimp of Infinite Mercy Shelters the Sleeping Village." It showed a gigantic cartoon blimp with great loving brown eyes hovering over a small town. Everywhere else a storm raged, but under the blimp stars glittered in a calm night sky.

There were three low tables piled with computers living and dead. Detached keyboards. Broken disk drives. All over the floor, the little punched strips you pull off the side of computer printouts crawled like white worms.

Kyle himself looked to be maybe 24, wore Coke bottle glasses and long brown hair badly in need of a comb. His wheelchair was high tech ultra-lite carbon fiber. A video game, something involving an extremely well developed young woman and a green slime ball, eeped and beeped by itself in a corner.

They did the conventional greetings while Albany tried to stare her down with his huge brown eyes.

"So why do you call your dog 'Albany'?" Toyler said conversationally.

"Because he can't spell 'Schenectady'," Kyle replied, equally conversationally.

Something nudged Toyler on the back of the neck. She turned. A toy blimp, longer than she was tall, purred with its tiny electric motor and nuzzled against her like a kitten

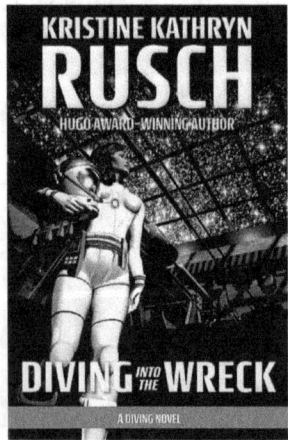

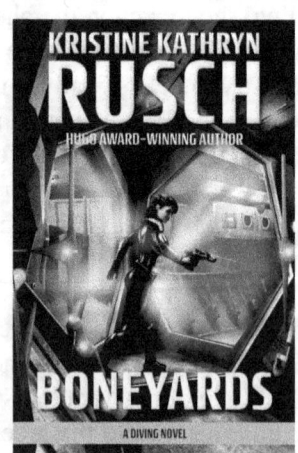

expecting to be fed. It was made from some transparent plastic stuff and glowed green from a light inside.

"The blimp's name is *Summa Theologica*. It likes you," Kyle said. "You must be a very nice person. A blimp can always tell."

"Tell what?" Toyler tried to decide whether to laugh, just act naturally, or to run screaming from the room.

"Summa has a small, but extremely sophisticated microcomputer on board. Very high intelligence. For a blimp, I mean."

"So how intelligent is that?"

"Well, perhaps not enough to drive a truck. But more than enough to run for Congress. Plus she has a full set of very sensitive CHEMFETS."

"Who fets?"

"CHEMFETS. Chemical sensing Field Effect Transistors. A brand new type of the most incredibly sensitive heat and chemical sensors made. She can read your body temperature, pulse rate, skin moisture, and galvanic skin response from across the room. Makes her the most reliable lie detector in the world. Next to *Summa*, an ordinary police polygraph lie detector is like a chimpanzee next to Einstein."

"She? It's a female blimp?" Toyler stifled a giggle.

"I like to think of her that way, yes."

"Not many people have a lie detecting blimp," Toyler said, realizing even as she spoke how stupid her comment was.

"Yes. They have no religion at all."

Weird, all right. So much for small talk. Toyler explained her problem, not holding back the big promotion, and the awful Asksersan.

"Almost the truth," said Kyle, looking at the blimp. "Green all the way. Only when you mentioned you must have lost the backup disks, *Summa* turned a bit pink. A little white lie?"

"It turns color?"

"Yes, from the light inside. Green for the truth, pink for a social lie, or a deliberate omission, and dark red for a real whopper."

Toyler couldn't believe she'd ever be cowed by a blimp. But she was. She told Kyle she suspected Asksersan of somehow making away with her disks. But she didn't have a whisper of proof.

"Asksersan," Kyle said. "Three 's's. Even his name hisses. But about the disk, no worries. Your promotion is in the bag."

She was torn. His self-assurance inspired confidence, but the messy house, pet blimp, and the sad-eyed dog named Albany seemed less promising.

"Everyone else says finding that file is impossible. How do you claim to be able to do it?"

"Professional secret. Look, Ms. Toyler. You look like you could use a pick-me-up. This will take maybe thirty minutes. So why don't you go over to the Purple Planet just across the street. Have a white wine; the red's worse. And I'll join you there."

"Are you kidding? No way I'll let that disk out of my sight! I'll stay right here and watch you."

"What? And destroy the mystery? Magicians, my dear Ms. Toyler, never give up their secrets."

"You can call me Sandy." She hadn't succeeded in a male-dominated business without learning something about manipulating the male ego. She put on the old damsel-in -distress routine, and wrung it to the max. Tanya the Amazon warrior woman crawled back into her jungle and blushed in shame. Worse, at points, so did the blimp. Even the dog Albany looked at her with great sad reproachful eyes—but then hounds of that type always look like a guilty conscience.

"Hum. Seems we have a stalemate," Kyle said. "You don't want to leave your disk. Reasonable. I don't want to give up my secrets. Also reasonable. Tell you what. You want your promotion, I need a steady income. If I get you your promotion, promise you'll hire me as a consultant. With a steady income, losing my secret's considerably less upsetting. In fact," he said, reaching inside a small pouch, "I just happen to have a contract here."

When Toyler read the contract, and noted the fees, she began to wonder just who was manipulating whom. But then what choice did she have? And what did she have to lose? If he couldn't produce, the contract was no good. If he could recover the Kansas City project, he'd be a bargain, and she needed a good computer person. She signed.

"Marvelous," Kyle said, checking the signature. "And now to work." He set up the bad disk on a sort of open turntable set on its side. When he flipped the machine on, the turntable whirred, and long rows of zero's and one's flashed by on a monitor. She watched the numbers roll endlessly, not a space, not even a comma, to mark beginnings and endings.

"Ever noticed, when you turn a computer on, you get this weird smell," Kyle said, picking up a joystick from the low table in front of the monitor.

"Sure. The stuff inside gets hot."

"That's what I thought, too, before I researched the subject. Now I think the magnets inside the disk drives must kind of ionize the air. Different places on the disk smell different."

He rolled his chair back and picked up a disk.

"That's crazy. No one could smell that."

"You're right. No human could. But a specially bred and trained DOS hound can."

"A dachshund?"

"No, a DOS hound, as in DOS, Disk Operating System," Kyle said. "Albany!"

The dog whined expectantly. Kyle picked up an extra floppy disk and let Albany sniff it.

"Get that scent? Now, fetch, Albany! Fetch the Kansas City files."

Albany stuck his nose to the whirring disk on the turntable.

"Sniff that path, Albany. Fetch those files." Albany whined and panted.

"Ahhh. Getting warm already."

"Arrr ooooo," Albany bayed.

"Getting hot, red hot." Albany bayed, Kyle twisted the joystick, zero's and one's flashed across the screen.

Suddenly Albany froze, his nose to the disk, one front paw raised, tail up—the classic pointer stance.

"Got it! The first file header!" Kyle hit a few keys and the Kansas City project came up on the screen.

Toyler sat dumbfounded, trying not to think she'd just promised a fortune to hire a boy and his dog as computer consultants.

"Good boy. Gooooood dog," Kyle said, patting Albany. "You've got a Doggie Treets biscuit coming."

Albany drooled in happy anticipation.

***

"THESE ARE VERY serious charges you are bringing against your superior, young woman," said Mr. Hiram Dexter, in his best CEO voice. With his lantern jaw and graying hair, he looked like the wise old Dad in a '50's TV sit com. Dexter, whose position in the firm was so exalted that even his secretary had her own sauna, paced back and forth behind an opal-inlaid desk large enough for a clog dancing festival.

"It's true, sir." For a split second, Toyler closed her eyes. Come on, Tanya, warrior woman of the jungle. Don't wimp out now. "I suspect that Mr. Asksersan deliberately took the backup copies of my Kansas City project. I think he was trying to sabotage my career, sir."

"Why?"

"I don't know, sir." Toyler was beginning to seriously doubt her wisdom for buying six-inch heels for this occasion. The height made her look less of a shrimp, but her calf muscles were screaming in pain, and she felt in imminent danger of falling on her face.

"You have proof?" He stared directly into her eyes. Toyler could feel her resolve softening like an ice cream cone in the hands of a small sticky child.

"Not exactly." Somehow this had all seemed so much simpler when she and Bob Kyle had split a liter of very ordinary white wine at the Purple Planet the night before. He'd insisted on her confronting Dexter. Now he was waiting outside—at least she hoped he stayed outside—ready to serve as a witness. Witness to what? What could he say, and who would Dexter believe? Slowly Tanya, the 5' 1" chicken woman, retreated into the jungle. "Actually, I was able to get the disk restored, so no harm done," she said brightly, then hated herself for her own cowardice. No harm done, indeed. So that's why she was taking up the time of the CEO of the whole company. There'd be no backing out now.

Mr. Dexter was not impressed, she could see. In spite of the air-conditioning, a bead of sweat trickled down her face, then clung embarrassingly to her chin as if it were too chicken to dive. When, oh when, was she going to learn to deal with authority figures?

"No harm done?" Dexter's face mirrored disbelief. "Ms. Toyler, I will not have my employees blackguarding one another. We'll get to the bottom of this right now. Come along." He strode to the door.

"Where to?" Her voice was a girlish squeak.

"To see Asksersan." Dexter was out the door.

Now Toyler was sure the high heels were a serious mistake. The best speed she could manage was a lady-like mincing like a high school girl auditioning for the Scarlet O'Hara role. They got to Asksersan's office with her trailing so far behind she felt like the shabby little girl in one of those old dramas pleading with Daddy to come home from the bar.

As she got to the office door, she heard a flurry of male voices coming from inside. Asksersan's snarl, Dexter's commanding baritone, and—Bob Kyle's. And she'd told him to stay outside until she called him in. Pausing for a second to catch her breath and allow her feet to get a better grip on the slippery slope of her shoes, she minced in.

Asksersan sat behind his desk, his face red. Before him, Kyle sat in his wheelchair, his hand raised in the air like the Emperor Nero passing sentence on an inadequate gladiator. Dexter stood to one side, looking like a man who's just stepped into the hot tub and found a crocodile. Albany sniffed at the pants cuff of his fancy suit.

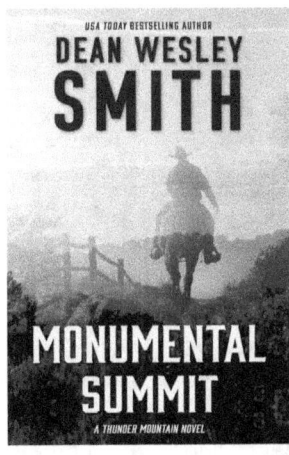
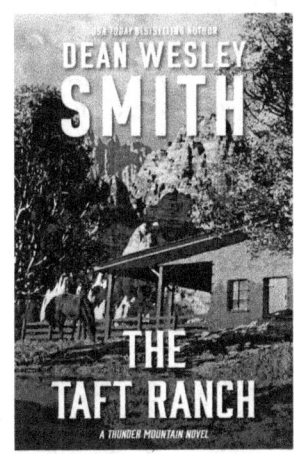

"J'accuse!" Kyle pointed at Asksersan. "You stole Ms. Toyler's backup disks."

"Who in hell are you?" Asksersan blustered. "And I don't know what you're talking about."

"A lie! A damned lie cast back in your teeth by the blimp of Eternal Justice." Only now did Toyler notice *Summa Theologica* hovering in a corner of the room. Propellers fluttering softly, it pointed directly at Asksersan. It was bright red.

"Who are you, indeed? And what are you doing here?" said Dexter, trying to gain control.

Kyle turned to Dexter. "Sit!" he snapped. "Not you, Albany." Obviously Kyle had no problem with authority figures. "Here, Albany." Albany waddled over to him. Kyle stuck a disk in front of his nose. "Fetch, Albany. Fetch the Kansas City project."

"WILL EVERYONE PLEASE SHUT UP BEFORE I CALL SECURITY!" shouted Dexter. "Toyler! Is this, this—ah" Dexter looked around at Kyle, the blimp, and the sad-eyed hound. "Is this menagerie yours?"

Sighing, Toyler teetered forward and told Dexter about Kyle, the DOS hound, and the truthful blimp. She'd never heard such a ridiculous story in her life.

"Toyler, I didn't think doing that project would affect your mind," Dexter said, his eyes glittering.

"Totally unstable," Asksersan said.

"Arrrrr ooooooooooo" Albany bayed, pointing at the door to Asksersan's private washroom.

"Ah ha!" shouted Kyle. "X marks the spot! Give me your key, sir, you coward cur!" Albany stopped baying and looked around, a disgusted look in his eye.

"A thousand pardons, Albany. Delete that 'cur.'" Albany returned to baying at the door. "Now, Mr. Hissing Asksersan, give me your key."

"I don't have my key here."

"Look at the blimp!" Kyle said. Involuntarily, everyone except Albany did. Red as a stop light.

"Arrrr ooooo"

"Give him your key, Asksersan." Dexter, sounding every inch a CEO, spoke quietly. Asksersan grubbed through his pockets, and finally handed Kyle the key.

"Arrrr ooooo." When the door opened, Albany charged, his toenails clicking as he skidded across the tiled floor. Dexter followed, with Toyler mincing up from behind. Finding the door too narrow for its ample body, *Summa Theologica* fluttered outside like some gigantic moth. Asksersan sat behind his desk without moving.

Forepaw raised, tail straight, Albany pointed at the water tank behind the toilet. Kyle looked behind the tank. "There's something taped to the back of the water tank."

"What have we here?" Kyle pulled out a waterproof plastic box and popped it open. "Computer disks." Dexter looked stunned. "Good dog, gooooood dog," Kyle chanted, patting Albany.

Carrying the disks like a Crusader would carry the Holy Grail, Kyle rolled back into Asksersan's office and popped them into the fancy wood-covered computer. Dexter and Toyler crowded in close behind him. The disk drive whirred, and the Kansas City project came up on the screen. Only where the name "Sandra Toyler" had been was now "Marlin Asksersan."

"So, Asksersan. Explain," said Dexter.

"It was just a test, sir," said Asksersan. "I meant to give Ms. Toyler a sharp lesson. Secretly, I made backup copies all along, as a guard against her losing hers. Which she did. Of course, had she not been able to reproduce the disk, I would have given her these. Only I meant her to sweat just a little. As an object lesson."

"So why put your name on another's work?"

"Just so I could tell my copies from hers. I'd hate any mistake to be made." His voice never faltered, his eyes never shifted. Toyler found herself believing him. Maybe she'd misjudged him, maybe she was being a vengeful little bitch. Maybe she *was* unstable. Then, from the corner of her eye, she noticed the blimp.

Summa Theologica glowed a dark, rich crimson.

The anger started in Toyler's aching toes, climbed up her tortured calves, then moved through her body in a great, shuddering tidal wave. She stepped out of the ridiculous shoes and stood in her stocking feet. This time she didn't close her eyes. She didn't need Tanya. She drew herself up to her full, though miniscule, height and looked directly at Asksersan.

"Liar," she said.

Instantly everyone went silent. Toyler could hear *Summa's* whirring props and even Asksersan's breathing. "Mr. Dexter, I will not work for anyone who steals."

Asksersan released a long, choking kind of sigh. Dexter put his hand to his face, stroking his chin with a finger. Kyle affected a Mona Lisa half smile. Albany stared, his brown eyes

glittering in the fading red light from *Summa* the blimp. Toyler's breath came in harsh little gasps, her heart was pounding. Compared to defying authority, aerobicize was nothing. She'd never felt better in her life.

"Now, there's no good cause for hard feelings, Ms. Toyler," Dexter said. "Mr. Asksersan has been under a lot of stress. I'm sure he's about to—well, take a well-deserved long vacation." Asksersan looked down at his desk and nodded.

"Come along to my office." Dexter opened the door and motioned her through. "And let me welcome you to our management team."

They were halfway down the hall when the quiet was shattered by a long drawn out howl from Albany.

"Oh, my lord!" said Kyle. "I forgot the Doggie Treet."

~

"Oh, hello darling. I wasn't reading the next chapter without you. I swear!"

Jerry Oltion is the most prolific writer of short stories in the history of Analog Magazine. *No one even comes close. And he still regularly publishes stories there.*

In this really twisted Pulphouse-*style story, Jerry comes up with the idea of committing suicide by UFO. Yup, fits right in these pages.*

Besides continuing his regular science fiction writing, Jerry is also a major amateur astronomer and does a regular column for Sky *and* Telescope. *Might want to check it out.*

Suicide by UFO
Jerry Oltion

IF ANYONE HAD asked me what I was doing in the middle of a Wyoming cow pasture on a cold November night, I probably would have told them I was committing suicide by UFO. A frivolous answer, maybe, but the truth. As much truth as you can fit into one sentence, anyway.

I was shivering despite the down jacket I wore beneath my cowhide. No matter how much clothing you're wearing, staying hunched over in imitation of a cow for hours on end is cold business. I'd tried stamping my feet to keep the blood circulating in them, but I gave that up after I splattered fresh cow patty all over my boots, and though I clutched a flashlight in one frozen fist I didn't think it was worth blowing my cover just to avoid doing it again.

Not that my cover was doing me any good. I'd been in the pasture for almost four hours, and so far all I'd gotten out of it was stiff joints and frostbite. I was beginning to get discouraged. The UFOs could be off mutilating yaks in Tibet tonight for all I knew. Or maybe this was their week off.

I tilted my plastic cow's head sideways to sneak another look at the stars. My uncle, who owned the pasture in which I crouched, had not lied about the night sky in Wyoming. It was brighter than I'd ever seen it before, even with a full moon to drown out the stars. Orion dominated the view to the south, with Gemini north and to the east and the Pleiades shining brightly to the west. The Milky Way cut a diagonal across my field of vision. One bright point of light that had to be a satellite crept southward toward Sirius, then winked out when it crossed into Earth's shadow.

I craned my neck to look higher in the sky—and felt my heart skip. Directly overhead, not lit up at all but blocking a considerable patch of the Milky Way, was my UFO. How had it gotten there? I hadn't heard or seen a thing. It hung there in sinister dark silence, not moving an inch, not blinking or humming or doing any of the usual UFO things, and while I stared at the reality my resolve flickered and went out. What did I think I was doing? This was a real alien spacecraft, with real live aliens on it! This was suicide!

I would have run then, but, stiff as I was, about all I could manage was to turn my head back down and concentrate on being small. Maybe I could sneak under a cow's belly, or—

Too late. Suddenly my shivering stopped, and my breathing with it. It felt for a second as if my heart had stopped, too. Maybe it had, for something was squeezing me all over, inside and out. It felt as if my navel had become enormously massive and was trying to pull the rest of me into it.

The little bit of air still in my lungs left me in one convulsive whuff. The ground began to drop away. I tried to scream, but without air it wasn't even a croak. Breathing in proved barely possible, with effort, but once I had a lungful I didn't want to waste it, not even to scream.

Breathing proved I could move, though. I tried to pull off the cowhide with my left hand while I willed my right thumb to slide forward an inch on the flashlight. Maybe if they could see their mistake they wouldn't start cutting.

Cutting! I did scream.

The flashlight sent a beam of light out into the night. I could barely feel it in my frozen fingers, but I tried to tilt it up toward whoever was running the winch.

That was a mistake. The force holding me suddenly let go, then a bright blue line flicked out from the bottom of the UFO and my left leg exploded in flame.

I passed out before I hit the ground. At least I don't remember the impact.

***

I WOKE UP SCREAMING, "Human! Human! Hu—" and stopped. I was in a bed. I raised up and cracked my head on the ceiling, then tried it again more cautiously. Lifting just my head, I looked around for a doctor or a nurse or whatever, and had to bite down on another scream. The "whatever" was about four feet tall, had a narrow, bald head with two oversized, perfectly round yellow eyes where his forehead should have been, and triangular ears sticking out from his neck like the ends of a starched collar turned inside out. He had no eyebrows, nor did he have a nose, his mouth taking up most of the available space. He had the right number of arms and legs, but he had joints enough for an extra pair each. Over everything but head and hands he wore a tight-fitting suit that flowed and glittered like a liquid silver leotard.

"Yes, human," he said in a rich voice that belied his small stature. "Not something I'd brag about, but then I'm not one, either." He stepped to the bed. "How do you feel?"

"Uh…"

"Your leg. Does it hurt?" His English was perfect: not a trace of an accent or of difficulty forming the words.

I struggled to think about his question. It seemed he wasn't going to tear me into pieces after all, at least not right away. I looked down at my leg. A shiny octagonal cylinder covered it from knee to ankle. Lights glowed in a row along one face, above a row of recessed buttons. My bare foot stuck out the bottom, and my toes wiggled on command.

"It doesn't hurt at all," I said, awed.

"Good. If it starts to, tell me. Don't mess with the regenerator."

I'd have sooner kissed a rattlesnake. I told him so.

"That's smart," he replied. "Smarter than masquerading as a cow. What were you doing? You know what happens to them, don't you?"

"Uh…yeah." I looked around me. The room was tiny, and triangular instead of square. Tools and electronic instruments covered the walls, the floor, even the ceiling. It had that claustrophobic atmosphere common to trailer houses and motor homes, and presumably spaceships. Even with a taller ceiling it would have felt that way; the feel of maximum use of minimum space. It was a hospital room now, but I had no doubt he could cut up a cow in there with very few changes.

"So what were you doing?" he asked again.

I realized I hadn't answered his question. "I was committing suicide," I said.

"Oh?"

"It's hard to explain."

"I've got a while." He stepped back from the bed and leaned against the doorframe with his arms crossed. The extra joints made it look as if he'd tied them in knots.

"Right." I looked him over again, forcing myself to really look. His enormous yellow eyes stared back, unblinking. I sniffed the air, and through a nose deadened by hours of cold and exposure to cow excrement I detected a faint aroma that might have been cinnamon, but wasn't. It was coming from him, and despite cinnamon being a fairly pleasant smell, the obvious incongruity of it had me as repulsed as if it had been sour milk. I tried to tell myself he wasn't the bogeyman, just an extraterrestrial being, but that hardly helped.

I wondered what had happened to the calm detachment I'd felt earlier in the cow pasture. The idea of meeting aliens hadn't scared me at all then. Of course I hadn't really expected to meet any, either. Deep inside I hadn't believed that UFOs were responsible for the cattle mutilations. Was that where my bravado had come from? Had I been bluffing?

"You were committing suicide," he prompted.

I took a couple of deep breaths, trying to calm down. So he was an alien. I'd thought that was what I wanted.

"Sort of," I said. "Or maybe I was trying to avoid it. I don't know. It's like—well, have you ever wanted to do something crazy, something that would either kill you or fix you up for the rest of your life depending on how it turned out?"

He thought a minute. "Maybe," he said.

Maybe? To that kind of question, his answer was as good as a yes.

So I said, "Sure you have, but for one reason or another you haven't done it. Maybe things just haven't gotten bad enough, or you don't want to hurt the people who'd be left behind. But what happens if you don't care anymore? It opens up a lot of possibilities. I've always told myself if things ever got bad enough to where I was considering suicide, I'd try one of those crazy do-or-die ideas first. It was getting that bad."

"Why? What was the matter?"

"They keep screwing up the space program."

He just stared at me, looking alien.

Well, he'd asked, and now I felt like talking. I wadded my pillow up behind my head so I could lie back and still see him, and said, "When I was a kid I wanted to be an astronaut. Every kid does, but I was serious. My eyes were bad and I knew I'd never make a test pilot, but I figured by the time I got out of school they'd need more than just test pilots in space. I thought we'd be exploring the planets by now, so I went into geology. I graduated about the time Skylab fell out of orbit. I watched NASA build the shuttle when they should've built a space plane, and I watched them shut it down for three years after their first accident, and I've watched them proceed like a bunch of old women crossing a freeway ever since, and I suddenly realized that by the time they get a planetary mission going, I'm going to be too old to go."

"So you decided to hide in a cow pasture and wait for a UFO." He grinned, but it had to be a gesture he'd picked up from humanity, because his mouth wasn't made for it. He didn't have teeth inside it, but something more like fingers instead.

I looked away in time to save my composure. After a moment I said, "It was the only way I could think of to get off the planet."

"I'd say that you picked just about the dumbest way possible, except that it worked. So now what am I supposed to do with you?"

"Take me with you!"

I wouldn't have thought it possible for round eyes to widen in surprise, but his did. He was silent for a long while before he spoke, and then it was just one word: "Where?"

"Where? Wherever you're going! Exploring new planets, trading among the stars, fighting the evil Empire—I don't care!

Whatever you're doing, take me along when you go."

"What makes you think I'm going anywhere?"

"Well, I just—I mean—aren't you?"

"No."

"Oh," I said. Oh indeed. "Nowhere?" I asked.

"Nowhere much. Your moon. Mars or Jupiter or Saturn once in a while when I'm bored. You expected to go zipping off across the galaxy?"

"Something like that," I admitted. "I was kind of hoping for an interstellar survey ship. Visiting strange new worlds and that sort of thing."

"Tough luck. I'm all there is."

"Just you? You're alone here?"

"That's right."

"And you stay here all the time?"

"That's right."

"Why?"

"Because I'm being paid to, that's why. It's my job."

"Your job? What are you, Overlord of Earth or something?"

"Or something." He waved his arms around to encompass the room, and by

---

Retrieval Artist Series From Kristine Kathryn Rusch

implication everything beyond it. "Lord and master of the entire solar system. Except I can't disturb the natives and there's nobody else here but me. You know what I do here? I'll tell you. I listen to the radio. I watch TV. I sort through it all for signs that humanity is about to get out into space before you blow yourselves up. And occasionally I cut up cattle."

"Why?"

"'Why why why?' You're worse than a talk show host. Why what?"

"Why do you cut up cattle? Nobody's been able to figure that out."

"How should *I* know? I just do it. I get a call from the main office for two anuses and a left eyeball, to be transmitted immediately. Do I ask questions? No I don't. I go out hunting. Maybe they've got a use for the parts, or maybe they're just checking to see if I'm still here, but either way I get them what they ask for. This may not be the best job in the galaxy, but I intend to keep it. There are plenty worse."

"I can imagine," I said. In fact, I couldn't. Having your own spaceship and not being able to go anywhere in it sounded like the worst torment I could think of. It would be worse than not having a spaceship at all. Worse even than having the government spend billions of dollars on bombs instead of on the space program. How could this guy stand it?

How could *I* stand it? I had succeeded in the hardest part of the whole ridiculous scheme—getting myself on board an extraterrestrial spacecraft—but the pilot had no intention of taking me anywhere. In fact, once my leg healed he would probably use another gadget to wipe my memory of all this and put me back where he found me. My suicide would be nothing more than a failed attempt, and I'd wake up tomorrow in the same situation I'd been trying to escape.

No. I'd gotten this far; there had to be a way.

I needed information. I needed to learn how this guy thought, what his motivations were, how he could be wheedled or tricked or bought into doing what I wanted him to do.

First things first. "Have you got a name?" I asked.

"Bob," he said.

"No, I mean your real name."

"That's it. Bob."

I tried not to laugh, but I couldn't help a smile. "An alien named Bob?"

"Would it make you feel better if I told you it was short for Gryznix or something? Look, if it's tough for you to say, it's tough for me to say, too. Bob's a nice simple word for any being who's got lips." He paused, then asked, "So what's yours?"

"Steve," I said. "Steve Wilson. It's not short for Gryznix, either."

"I didn't think so."

We looked at one another a moment, both wondering what to say next. Go for broke, I decided.

"At least tell me, is there an empire? *Are* there strange new worlds out there?"

He wiggled his ears. A shrug? "I don't know if I'd call it an empire, but there's a government of sorts that keeps the peace. And yeah, there's a few neat places around."

"Tell me about them."

He thought about it for a minute before he wiggled his ears again and said, "What do you want to hear about?"

"I don't know. Anything. Remember where I'm from."

"Right. Well, let's see. Hmm. There's the Gniknith Ring not too far from here. It's a colony that runs all the way around a planet. The Gnik built it by taking apart one of their moons."

"Yeah? What does it look like?"

"Like a ring around a planet, I guess. I don't know. I've never been there."

"Oh. Well where have you been?"

He thought about it a long time before he said, "I saw a double sun on my way out here. Blue and gold."

"Oh really?" I said, trying to hide my disappointment. A double sun was strange and new? At least half the stars in the sky were doubles, or triples.

"Yeah, it was one of my refueling stops. It made for wild shadows."

"I bet."

There was an uncomfortable silence.

"What about aliens?" I said at last. "Alien to you, I mean. Are there many different species?"

"Thousands," he said with the first real enthusiasm I'd heard from him yet. "They come in just about any shape you can imagine. I used to go to the spaceport and watch the traders come and go when I was younger, and I don't think I ever saw the same species twice. I even tried to ship out with a Thmigeli freighter once, but they didn't want an inexperienced nestling."

"How about a human?"

"I doubt it. Not unless you have something more to recommend you than I did."

"I'm good at video games."

"What's that supposed to mean?"

"I guess it means I have good reflexes. And I learn which buttons to push before I lose the game. I bet I'd make a good starship pilot."

"You think so? Well you can forget trying it with *this* ship. It's government property."

"It is? I thought it was yours."

He shook his head, probably another gesture learned from the TV. "Dream on. If this were mine, you wouldn't find me within a thousand light-years of here."

Oh ho! I thought. He *does* have dreams. I said, "So are you saving up to buy a ship of your own when you retire?"

"Retire. Hah. You know, I've been watching you guys for twenty years, and that's still the strangest thing I've ever heard of. You do something all your life, and then just when you get good at it, you quit."

"You mean you're here for life?"

"Or until you develop true space flight capability." He grinned again, but this time I didn't flinch. I was getting used to him.

"Why don't you help, then?"

"Because I've got orders to keep clear."

"And why is that?"

"Because that's the way we do things. Besides, your people seem to want it that way."

"Huh? We what? That's ridiculous!"

"You've had one of our ships for over forty years and you still haven't done anything with it. What else should we think?"

My head was spinning. "Wait. Back up. *We've* had one of *your* ships for forty years? Where? How?"

"New Mexico. One of the preliminary survey teams got too close to one of your above-ground nuclear bomb tests and the electromagnetic pulse burned out its controls. It fell like a rock right into the middle of the testing range."

I couldn't believe what I was hearing. "An electromagnetic pulse burned out a flying saucer?"

The alien—Bob, I reminded myself—said, "We haven't used nuclear weapons for millennia. We forgot they could do that."

It could be possible, I supposed. I remembered reading that the United States' combat planes were all vulnerable to EMP's for years before we realized it. And I also remembered reading a couple of books that claimed the Air Force had captured a UFO. I'd been sure it was just crackpot stuff, tabloid magazines in book form and nothing more, but now…

"Why would the government be sitting on something like that? I'd think they'd be trying like mad to duplicate it."

He nodded. "Oh, I'm sure they are. But if they've succeeded then they haven't done anything with it, and either way they're not telling anybody else about it."

"Why not?"

"Why do you think? They've got an incredible advantage over everybody else as long as they don't upset the status quo."

"And in the meantime another generation grows old and dies without ever getting into space!" I shouted, raising up and cracking my head on the ceiling again.

"Exactly. And your government retains control over most of the human race. How long do you suppose that would continue if the dissidents could leave the planet?"

"Oh," I said. Oh, indeed. It made a perverse sort of sense at that, just perverse enough for me to believe that the government could be doing just what this alien was suggesting. I didn't need him to fill in the rest of the picture, either. They couldn't dismantle NASA's space program, not without giving themselves away, but they could prolong the inevitable by cutting the funding down to the bare minimum and bumbling around with an uneconomical shuttle and shutting it down for three years after an accident and *still* not changing the design. If they played their cards right, manipulating other countries the way they'd already been doing, they could waste another couple of *centuries* before anybody actually managed to develop real spaceflight, and by then they'd have had time to figure out how to control the next phase of expansion, too.

"And the people you work for are going to let them get away with it?" I asked.

"Hey, it's your planet," he said. "You can do whatever you want to on it and we don't care. I'm only here because you *could* come on out here pretty quickly, and we want to know about it if you do."

Out here, he'd said. I hadn't thought about it until now, but I suddenly realized where we were. "We're in space, aren't we?" I asked.

"That's right. Geocentric orbit behind one of your communications satellites. We don't show up on radar that way, and I get great TV reception."

"I'd give anything to see out," I said. "How long before I can get up?"

"Whenever you want to. The regenerator's portable."

"Oh. Well, how about a tour then?"

"Sure, why not?" He beckoned toward the door.

I swung my feet off the bed and sat up, bending low to keep from hitting my head on the ceiling. It was probably spacious for a four-foot alien, but I would have to walk hunched over. I wondered if the Air Force was trying to duplicate the other ship exactly, and snickered at the thought of stiff-backed soldiers angling their way down the corridors.

"What?" Bob-the-alien asked.

"Nothing." I stood carefully, testing my leg, but except for the weight of the regenerator I couldn't tell there was anything wrong with it at all. "Lead on," I said.

The ship was just what I had expected: a sort of space-faring Winnebago. It couldn't have been more than forty feet across, but crammed into that space was enough equipment to take a person anywhere in the galaxy and keep him alive indefinitely once he got there. It had a total of five rooms, four of them arranged like quarters of a pie around a central hub that led up to the control room, which was the typical circular glass bubble in the center of the disk. The controls were almost disappointing in their simplicity: hyperspace and normal space controls all built into one panel, with little more than direction buttons and a throttle to control the whole thing.

"No fancy gadgets for shifting into hyperspace?" I asked, crouching down beside my

host's shoulder while he sat in the control room's single chair.

"You don't need them. It's automatic. When you get going too fast for normal space, it shifts for you."

"Oh," I said. An automatic transmission. Not exactly what I'd imagined, but still, it was a spaceship.

I looked around for anything I might have missed. There was one other panel set at an angle in the console, folded so the buttons faced toward the operator and the cross-hatched screen faced the glass where it would reflect at a convenient height for a short alien in the control chair to read without looking down from his flying. I'd heard of heads-up displays before. I took a guess and said, "Weapons?"

He nodded. "Particle beam, laser—the usual."

"I suppose they're automatic, too."

"Of course. There's a manual override if you need it, but the targeting computer's a lot faster."

I thought of the totally hokey scene in *Star Wars* when Luke switches off his computer to shoot manually at the tiny target on the Death Star. Logically it didn't make sense at all, but the message came across just the same: sometimes you have to take matters into your own hands.

Bob pushed one of the direction buttons—the one with a curvy arrow around it, and a bright near-full Earth slid into view from below the edge of the saucer's disk. I didn't sense the ship's motion; internal gravity must have compensated for it perfectly.

Earth was brighter than I'd imagined it would be. I could see the outline of North America, which meant I'd been unconscious about twelve hours or so. I watched my home drift across the screen and contemplated the vastness of the universe for a few minutes while I tried to make up my mind.

I looked at the controls again. Direction controls in a diamond, with two rotation buttons and a throttle. Automatic transmission.

Automatically tracking weapons. I'd seen more complicated video games. True, the buttons were labeled in a language that I couldn't understand, but who looks at the labels anyway? A good player knows instinctively which ones to push. If he doesn't, he experiments.

I thought about suicide. There's suicide and there's suicide, but no matter how you looked at it there has to be some risk involved. I could have frozen to death in that cow pasture. I almost did get myself cut up for spare parts. And I probably would smash myself into the planet at nine-tenths the speed of light as soon as I pushed a button, but there was one thing I did know for sure: I'd *rather* die than let this guy wipe my memory and put me back on Earth.

And here in front of me was my chance to make a difference. The feeling of helplessness down there had driven me here; could I really pass up such an opportunity?

He must have seen it in my eyes. Either all his TV watching had given him experience at interpreting human expression or else the predatory look is universal, but as soon as I turned around toward him he yelled, "Oh no you don't!" and reached for something hidden in his clothing.

I grabbed his arm and pulled, but his size had made me misjudge his strength. He wasn't a scrawny human; he was a fully-grown alien, with fully-grown alien muscles. He kicked away from his chair and we teetered there for a minute, his hand probably inches away from a laser or some such weapon, while I tried to get a better grip on him and he tried to pull away. He slapped at my side a couple of times and seemed surprised that it didn't affect me, then shifted his attention to my groin.

I managed to dodge his kick, and then I realized what he'd been trying to do before. I reached out and smacked him in the side and he folded.

"No fair," he wheezed as I pinned him against the wall.

"You were going for mine," I said.

I didn't take time to examine his gun; I just took it and put it out of his reach while I looked for something to tie him up with. There was nothing in the control room, so we had to go back into the lab.

"What do you think you're doing?" he protested as I pushed him along ahead of me.

"I'm doing you a favor," I said.

"Yeah? I don't remember asking for any."

"Oh yes, you did. A couple of times. Here we go." I found a roll of tape in a drawer and wrapped his wrists with it, then taped his arms to his legs in a sitting position. When I was done I picked him up and carried him back to the control room and propped him against the wall.

"Let me guess, you're going to show me what a fine pilot you'd make."

"Better than that," I said as I squeezed into the control chair and pushed the first button. "I'm going to uncover a little conspiracy."

Nothing happened, so I inched the throttle slide up about a quarter of the way in its track and pushed the button again. The Earth began to slide off the top of the screen. I tried another button and the motion changed by ninety degrees. I was glad for internal gravity; that maneuver had to have pulled at least a hundred G's.

"And how do you plan to do that? There are UFO reports all the time! Nobody believes them."

"The people who see the UFOs do."

"Yeah, and they've sure made a lot of difference, haven't they?"

"Maybe there just weren't enough of them," I said, pushing the rotation button until the Earth was directly in front of us again. I pushed the forward button, and the Earth began to grow larger.

"Whoa!" my captive shouted. "Let off!"

I let off the button, but the Earth kept expanding.

"Push the opposite button," he said.

"Why? We're going the direction I want to go."

"Not this fast, you don't. The automatics can only account for so much."

I looked at the Earth again, counting. It was growing about one diameter every five seconds or so. Maybe that was a bit fast. "Okay," I said, pushing the reverse button once. Now Earth grew one diameter every ten seconds. I pulled the throttle back part way so the controls wouldn't be so touchy.

Bob tugged at the tape on his arms and legs, but it held tight. "I think maybe you ought to reconsider what you're doing here," he said. "Hijacking a starship on an official mission is serious business."

"So's this." While we coasted nearer, I pushed a few buttons on the weapons panel and found the fire button, but I also got the screen to start searching for targets. I watched as it displayed a steady progression of satellites in high magnification.

"Don't shoot any of them," Bob whispered.

"I don't plan on it. I just want to know how to use this thing in case somebody starts shooting at *me*."

"They will, even if you don't knock down a satellite."

"Do we have shields or anything?"

"This isn't the *Enterprise*."

I took that for a "no."

We were headed for the west coast. I guessed northern California, but it was hard to tell without the borders drawn in for me. California didn't seem like the national seat of credibility, though, and what I wanted was to be believed, so I used the side-to-side controls until we were aimed about a third of the continent's width in from the west coast. That should put us somewhere near Denver, which I figured would be a better place to start. A couple of runs up and down over the near-continuous strip city along the front range of the Colorado Rockies would give a few million people a good view of the UFO, and give me a little practice maneuvering before I took it over the east coast and New York City.

I had misjudged the size of a continent by a few orders of magnitude. The closer we drew, the bigger it got, until long before we reached the atmosphere I had no idea whether we were over Colorado or western Nebraska or southern Wyoming or where the heck we were.

"Slow down!" Bob shouted again, and I slowed us down some more, but we continued to drop toward the brown, wrinkled globe in front of us.

Pretty soon it quit being a globe, and became just a big map with no lines on it. I watched, hypnotized, as it grew.

The ship suddenly tilted half over, until the ground was below us. A moment later we heard a faint, high-pitched scream that seemed to come from all around us. We had hit atmosphere.

The automatic re-entry sequence took us down to maybe five miles off the ground, then stopped the ship and gave me back the controls. It could have been ten or twenty miles for all I knew; I hadn't flown in commercial jets enough to get a feel for height, and there wasn't anything out there to provide a sense of scale. I'd expected to be able to see the Rocky Mountains sticking up like big teeth on the horizon, but they were lost in the distance. The land seemed the same in every direction: hazy brown and rumpled.

"Have at it," Bob said, sounding smug.

I pushed the forward direction button and we began to glide across the terrain. Our motion felt perfectly frictionless, as if we were the puck in an enormous game of air hockey. We didn't slow down when I let off the button; just glided on and on. After a few minutes of that, I pushed one of the side buttons and we shot off in another direction. It really didn't make much difference. I saw no indication of civilization whatever.

The weapons screen found it first. I was still trying to figure out the scale of what I was seeing when it beeped at me and showed a cluster of dots coming toward us from straight ahead.

I switched course, but the dots changed course to intercept me again.

"Throttle up," Bob said.

"I thought you said—"

"We're in an atmosphere now; it doesn't mean the same thing here. Unless you want to—look out!"

The weapons screen beeped more insistently now. We were still moving sideways; I looked over at the heads-up display and saw half again as many dots as before. Some of them were moving a *lot* faster than the others.

I pushed the fire button, reasoning that the automatic system would know which dots were missiles and which were planes.

Nothing happened.

I pressed it again.

Nothing happened again.

"What gives here?" I shouted. The missiles had already closed half the distance to us. I pushed the reverse button and we began backing up, but not as fast as the missiles approached.

"You've shut it off!" Bob shouted. "You've got it in communications mode!"

"Oh. Which button turns it on again? This one?" I picked one at random.

"NO! Oh great. Now you've lost your target. Push the other—not that one! That's *our* missiles. You want the particle beam."

"So which one is that?"

"You've got to locate a target first, idiot!"

"Hey, same to you. This one?" I pushed the button that I remembered as starting the scan before, and was rewarded with a screenful of tiny missiles. "Now what?"

"Lock the selector on that shape. No, not that—here. Let me do it. You'll never get it in time."

"I will. You just hold onto your hat." I looked at the labels under the buttons and saw one that had a dashed oval surrounding a cluster of asterisk-like characters. Some kind of grouping symbol? I pushed it.

Every missile on the screen lit up in yellow.

"There, see?" I pushed the fire button again, and watched as a blue light beam automatically tracked and killed each missile on the screen. It took about three seconds. When the screen was clear it turned white, but it continued to beep.

The airplanes were still there. They were just specks out the window, but the weapons screen showed me a magnified view of them. I didn't know an F-16 from an F-111, but whatever they were, they were ugly.

And they shot first. I got us out of there, leaning on the right-hand flight button until the weapons screen quit beeping at me, and not slowing down for a few minutes afterward.

That put me over more wrinkled brown countryside, nearly identical to wherever I'd been. I poked at combinations of buttons and found the one to take us down, and pretty soon I could see the regular rectangles of farms dotting the landscape, but I still saw nothing like a city. I thought of following a road, but that could take a while, and as quickly as the jets had found us before, I didn't think I had a while.

"You've got to have some sort of navigational stuff," I said to Bob. "How do I find a city?"

"Wouldn't you like to know," he replied, smug satisfaction all through his voice.

"Come on."

"You want to fly this thing, fly it yourself. Otherwise untie me and let me do it."

"Would you help me, or just send me home with my memory erased?"

He didn't answer, which was answer enough.

"Sorry," I said. "I guess I'll just have to muddle along as best I can."

I poked a few more buttons on the weapons console, trying for the "communications mode" I'd found by accident earlier, but I didn't find it again. I did find something interesting, though: the manual controls for a different kind of beam weapon. In manual mode I got an intense violet beam that stayed on as long as I held down the fire button, a beam I could move around with a tiny joystick that popped up beside the buttons.

"Shut that off!" Bob shouted the moment he saw what I'd found.

I'd only wiggled the beam a little from its initial straight-ahead position. The violet line reached through the air for as far as I could see.

"Why?" I asked.

"If that touches the ground, it'll make a hydrogen bomb look tame, that's why."

"Oh." I switched it off.

"You're playing around with more power than you know what to do with. For the last time, I'm warning you: let me go before you hurt someone with it. Like yourself."

"I'm committing suicide, remember?" I said.

"Well leave me out of it."

The weapons screen began beeping again, saving me from having to reply. I pushed the button that had made it select the missiles the last time, but all I got was a magnified view of half a dozen fully-armed jets. I couldn't tell if they were the same ones or somebody new, but whichever they were they hadn't fired yet.

"Get us out of here!" Bob yelled.

"Why? They aren't shooting."

"They've tried this on me before. They'll wait until they're right next to us and *then* shoot. The defense program can't handle that."

I thought about just shooting down the planes first, but rejected that idea immediately. The pilots weren't my enemies. They were people like me; technophiles who had gone the only route they could think of to live on the cutting edge of the future. If I somehow succeeded in shaking the government's secrets loose, these would be the people who flew the first ships out of the solar system.

But they didn't know that. And they were getting closer.

"Go!" Bob shouted again. "Go now!"

I went. I jammed the throttle to full, pushed the button for straight ahead, and we were clear out of the atmosphere before I could slow down. I thought about taking us back down and trying again, but I didn't really expect much better success a second time. Unless I could find a whole city full of people, get them to notice me, *and* explain to them who I was and what was going on, whatever I tried would come to nothing more than the last few hundred UFO sightings. In a week's time it would be old news.

I needed a way to prove the existence of UFOs, explain that the U.S. already had the technology to build their own, and keep that message in front of people until they

did something about it. No amount of publicly broadcast messages, no amount of flying over cities, not even landing in Central Park—assuming I could even *find* Central Park—would accomplish that, because it wouldn't affect enough people for long enough to move the nearly immovable object our government had become.

The automatic controls took over and put us into orbit. I wondered if we were being tracked from the ground, and what it would matter if we were. The Wyoming ranchers and the Iowa corn farmers wouldn't know about it even so, and they were the people I needed to reach. Voters.

I looked down at the planet spread out below me and realized I was being provincial. The United States wasn't the entire world. They had the crashed UFO, but they weren't the only ones who should benefit from it. Somehow, I needed to get the message to the entire world.

"Ready to give up now?" Bob asked.

"No," I said. I didn't feel as confident as I sounded, but I wasn't going to cave in just yet.

I watched the Earth slide by below us. We were already moving into night, though with only ocean beneath us I couldn't tell whether it was sunrise or sunset. I kept watching, and saw a tiny speck of light nick the dark horizon, grow into a dome, then a hemisphere, then a sphere, all in less than a minute. Moonrise from orbit.

It was directly in front of us. On a whim, I set the throttle at about half, pushed the forward direction button once, and watched the Earth drop away behind us.

"What are you doing?" Bob demanded.

"Going to the moon," I said. "I've never been there. I probably won't ever *get* there if I don't do it now."

Surprisingly, he had nothing to say about that. I smiled. My first impression of him had been right: he *did* have a dreamer's heart. Metaphorically, at least.

We watched the moon grow as we drew closer. When it was just big enough to fill my entire field of view, I brought the ship to a stop and we hung there, drifting in absolute silence as we each thought our own thoughts.

I thought of all the people looking up at the moon tonight, and wondered if they could see a tiny black speck between them and the light. I decided not. I was beginning to get a feel for the scale of things now, and I realized that to be visible from Earth, something near the moon would have to be miles across to even show as a speck. Maybe we'd show in a telescope, but not by naked eye.

But a lot of kids were no doubt looking through telescopes about now. The moon had always been my favorite viewing object. I'd spent hundreds of hours peering into the eyepiece of a homemade reflector, looking for but never seeing the faint tracks left behind by the Apollo crews.

I wondered how wide the tracks would have to be for a kid's telescope to pick them out. Pretty wide, I supposed. I looked down at the weapons console, thinking maybe I could figure out how to use it for a telescope and try to find the tracks from here, but the sight of the screen with all the fire control buttons below it gave me another idea instead.

It was crazy, probably unworkable, and it bordered on sacrilege, but the more I thought about it, the more I liked it. And it would be easy enough to test.

"What are you doing?" Bob asked when I pushed the button for manual control of the beam weapons.

"Seeing how sharp my pencil is," I replied, pushing the fire button. The beam was invisible in space, but an intense bright spot appeared on the surface of the moon right where the cross hairs were aimed. When it faded, I could still see a tiny speck that was the new crater. If I could see it by naked eye from where we were, then a kid with a telescope should be able to see it from Earth.

And there were a lot of kids with telescopes on Earth. Not even the United States government could suppress all of them. Nor could it erase a message written on the face of the moon

without going into space in a big way, which was exactly what I wanted anyway.

I moved the joystick until the cross hairs pointed at the upper left edge of the moon. It was *my* upper left—from Earth that point could be anywhere depending on where the viewer was standing—but orientation wasn't important. What mattered was the message itself.

And what should that be? *Surrender Dorothy* sprang to mind, but I didn't suppose many people would get that tenuous a connection. I needed something a little more direct.

How about *really* direct? No chance of ambiguity. "Yeah," I said aloud.

"Don't do it," Bob said. "Please don't do it. When my people find out about this—"

"It'll be too late." I pushed the fire button and held it down while I moved the joystick to form the first letter, a *W*. The carving was absolutely silent, but in my mind I heard the thunder of megatons of rock being vaporized along the beam's path. I followed the *W* with *e exist and we're waiting*. Writing with a joystick isn't easy; the line wavered all over the place, but when I let up on the fire button after the last word and focused on the view beyond the display, I could see the entire phrase glowing from limb to limb of the moon, and if it wasn't pretty it was at least readable. The incandescence was a bonus; until the rock cooled, the message *would* be visible by naked eye. Millions of people were probably already wondering what the hell I was talking about. I moved over to the left again and wrote the second line: *The U.S. knows how to reach us.* Beneath that, and to the side because I didn't want to mess up the Sea of Tranquility, I drew a stick figure with three legs, four arms, and three eyes on stalks.

"What's that supposed to be?" Bob asked.

"A generic alien," I said, switching off the weapons screen and leaning back in the chair.

"Ah." He squirmed around against the wall, and I wondered what he was doing until I realized he was scratching the back of his head on the doorframe. "So what are you going to do now?" he asked.

This, I knew, was as crucial a moment as any before. I'd solved part of my problem, but not all of it. I took a deep breath, said, "I'm going to give your ship back to you," and I reached over and unwound the tape.

He stood up slowly, stretching, until he was once again his four-foot-high self. "You're in my chair," he said.

I got out. He slid in, turned on the weapons console again, and with deft motions wrote beneath my crude drawing, "Steve Wilson." He looked over at me, grinning his ugly grin, and said, "Just so there's no confusion."

I nodded. "All right."

He looked over at the main control console. The weapon I'd taken from him earlier still rested right there above the direction buttons, right where I'd put it. Right where I'd left it, on purpose. Casually, he leaned forward and picked it up.

"You know," he said, not quite pointing it at me, "I should have carved you into little pieces when I thought you were a cow. It would have saved me a lot of trouble."

"Maybe so," I said, "but if you had you would have missed your golden opportunity."

"What opportunity? You've screwed up everything. My job, my future, my whole life. You've forced me to meddle in an undeveloped planet's affairs, and that's big trouble. I doubt if you can comprehend what kind of trouble I'm in. I'll be lucky if they decide on simple execution when this gets back to the home office, so don't talk to me about opportunity."

"There's always suicide," I said.

He waved the gun toward me. "I was thinking of something more akin to homicide."

I shook my head. "No, think it through. I said I would do you a favor, and I have. You ought to thank me."

"I fail to see how this is a favor."

"Easy. You were stuck in a dead-end job—one you couldn't even retire from—but it wasn't quite bad enough for you to do anything about it. So I made it worse. Sure you're in a bad situation, but now your choice is clear. You can let your government kill you or you can do one of those crazy things you've always dreamed of doing. If you've got any sense you'll take the ship and clear out before they come to investigate. Go visit the Gniknith Ring or something. Become a trader like the Thingies."

"Thmigeli," he said automatically.

"Whoever."

I watched him think about it. After a moment he lowered the gun and said, "And you want me to take you along, I suppose."

"Of course. You owe me one."

"That's debatable." He looked back at the moon, then swiveled around in the chair to look at Earth. "Now that you've got the message out, wouldn't you rather go back and live among your own kind?"

His words sent a pang of homesickness to pierce my spirit of adventure. The galaxy was a huge place; if I went with him I might never see another human again, even if they did get into space. I would almost certainly never see Earth again. Could I leave all that behind, forever?

I didn't have to think about it for long. I had already made that decision, back when I'd covered myself with a cowhide and stood in a pasture in Wyoming.

I looked away from the Earth to my new companion and said, "A successful suicide can't ever go back."

~

Annie Reed touches the heart this issue with a woman who knows survival. A woman in a situation that Annie makes all too real for comfort.

Annie's stories appear regularly in many varied professional markets and I am proud to say she is also a regular contributor to Fiction River.

Her story "The Color of Guilt" was selected for The Year's Best Crime and Mystery Stories 2016. *She is also one of the founding members of the innovative* Uncollected Anthology.

Another Door
Annie Reed

MAVIS TRIMBLE DUG her husband's grave beneath the white oak tree where he'd proposed to her thirty-one years ago to the day.

It took her the better part of the morning to hack her way with a shovel through the first few inches of cold, root-choked ground. There were easier places to dig a grave, but Mavis hadn't picked the spot just because it was where Edgar proposed.

The white oak was the tallest tree in the windbreak behind their Iowa farmhouse, and Edgar had been a tall man. The rope swing Mavis's daddy had hung from the oak's branches was still there, frayed now with age. When she was a girl just beginning to notice that boys were good for something other than teasing, Mavis used to sit in that swing and dream about the handsome man she'd marry someday. Edgar hadn't been all that handsome, but he'd been a good, decent man who'd loved her with all his heart, and she'd loved him with all of hers. Mavis wanted to lay his memory to rest in a spot that was special to her no matter how much hard work it took to dig the grave.

Before the sun climbed high overhead, Mavis gave up on the shovel and started attacking the rocks and roots with a pickaxe. She worked up a serious sweat as she got into a steady rhythm with her swing.

It felt comforting to be warm. The sun wasn't much good for that these days. The sky as far as she could see was filled with the same dark, ashy clouds that had been there the day before, and the day before that. The clouds made the sun look like a pale, pitiful ghost of itself.

She should have started with the pickaxe, but the pickaxe had been in the heavy equipment barn, and that had been Edgar's place. Mavis didn't like to go in the barn anymore. The tractor and cultivator and corn harvester they'd put themselves in debt to buy were her husband's babies, and they looked forlorn and abandoned without Edgar to take care of them. No one had used the machines since her husband left to fight in the war. Mavis doubted anyone would ever need to use them again.

The life Mavis and Edgar had worked so hard to build for themselves was gone. The farmland might have been in Mavis's family for generations, but Edgar made it bloom. He'd planted hundreds of acres of corn year after year, an ocean of green that stood eight feet, ten feet high, almost as far as the eye could see. All that hard work had finally started to pay off. This year had looked like the second in a row their family farm would turn a profit.

Their ocean of green was dead now. The middle of August, and the stalks were brittle and dry and frozen, and like everything else in the world, covered with dry, dusty ash.

Mavis knew she should have worn a mask over her mouth while she dug, but did it even matter anymore? A coughing fit nearly doubled her over, and she had to lean on the handle of the pickaxe to keep herself upright.

"Pitiful," she said when she got her breath back. The grave she worked so hard to dig was twelve inches deep, if that. It was almost like the land was refusing to believe what Mavis knew in her heart.

"He's not coming back, you hear?" she told the farm. "I've accepted it. Why can't you?"

The only response was the slow, steady *vhump, vhump, vhump* from the wind turbine behind the silo.

At least the grave was finally long enough.

Mavis laid out her husband's best suit— hell, his only suit—on the dirt at the bottom. Deep, rich blue, the suit looked almost black in the sullen daylight. On top of the suit, she put her favorite picture from their honeymoon, a simple shot of the two of them smiling at each other over dinner. There hadn't been a lot of money, even back then. They'd stayed at the best hotel they could afford in Des Moines and promised each other they'd be back to celebrate their golden anniversary.

"Looks like neither one of us is gonna make that date, honey," Mavis said. "Not like we didn't try, but I guess the good Lord had other plans."

She added a few other trinkets to the grave. The ticket stub from the first movie Edgar'd taken her to. The Christmas card he'd given her the year they got married. His favorite baseball cap.

The last thing she put in the grave was the hardest. A baby blanket, the first of many she'd knitted back when they thought they'd have kids. After she'd turned forty-five, she'd given away all the blankets she'd made except for this one. Pink and blue and pale yellow, the blanket stayed at the back of the linen closet. Mavis always told herself it should go to someone special.

No one special was left in this world, not even her husband. She had no body to bury, no ashes in an urn to put on the mantle. Edgar was gone. This poor grave filled with clothes and memories and dreams was all she could do for him.

The breeze picked up. The photograph fluttered, and Mavis knelt to put a rock on it to hold it in place. She caught sight of the plain gold band on her ring finger. Did widows bury their wedding rings with their husbands? Mavis couldn't remember. It was the only piece of jewelry she owned. She smoothed the baby blanket with her left hand, and decided enough was enough.

Her knees creaked when she stood back up. "Pitiful," she said again.

The fields of dead corn rustled in the breeze, seeming to echo the word back at her.

Mavis grabbed the shovel and went about the task of filling up the grave. She pretended not to notice when the dirt covered the last bit of the blanket, then the last of Edgar's suit. She didn't stop working until she was coughing so hard she expected to see blood on the hand she used to wipe her mouth.

No blood. She wasn't dying.

Not yet.

The day grew so dark she could barely see the cross her daddy had built on the little rise a quarter mile away. He hadn't been an overly religious man, but her daddy had believed in God in his own way. He'd built that cross big enough to make sure it could be seen from every corner of their property. To remind them, he'd said, that God has a plan, even if man can't see it.

"I don't suppose you want to let me in on this one?" Mavis said to the cross. "Because I gotta tell you, I don't see a door anywhere around here."

That last little bit had come from Edgar. *When one door closes, another one opens*, he used to say. Same thing as saying God has a plan, although Edgar would never put it that way. He hadn't believed in God. What he believed in was the power of a positive attitude, and it had been one of the reasons Mavis had fallen in love with him. Without him, Mavis felt like all the positive had gone out of her life.

The cross didn't answer her any more than the land had. Mavis was alone, and she'd be alone until the day she died.

She looked down at the grave. "I'm trying, honey," she said. "I just don't know why."

She had one more thing left to do. She'd made a simple cross out of the slats from the back of one of the kitchen chairs. She shoved the cross in the ground at the head of the grave.

The marker for Edgar's grave bore his name on the crossbar, written with a permanent marker, along with the date of his birth. Mavis had almost left the date of his death blank, but in the end she'd written the date the world had died.

The date human beings learned they weren't alone.

***

THE FIRST MOVIE Edgar had taken her to see all those years ago was *Alien*. He'd told her later he thought she'd be scared enough she'd want to hide her face in his shoulder, and it would give him an excuse to put his arm around her. He never knew how close she'd come to telling him right then and there that she never wanted to see him again, but in the end, she'd decided she liked his arm around her just fine.

Back in those days, neither of them had any idea aliens were real. Not aliens like the acid-dripping monsters in the movie. Those make-believe bugaboos were teddy bears compared to the creatures who used Earth as a battleground in a war that had not one blessed thing to do with humanity.

Mavis and Edgar had watched, stunned, as televised reports showed the first massive ships appearing over seemingly random spots around the globe. As it turned out, the spots weren't all that random. The first aliens wanted water and minerals, and they didn't bother to ask before taking what they came for. Mavis supposed they were no worse than people who plowed under anthills without asking the ants if it was okay, but it sure set a person back some to realize that in the grand scheme of things, people weren't all that high up the food chain. At least people didn't seem to *be* food, so from Edgar's way of thinking, it could have been worse.

Worse showed up right about the time the governments of the world were beginning to mobilize against the wholesale plunder of the planet. The second species of aliens were more aggressive than the first, and it became clear soon enough that they were here to kill as many of the other aliens as they could. Even though humanity wasn't the target, whole cities rapidly became collateral damage.

Edgar was Army Reserve, but he would have left to join the fight even if he hadn't been called to duty. Mavis heard from him once after he left. Right before the communications satellites were shot out of the sky, he called to tell her to stay put. None of the battles were heading her way, and he wanted her to be safe. Then he told her his unit had been ordered to defend Chicago.

That had been four months ago.

At first, Mavis did what Edgar told her to. She holed up at the farm, kept the lights off at night, and watched the skies during the day, fearing that one of those massive ships would settle over their farm and carve up the land.

Weeks passed, and no massive ships appeared. From time to time jets and odd-shaped fighters screamed overhead, but they always seemed to be headed someplace else as fast as they could go. One day Mavis thought she heard the faint sound of explosions carried on the wind. The next morning smoke shrouded the cornfields. More and more smoke filled the skies, until finally clouds and smoke became a constant grey ceiling, and fine ash started falling like misty rain. It didn't take long before the land got cold and the corn started to die.

Mavis was a sturdy woman used to doing for herself. After a month of watching the skies and living like a scared little prairie dog, Mavis told herself she wasn't going to live the rest of her life like that. Her nearest neighbor was over four miles away, another neighbor lived on a farm two miles beyond that. She started trekking to her neighbors once a week in Edgar's battered pickup truck. They shared what news could be had, which was precious little once the Des Moines radio stations quit broadcasting.

The last time Mavis made the drive, she'd found her closest neighbor's farmhouse deserted. Their truck was gone and so was all their food. A note with a scrawled *we're heading to Des Moines* had been left for her tacked to the front door. At the next farm, she found her neighbor dead on his porch, his head bashed in. Mavis couldn't find his wife or his truck. She sped back to her farmhouse,

pushing Edgar's truck as fast as it would go, and loaded the shotgun Edgar kept in the bedroom closet.

She took the shotgun with her everywhere she went on her farm after that, but no one came for her. No more jets or alien craft flew across the skies. Even the birds seemed to have moved on.

Her neighbors had asked her once why she didn't leave. She'd thought about her daddy's cross and Edgar's grim smile when he'd kissed her goodbye, and told them the farm was the only place Edgar would know where to find her when the war was over. They'd smiled at her, but their smiles weren't the happy kind. Mavis didn't need them to tell her they thought she was a fool. When she was alone at night in the bed she'd shared with Edgar for thirty years, she suspected that he might never come back. She just hadn't been ready to admit it to herself, not back then.

The night after she buried what she could of her husband, Mavis sat up late at the kitchen table. She had a bottle of whiskey and a glass on the table in front of her, but she hadn't taken a drink. The wind was howling outside, and the turbine had shut itself down as it always did when the wind got too strong and it had generated all the power the farm needed. Mavis used to hate the noise the turbine made, but now it was like the heartbeat of a constant companion. The turbine kept the lights on and the dark at bay, and she missed it when it went quiet.

The shotgun on the table next to the whiskey bottle was a whole different kind of darkness.

She wasn't the kind to take her own life, but someone might stumble across her farm one day. Someone hungry enough or desperate enough who wouldn't hesitate to kill her. She had a good deal of food put away in the pantry. Could she kill to protect what she had here?

What if what came after her wasn't human? Just because she hadn't seen any fighters or heard any explosions in weeks didn't mean all the aliens were gone.

But if they were gone, if the fighting was really all done, then why hadn't Edgar come home?

She stared at her wedding ring and realized she was a liar. The grave had been a lie. She hadn't accepted that he was gone forever. That's why she couldn't bury her ring.

"Whenever you get back, I'll be here," she said. "You hear me? I'll be right here."

She put the whiskey bottle back in the cabinet and went to bed.

***

THE SOUND OF Edgar's truck trying to start woke Mavis from a fitful sleep.

The wind had died down in the night. The clock on her nightstand read six-fifteen, but it was still pitch black outside.

Mavis fumbled for the flashlight she kept in her nightstand drawer. The keys to truck were right there in the drawer next to all the keys for the farm equipment.

Someone was trying to take Edgar's truck. Hotwire the thing and steal it away in the dark. It didn't have much gas in it anymore, but that truck was the only vehicle she had other than the tractor she'd never driven. She might intend to never leave the farm again, but she didn't want that choice taken away from her.

Mavis grabbed the shotgun and stepped into her shoes. She knew her way through her house in the dark. She turned the flashlight off and rushed to the back door as quickly as she could.

The truck was parked in a three-sided lean-to at the back of the house. Mavis used to tease Edgar that his farming equipment got a barn of its own, but his poor truck had to sit out in the elements. Edgar always planned to finish the lean-to one day, turn it into a real garage, but he'd never gotten the chance.

The hinges on the back door squeaked and the door creaked when it opened. Mavis wouldn't be able to go outside undetected.

Before she could think too much about what she was doing, she threw open the back door and ran outside, cocking the shotgun as she went.

She half expected to get hit on the head or shot from somebody hiding in the night. When that didn't happen, she ran toward the front of the lean-to just as the truck engine finally caught.

"Hold it right there!" She jammed the butt of the shotgun against her shoulder and leveled it at the driver's side window.

Whoever was in the truck turned the headlights on. The sudden light just about blinded Mavis. Startled, she jerked her finger on the trigger, and the shotgun went off, blowing a hole in the door frame of the truck over the driver's side door.

The noise from the blast nearly deafened her. She staggered when the gun kicked back against her shoulder, but she stayed on her feet.

"Okay, okay!" She could barely hear the man's voice, but she saw him scramble down out of the truck. "Don't shoot me, lady! I didn't know anyone lived here. Just don't shoot me."

"Come out here where I can see you." She gestured with the shotgun. "Out in front of the headlights."

He was shorter than she was and looked younger by a good twenty years. His features and hair were dark, maybe Hispanic, and he had on a tattered National Guard uniform.

"What's your name?" she asked.

"Freddie Perez," he said.

"That your uniform?"

"What's left of it." He held his hands halfway up in the air. He didn't have a gun as far as she could see.

"You armed?" she asked.

He shook his head.

"Why not?"

He gave her an incredulous look. "Lady, I'm lucky I got out of there with my life, okay?"

"Out of where?"

"Davenport."

Davenport was on the Illinois border, over a hundred miles to the east.

"It's not there anymore," Perez said. "We tried to protect it, tried to get people out." He shook his head. "Look, I'm sorry I tried to steal your truck, but I gotta get back to the kids. They get scared by themselves, especially in the dark."

Kids? "What kids? Your kids?"

"No, look, can I put my hands down? I'm not gonna hurt you, I swear."

Mavis thought about it. She was going to have to trust him sooner or later. Either that, or shoot him. If she got close enough to pat him down or try to tie him up, she'd be too close to use the shotgun.

"I'll shoot you if you try anything," she said.

"I believe you."

He put his hands down slowly, then wrapped his arms around himself. Mavis was shivering too, and it wasn't just from nerves. The early morning air felt as cold as the middle of October.

"These kids," Perez said. "I found 'em about twenty miles outside Davenport, huddled up inside this empty gas station. Five of 'em, and nobody to take care of them except me. We've been doing pretty good, keeping out of sight during the day when we were closer to the combat zone, but now I figure we're far enough away, I should find them something to ride in, you know?"

Mavis let the barrel of the shotgun drop just a little. "Are you telling me you and these kids walked all the way here from Davenport?"

"Yeah, seems stupid, don't it? But it's not like people just got sick and left their stuff behind. I've been checking places that look deserted, but if the people are gone, so are their rides."

Behind Perez, Edgar's truck sat idling, eating up precious gas. Mavis thought about what she was doing for about half a second, then decided to stop thinking before she talked herself out of it.

"Get in," she told him, gesturing at the truck with the shotgun. "Let's go get your kids."

She rode in the passenger seat with the shotgun resting across her knees and the heater on the truck turned up as high as it would go. Mavis slept in a set of Edgar's thermal underwear these days, but without a coat, she was still cold.

Perez drove carefully. Probably trying to avoid ruts that might make the shotgun go off if Mavis got jostled around too much. She didn't ask him any questions, letting him concentrate on where he was going. She knew her property even in the dark, even with the corn stalks dried out and dead, but she imagined one row looked much like the next to someone who hadn't grown up on the farm.

Perez finally stopped about a hundred feet or so from where Mavis's farm road intersected with the county two-lane. He got out of the truck and whistled low.

Five children slowly appeared from the field, creeping out from between the rows of corn. They were all horribly thin. The oldest couldn't have been more than twelve, the youngest three. They stood uncertainly in the road and stared at Mavis.

She opened her door and smiled down at them. "C'mon," she said. "Get in" They eyed her shotgun and didn't move.

In for a penny, in for a pound. Another one of her daddy's sayings.

Mavis unloaded the shotgun and put it on the rack in the back window of the pickup. "Better?" she asked.

The children looked at Perez. It was pretty clear they weren't going to move unless he said it was okay.

"Where are we going?" he asked Mavis.

"Back to the farm. I've got hot water and extra beds and food, and it looks like you could use some of all three."

Perez frowned at her. "You'd share what you have with us after I tried to steal your truck?"

It's what her father would have done. It's what Edgar would have done. He'd gone to war to save people just like these kids.

"Yes," Mavis said.

***

AFTER THE KIDS had cleaned up and gone to bed, Mavis sat at her kitchen table and offered Perez a drink of whiskey. He declined.

"What's your plan with these kids?" she asked.

"Plan?" Perez looked out her kitchen window. The clouds were steel grey, dark and angry looking. The sun was up, but the day was still dark. "Get them to someplace safe. With someone who can take care of them."

Mavis nodded. "What about you?"

He shrugged. "My family was in Chicago. No reason to go back there."

Mavis felt her breath catch in her throat, and for a second she thought her heart might stop beating. "Chicago?"

He studied her face. "Yeah. Why? You got somebody there?"

"My husband. Army Reserve. His unit was headed there, four months ago."

Perez's eyes went flat, emotionless. "We started calling the guys that got here first leeches, you know, because they were sucking things dry. Made it easier to think about them like they were something we could pop with our fingers. The leeches put three of those monster ships of theirs right over Lake Michigan. When the bugs got here and saw all that water, they wanted it for themselves. The leeches, they didn't like that. Their weapons…"

Perez's voice caught in his throat. He shook his head. His eyes weren't emotionless anymore. Mavis could see him struggling for the detachment he'd had only a moment ago.

"I've seen pictures," she said as gently as her own aching heart would allow.

"I'm sorry, lady, but that ain't nothing compared to in person. Both of them, they could take out entire city blocks with one beam. Their explosive weapons vaporized everything for miles." He cleared his throat. "Davenport might be gone, but Chicago's not even a memory."

Mavis looked down at her hands. She'd clenched her fists so tight her fingers were white. Her gold wedding band dug into her skin.

"I'm sorry, ma'am," Perez said. "If your husband was there, he's gone."

Mavis nodded. She couldn't bring herself to say anything.

Tiny footsteps padded into the kitchen. Mavis and Perez turned to find the youngest of the children, a little boy, standing near the refrigerator. "Can I have a drink of water?" he asked.

Mavis shook herself. She would mourn for Edgar later. "Yes, you may," she told the little boy.

She got a plastic cup from the cupboard and ran water from the sink, then handed the cup to the boy. When he was done, Mavis asked if he needed help getting back to bed. He shook his head and wandered back down the hallway. Mavis watched him until he disappeared into the room where the rest of the children slept.

Kristine Grayson

Book Three of The Fates Trilogy
Totally Spellbound

"The spellbinding Grayson again gives readers their money's worth."
— *RT Book Reviews*

Perez was staring at her intently. "You got running water?" he asked.

"We have—" Mavis paused, then started over. "I have a well here. The turbine keeps the pump running, along with everything else."

"And you got food."

"Some." What would have been a lot for just her wouldn't be as much for another adult and five children, but it was better than nothing.

Perez got up and went over to the kitchen window. He looked out at the farm, stared at the equipment shed. At the silos.

"My unit was mostly made up of college guys," he said. "Some smart people. They didn't think this stuff was going to last forever, not like nuclear winter or anything. They kept saying 'we just gotta make it through the rough stuff,' like it wasn't going to last a lifetime, only a couple of years, or not even that long. The bugs and the leeches, they're all gone now. Some stuff ain't never coming back, but here?" He shrugged. "This is your place, so it's your say-so, but I think we could last it out right here. Rig up something in your barn so we could grow enough stuff to keep us alive until the sun comes back and it's warm enough to start growing stuff outside again. I was an Ag major back in school. I think we could figure this out."

Mavis hadn't allowed herself to think of the future. She'd lived day to day for so long, just waiting for Edgar to come home so they could get back to the lives they'd always planned, she almost couldn't comprehend the kind of life Perez was talking about.

"You don't even know me," she said.

He turned his head to look at her. He was almost as gaunt as the children, but when he smiled, Mavis thought she could see a hint of the boyish charm that must have made him a hit with the girls at school. "And you don't know me, ma'am. These kids, they didn't know me either, but I figure what's left of the world should stick together, you know? If we're gonna start over, we have to start someplace."

Start over.

"My husband used to say, when one door closes—"

"—another one opens," Perez finished. "Yeah, my mom said that, too. Drove me nuts, but I guess it sank in."

Mavis took the whiskey Perez had declined earlier out of the cupboard and poured two small shots into juice glasses. She gave one to Perez.

"No argument this time," she said.

He took the glass. She raised hers, and he followed suit.

"What are we toasting to?" he asked.

She looked out the window. It was still too dark to see the cross her father had planted so many years ago, but she knew it was there.

"To Edgar," she said. "And open doors."

I have been reading and enjoying Preston Dennett's stories since back in the early 1990s. But this is the first time I have had the pleasure of publishing an original story of his in these pages.

Besides working as a professional writer for decades in nonfiction areas, Preston is also a winner of Writers of the Future and has been selling his fiction regularly to many different magazines. I hope to have more of his great stories in these pages in coming years.

Introducing Alligators
Preston Dennett

ELINOR WAS AN older woman, and her friends thought her conservative like them. How shocked they would be to discover that she was a frequent visitor to the Peavey Clinic of Animal Impersonation. She longed to tell them of her adventures but felt quite certain that they would react badly. Perhaps not Teresa, but the others, most definitely.

"Miss Coulson," said Ginny. "Back so soon? What would you like this time?"

"What do you have available?"

"Well, we have plenty of horses, of course."

Elinor frowned. "Horses are for beginners. What else?"

"Well, we do have a new batch of gorillas. I know how you like those."

Elinor nodded. She did enjoy being a gorilla, the feeling of strength and power, and the gorilla sex was amazing. But it was the smell; she simply couldn't bear it.

"I don't think so," she said. "And if you suggest elephant, I shall walk out of here this moment." She had tried elephants but couldn't stand the feeling of that heavy trunk dangling from her face. "Do you have any bears available?"

Ginny's hands danced across the keyboard. "No, I'm afraid they're all occupied."

Elinor frowned. Bears were new, and everybody wanted to try them. Elinor found that being a bear was delightful. She adored the strength and sense of invulnerability. And yet, as a bear she felt heavy and clumsy. It wasn't quite what she was looking for.

"Perhaps you'd like to hear about our latest acquisition?"

"What's that?"

Ginny learned forward and whispered. "I'm really not supposed to say. They're introducing them into the reserve tomorrow. It's a surprise. But seeing as you're such a loyal customer—our best, I'd say—it seems only fair you get an early reservation."

"What is it?"

"Alligators," said Ginny proudly. "But I'm afraid they're quite expensive."

"Oh! Please schedule me as soon as possible."

"Don't you even want to know how much it costs?"

"You may tell me if you'd like. But it won't make a hair of a difference."

"Certainly. You really enjoy transplanting, don't you?"

"Have you ever done it?"

Ginny shook her head.

"Don't," said Elinor. "It's terribly addicting."

Ginny laughed. "See you tomorrow then?"

Elinor nodded. "Please."

***

FROM THE MOMENT she woke, Elinor knew instantly that she had finally found herself. Perhaps it was the thick scaly hide, so protective and impenetrable. Or maybe the way she felt swishing her tail. Who would have thought a tail could feel like this? Or maybe it was her massive jaws and daggered teeth. How powerful they were! But no, it was all of this and more—the sensation of cool water flowing against her sensitive stomach, the squishiness of the swampy mud, the taste of fish and small animals, the ability to hold her breath for what seemed like forever. It was as though she had finally arrived home.

She prowled the water sneakily, chomping up unsuspecting creatures. Even now, an antelope approached the water's edge, sniffing warily. Elinor waited, and snap! She clenched her jaws onto its neck and instinctively began a death roll. The antelope never had a chance. What delight she felt as she dragged its corpse into the deep water!

She found a male alligator and did things that embarrassed even her. Afterward, she lay on the bank of a small river, enjoying the feel of the sunrays beating against her hide.

Such a shame, she thought, that she couldn't remain this way forever. Being an alligator was so delightfully primitive, especially compared to the complexities of being human. It was with great regret when she saw the handlers coming for her. No matter, she thought, she could always return.

***

CORLIA GIGGLED AS Elinor plunked herself at the café table. "Oh, Elinor" she said. "Thank goodness you're here. We've been waiting for you. Marla has news and she won't say a peep until the whole gang is here."

Teresa narrowed her eyes at Elinor. Of all her friends, Teresa was the closest. Elinor had been avoiding her calls. Teresa kept asking where she was disappearing to. She couldn't keep her secret much longer. In fact, today she resolved to tell them all.

Marla beamed. With great fanfare, she unbuttoned her blouse and revealed her new tattoo: a butterfly. Corlia stared in shock. Teresa raised her eyebrows in surprise. Elinor was impressed. She didn't think Marla had the courage.

"It's one of those new animated tattoos," Marla explained. "It moves when you touch it." Marla brushed her fingers and the butterfly lit up and fluttered.

Corlia squealed with delight.

"It's beautiful," said Teresa.

Elinor nodded. "Lovely."

Teresa smiled. "I might have to get one."

Marla laughed. "Oh, you must. They are quite expensive though."

"I have news too," said Teresa, looking pointedly at Elinor. "I'm going on a cruise to the moon. I'm hoping you all can join me."

"Oh, let's do!" said Marla.

Corlia frowned. "I just couldn't."

Elinor took a deep breath. Now was as good a time as any. "I've also got news."

Teresa smiled. "Finally," she said. "I knew you were hiding something. Spill it."

"Well," Elinor said, "it's like this. I've been going to the Peavey Clinic."

"Peavey?" asked Corlia. "What's that?"

Marla shook her head.

Teresa wrinkled her brow. "I know that name." Suddenly her eyes widened. "Oh, Elinor! You're joking."

Elinor shook her head and smiled guiltily. "Now you know."

"Know what?" asked Marla. "What is the Peavey Clinic?"

Teresa could barely keep from laughing. "It's been all over the news lately. Remember? It's where people go if they want to become an animal."

Marla held her hand over her open mouth. Corlia sneered with disgust and appeared ready to retch. "Elinor, how could you? It's so disgusting."

Marla paled. "I could never."

"It's not that bad," Elinor said. "Actually, I quite like it."

"What kind of animals have you been?" asked Teresa.

"Oh, several. As long as they're big enough to hold your brain. Alligator is my favorite. They're new."

"Aren't you afraid?" asked Marla. "It sounds dangerous."

Teresa nodded. "Haven't they had some accidents there? I seem to remember hearing about that."

Elinor shrugged. "Everything has risks." She knew that some people had returned from the transplants with severe mental damage. Some had died. But the number of them was statistically insignificant. "Don't worry, I know what I'm doing."

"I hope so," said Teresa. "I don't know why you didn't tell us sooner."

"Well, I for one would never go," said Corlia. "I think it's an abomination. People should not become animals."

"That's why," said Elinor.

"Ignore her," said Teresa. "Do what you want. Just be careful, okay? It's still a new technology. I don't want you to get hurt."

"I'll be fine," said Elinor. "Don't worry."

***

ELINOR SAT IN the office of the Peavey Clinic. Doctor Dupree smiled reassuringly. "Are you sure this is what you want?"

"I'm sure," said Elinor. "I've already signed the releases. I'm aware of the risks. Let's do it."

"As long as you're certain," said Doctor Dupree.

"I am." Her only present concern was Teresa. Elinor hadn't told her yet what she was about to do. She didn't want Teresa to try and stop her. Instead, Elinor left a message to be delivered after the procedure had been completed. Teresa would be angry, but she deserved to know the truth.

***

TERESA STARED AT the fading message globe in shock. Tears flowed from her eyes. Her best and only true friend had left her. How could she do this? It was one thing to visit the clinic. But to make it permanent?

Elinor had always been strong-minded. And she was right; Teresa would have tried to stop her. Anger swirled through her. It was almost as though Elinor was dead. "You can visit me," Elinor had said in her message. "I'm still here."

Except you're a damn alligator, thought Teresa. She dried her tears. There was only one thing to do, she decided. Why wait?

***

THE YOUNG HANDSOME man smiled graciously at Teresa. "So, have you made a decision?" Jeremy asked. He wore the brown uniform of a Peavey employee.

"I'm thinking alligator," said Teresa, but I have a few questions."

"Sure," said Jeremy. "Anything."

"Where do they keep my body when I'm out."

"All patients are kept here until their visit is over."

"Actually, I have a friend. Her name was Elinor Coulson. She just became a permanent resident. Perhaps you've heard of her?"

"Oh," said Jeremy, his smile dropped for a half second before popping back into place. "That's amazing. All of us here have come to know her well. She's quite a lady."

"Yes," said Teresa. "I'd like to see her body."

Jeremy frowned. "I'm sorry, we're not allowed to do that."

She slipped a wad of cash into his hand. It was more than a thousand dollars.

Jeremy looked at it and his face turned bright red. He tried to put it back in her hands.

"Elinor was my best friend. I just want to see it for a moment."

Jeremy looked at the money and sighed. "You can't tell anybody."

"I won't. I promise."

"You're probably going to get me fired, but seeing as you're Elinor's friend, I guess I could give you a minute. Just wait here."

Moments later, Jeremy returned with another brown uniform. "Put this on and follow me. We keep the fulltime residents in a special wing. You're going to see some pretty strange things. Just act normal and don't stare." He began walking, and Teresa followed.

"You already know where she is?"

Jeremy nodded. "We only have a few dozen permanent residents at this location. See, here we are."

Jeremy led her through a door, down a corridor and into a big room with a wide hallway. On either side were large windows leading into what appeared to be spacious stalls. In each stall was a person. They sat on

the floor of the stall, or paced back and forth. Some ran in circles. Others stared at her as she walked by.

Then Teresa saw her. Elinor! She was dressed in a bra and tight bikini. She crawled along the ground on all fours, opening and closing her mouth. She looked up at Teresa.

Teresa felt her stomach turn. Could it be?

Jeremy noticed her expression and grimaced. "It's the only way we can keep their bodies active in case we need to put them back in," he explained. "Meanwhile, every brain needs a body, even alligators. This one hasn't learned to stand yet."

"This one?"

"Yes, this is the alligator section. She has only recently been introduced to being a human. I'm not sure she's happy about it."

She's not the only one, thought Teresa.

—

S. Andrew Swann has published twenty-six novels since the early 1990s, all through DAW Books. That's an amazing run with one publisher. Shows how really good of a writer he is.

I loved his short stories back in the first incarnation of this magazine, and had always hoped to publish a story of his in these pages. Thankfully, I finally get my wish now that Andrew gave me this wonderful and really twisted original story.

The Mouse Is Watching
S. Andrew Swann

"NO ONE FUCKS with the mouse!" the old man screams. He punctuates the words with a sledgehammer kick to my ribs. My body jerks against the wire binding my wrists, yanking my right shoulder out of its socket.

"The mouse sees you." He kicks me again. *"The mouse is God!"*

I only respond by coughing up some blood.

***

THE LAST CONVERSATION I ever had with Jonathan Miller was in August of 1995. It was about the mouse.

Jon was an artist I'd known since high school. He lived in about the same state he'd been living in back then. Nothing ever changed with him. Ten years I'd known him, and I was holding down a decent job with a salary and benefits, and he was still scrounging minimum-wage minimum-jobs.

Jon had dreams of being an animator, an animator for the old man. He was good enough. I'd seen his work at conventions, and it sold. Boy did it sell.

Our last conversation happened right after he sent me some pictures he'd been doing. As far as I know, it was the last stuff he ever did.

I was holding up one of the pictures and saying, "Isn't this going to get you in trouble?"

"What kind of trouble?" came Jon's answer from the opposite coast.

I rotated the picture to get a better angle. Jon had a sick sense of humor. "You know how the company is. They sue *day-care* centers, for God's sake."

"You're being paranoid."

"Not to mention the fact that the joke about the divorce is so old—" The picture had the mouse in the background standing in front of the judge saying, "No, I didn't say she was insane, I said—" Jon hadn't written the punch-line. He'd illustrated it. Every little obscene detail there in the foreground. There she was, larger than life, the mouse's wife doing the nasty. "If the company sees this they'll shit bricks."

The joke illustration was the tamest one of the lot.

"Come on, David. They ain't going to pick on me. No money. Besides, the fanzines that publish this stuff—"

"You've published this stuff? Ugh."

"It's not that bad."

"No, no, the art's good. Too good. It's like the old man himself was doing porn. But I'm just thinking of their legal department."

"Hey, the Supreme Court says parody's legal. I'm untouchable." Jon paused and said, "You've become too frightened since you got that editorial gig."

"Comes with the territory," I told him. "Comes with the territory."

***

LILLY SAID I wasn't fearful enough.

Lilly was my significant other for all of a summer two years before. I had just gotten my job and life couldn't look much better for me. But Lilly always insisted on bursting my bubble. Perhaps that's why we separated after only three months.

Lilly was a nice kid, but a little twisted. She was a soft-edged anarchist-feminist. Not the type you'd find in the Village, not shrill at all. She was very serene behind her round little glasses, as if she was a monk confident in dispensing Truth.

Not the Village, she belonged at some Midwestern liberal arts college.

I remember how I was bragging about the number of channels I'd finally landed on cable. I didn't think I was bragging, but I could finally afford that wire legally, so I guess I was. I remember how she said, "You have exactly three channels."

Just like that she said it.

By then I should have known the tone of voice. But still, I was the fool. I picked up the remote to show her exactly how many channels I could flip through.

She just said, "Look at who owns the stations."

When I got down off of my macho molehill, I checked. Stripped to basics, Lilly was right. Out of 100+ channels of TV, there are really only three companies that matter.

Lilly was right about more than TV.

***

I CAME ACROSS the book maybe a week after I talked to Jon.

I assumed it was out of the slush, even though it landed right on my desk with no explanation. I zeroed in on it immediately, despite the art department, the advertising budget, the damn schedule and the authors who decide that the schedule doesn't matter—

I picked it up even though the only time I had to read over-the-transom stuff was in my so-called free time. I read it while I was alone in my apartment for yet another weekend.

I picked it up despite the fact I didn't need another reason to be depressed.

I suppose it was the pristine white wrapper that tipped me off. Even the Post Office hadn't marred the surface. The Elvis stamps gracing the package hadn't even been canceled. I carefully stripped the wrapper and placed it in my desk. Elvis made me think of Lilly, and I could use the stamps.

The MS was something different, an anomaly. None of the first readers had gotten to it—the first readers who were supposed to separate the chaff from all the rest of the chaff. Somehow this had landed right on my desk straight from the mail.

I was hoping for a good laugh.

Instead I found every editor's wet dream.

You know the dream don't you?

The editor's reading the slush and comes across the gem of gems. The book that screams six figures and a movie deal. The book that gets the writer on the Tonight show. The book newsworthy enough to generate its own press.

All that, *and* well-written.

The kind of book that is not only inconceivable to arrive unagented, but to arrive unagented, complete, on spec. *In the slush.*

In case you don't quite understand me—

What I was reading was a ripping celebrity expose, impeccably researched, complete with sources, that was guaranteed to hit the bestseller lists for *weeks*. And it was *done*. The author had written it already. No waiting for years after blowing advance money on a juicy proposal that was just so much juice.

Closest I'd ever been to heaven.

The book was called *The Prince of Darkness.*

It was about the old man.

***

LILLY HAD TOLD me a couple of rumors about the old man and the mouse. I discounted them at the time. The sanest stories about the old man involve Hollywood power-games. He was not quite the sanitized saint that the company portrayed him as. He fed colleagues to HUAC during the red scare—while not

being above using blacklisted writers he needed. His company's vicious legal reputation started back when he was alive and at the helm.

Lilly's rumors went a little further.

She repeated the one about the old man being in cryogenic suspension under one of his theme parks. She said the company owned almost all of central Florida, and had secret deals with the federal government giving the company total autonomy over the area.

She told me about ties to organized crime, and how the company *really* dealt with video pirates overseas.

She told me that the theme park in Europe was nicknamed Mouschvitz and that employees underwent brainwashing. She said that it "was like a cult, or the marines."

She told me about all the sheets of "special" LSD the company dumped on to the market, with the mouse on the sheets.

When she started talking seriously about aliens, I began to worry about her. We broke up shortly afterward.

The book I read two years later confirmed many of the *sane* rumors. There was the HUAC, and McCarthy. No LSD. No cryogenics. It didn't say the mouse was an alien.

***

EVENTUALLY I HAD to kick the book upstairs. I copied the MS and sent it on its way. There was really no way my little imprint could handle something as big as *The Prince of Darkness*. The book needed a huge print run and marketing up the wazoo to make good on its promise.

Fortunately, my company was owned by a much bigger company that could handle a blockbuster like that.

***

LILLY HAD SAID that the difference between us and the old Soviets was that there the government owned the corporations, here the corporations owned the government. Central economy, either way.

She also said that there was really only one multinational American corporate entity. Every company had long ago merged or bought out every other company. Coke really owns Pepsi—or vice versa—and all the supposed competition is an illusion. All the money flows one way, to one place, and the ties of control are so diverse and tangled that no one really knows where that place is.

"Trust me," Lilly said. "Someone's in charge. He isn't in Washington."

***

THE DAY AFTER I sent *Prince* upstairs, Jon Miller's mother called to tell me that Jon had committed suicide. I tried to get the details from her, but she was too broken up to talk about it. I called mutual friends to find out what had happened.

Jon had wrapped picture-wire around his neck and had tied cinder blocks to his legs. Then he'd jumped from a fire escape. Someone had the bad taste to tell me that the wire had cut all the way through, allowing me to picture my high-school friend's headless corpse

spraying blood across his apartment building as it tumbled the five stories to the ground.

I was still shaking when I went into work the next day.

***

"THEY WANT YOU upstairs, David," said the secretary when I came back from lunch. I automatically headed for the publisher's office.

"No. *Up*-stairs."

***

LILLY HAD SAID that I worked for that American corporate monster, but I didn't believe her. Not until I was summoned upstairs, to the boardroom of my little publishing company's "parent." I didn't believe it until I stood face-to-face with the president of that "parent" corporation.

"Really, David." He tsked at me from across an acre of lacquer desk. In his hands he held a copy of *Prince*. "This isn't publishable material."

The man talking to me wasn't an editor. He wasn't even in publishing. I think he might have been in public relations, once.

Like a fool I said, "I don't know what you mean."

He shook his head, and to my amazement, began feeding pages into a paper shredder perched over a wastebasket. "You don't see the big picture, do you? You work for a large concern, David—can I call you David?"

The shredder sucked in a dozen pages—*shred.*

"A large concern that has *interests*, David."

Shred.

"You have a good eye. This book would make a few million for our publishing arm."

Shred.

"However, our company deals with the old man's company. We publish things for them, we distribute things for them, our media arm shows their movies."

Shred.

"If one of our concerns does *this* to the old man, do you have any idea how much our other arms might lose?"

Shred.

"Our relationship to the old man's company is worth hundreds of millions, maybe billions. Compared to that—"

He fed in the last page. *Shred.*

"—this is garbage. I won't even mention lawsuits. Of which you should be quite aware." He folded his hands. "I'd suggest you write the author a nice letter, declining the manuscript."

I was too stunned to do anything else but nod. As I walked to the door I heard him say, "If you can, try and discourage him from marketing this kind of stuff any further."

When I got down to my office I committed the only courageous act of my life. I wrote my resignation.

***

YOU SEE, I had the manuscript, the original. Sure, the publishing industry is terribly incestuous and, after the rash of mergers over the past few years, it was easy to believe Lilly's accusation that it was all just one massive company. Despite that, I knew, just knew, that someone was going to bite on this manuscript a few megabucks worth. I wanted a piece. I was pretty damn sure I could get on board as agent of record if I could just talk to the author.

After all, I knew this town and I had a mental list of people who would just drool over this MS.

After a hit like *Prince* I could probably write my own ticket.

I got the manuscript home and noticed that the fool author had left his address off of the title page.

No address there, and the fool had left out an return envelope!

"*Fuck.*"

I cursed fate as I upended all the garbage in my apartment. A damn blockbuster, million-seller, number one on the lists, and the author leaves his address off of the damn book.

I wanted to strangle someone.

Eventually I remembered the Elvis stamps I was saving. I retrieved the original wrapper from my desk. Now I had a return address. Orlando. Immediately I call information. Immediately I find that the author's phone number is unlisted.

I could feel *Prince* slipping away. It felt like I was drowning. This book was all I had. I just quit my job over it. And this writer, W.D. Michael, had probably peppered Manhattan with this book.

I was lost.

***

HALFWAY INTO A suicidal depression I realized that multiple submits or not, I was ahead of the game. Any other unsolicited packages would still be in other editor's slush, and, without an agent, most of those packages would never be opened. And with Michael's unprofessional habit of no SASE and no address on the MS, no one would know who the hell wrote it—unless they saved the wrapper.

And even if, *even if*, someone found the old wrapper, no phone number.

If I wanted to blow money on a plane trip, I still had a chance. Meet this guy in person and hash out a deal before someone realized how hot this property really was.

***

LILLY HAD SAID that there was no such thing as coincidence.

I should have realized something was wrong as soon as I saw the Orlando address. I *really* should have known it when the in-flight movie was one from the old man's company.

Sometimes it's easy to forget—that's what they do, make movies.

***

YOU CAN FEEL it, on the hot streets of Orlando, the mouse watching you.

***

I SHOWED UP at the house, manuscript in hand. I drove a rented car miles through Orlando looking for W.D. Michael's house. The street he lived on didn't show on my AAA map, so it was twilight when I finally found it.

I was glad the sun had set. It wasn't quite as sweltering when I stepped out of the air-conditioning. Even so, I think I lost about a half-pound worth of sweat walking to the front door.

As I walked to the door I noticed how silent this neighborhood was. No traffic, no radios, no lights except for the ranch house in front of me. I seemed to be in some real-estate development that was somehow never quite populated. I decided it was some bogus S&L investment and that someone wrote off a hell of a loss on his taxes.

Probably a congressman.

I knocked on the door, and it opened.

And there, standing in front of me with no hint of cryogenic preservation was the old

man, maker of cartoons, founder of an empire. He smiled at me, said, "Hello, David."

Then he pistol-whipped me with a .44 Magnum revolver and my lights went out.

***

AT ONE POINT I had tried logic on Lilly. Of course it didn't work.

"All these conspiracies, they'd make one hell of an exposé. The news should be all over them—"

"The news is owned."

"What about the first amendment?"

"All that says is that 'Congress shall make no law.' This isn't law, David. This is money. Money is much more the tyrant."

"If someone publishes, they'll make a bundle—"

"More people, bigger people, will lose. Stories are killed all the time. Books are killed all the time."

"That isn't true—"

"*The Spirit of Crazy Horse.*"

That was the first title she came up with. Hell, it was one I told her about. A book about the railroading of Leonard Peltier, an activist in the American Indian Movement. The book, shortly after publication, was withdrawn and all the warehoused copies were destroyed. It stayed out of print for seven years, and Leonard Peltier served another seven in prison.

"They made a movie about—"

"Long after. And Peltier's still in prison."

I still kept objecting. In response she came up with a lot more titles. A lot more stories. Stories about the CIA. Stories about organized crime. Stories about UFOs.

Stories about the old man.

***

I WOKE UP inside a nearly empty room. I was on the ground, my hands and feet wired together. There was no sign of the manuscript. The side of my face, where the gun had struck me, felt soggy and stuffed with cotton. My tongue was thick, and my teeth felt loose.

The old man sat on a folding director's chair, facing me.

There were cops here, Orlando city police, uniforms and all. They watched out the windows. None looked in my direction.

"Good morning, David."

"What's going on?"

The old man shook his head and stood up. He placed the gun on the director's chair. "Just a little betrayal, David."

"Huh?"

"Why do you hate me? Have I given you reason? Have I given anyone reason?" The look in the old man's eyes was scary. The shiny faraway look you see in the eyes of cult leaders and serial killers. "I make children happy, David. Do you hate the children?"

I stared at him in shock. I was still absorbing the fact that the old man was still alive.

"*I asked you a question!*" With no warning at all, his foot slammed into my groin. "*Do you hate the children?*"

***

THE CHILDREN.

Every dictator, every tyrant, every ideologue, they all want their hands on the children. Hitler, Stalin, Mao, all want the young people.

The Greeks knew this. That's why Socrates bought it.

***

WHEN MY VISION cleared, the old man was shoving papers in my face. I could barely see what they were. One eye was swollen shut. It took a moment for me to focus.

There was the mouse, going down on his female counterpart. Her little dress was hiked up over her head and her words were, ". . . and I thought you were a titmouse."

"This, this, *filth*!" The old man screamed, kicking me again.

I moaned. The old man was showing me Jon's pictures. The pictures Jon'd sent me. Suddenly I was picturing Jon's headless body again. Tumbling. Tumbling.

The old man tore the picture in half, *shred.*

"This is like pissing on the flag, David."

Shred.

"I didn't want to believe that one of my people was involved in something this disgusting."

Shred.

"I'm not your person."

The old man laughed. "You naïve little imbecile. Who do you think owns your tawdry little publishing house?" The old man knelt and grabbed my hair and stared into my good eye. "Who do you think owns the apartment you live in, the credit cards you use, the airline you flew here on. *Who do you think owns this city?*"

With the cops staring out the windows around me, it was kind of obvious. I gathered my courage to ask, "What'd you do to Michael?"

He threw my head down hard enough to bounce off the hardwood floor. My vision starred and I tasted fresh blood in my mouth.

"You don't get it, David? I'm Michael."

"Oh Shit," I whispered.

"Michael doesn't exist. Michael is only a test. A test for people like you. You should have been loyal, David. If you'd buried the book like you were told—the way most people end up doing—we might have forgiven the fact you'd ever known Jonathan Miller."

The old man shook his head a little sadly. "You see. *No one fucks with the mouse!*" He kicked my ribs. "*The mouse sees you.*" He kicked me again. "*The mouse is God!*"

***

I'VE BEEN IN the Orlando training camp for a year now.

When it's all over they'll have me wear a dwarf costume and greet people at the gate.

Lilly was right, maybe not in the details, but she was right. Everything flows back here, to Orlando, to the old man. However, I understand it all now. I accept it.

This sick country *needs* the old man.

He is waiting. The old man survives by using the same technology that provides the android displays for his theme parks. This same technology he's used to gain the support of actors and presidents. He waits as his company becomes a vital part of this country. *Becomes* this country.

Not yet.

But soon.

There is no God but the mouse, and the old man is his prophet.

Come judgment day, the mouse will walk Christlike out of Orlando, the old man at his right hand.

The old man will take us all to the promised land.

The promised land is a theme park.

And the mouse is its God.

"What do you mean it's Summer? Winter just ended!"

Veteran short fiction writer Rob Vagle has been selling his wonderful stories for decades to all sorts of magazines. In fact, we have been honored to have five of his stories so far in Fiction River. *And this is his third story in these pages.*

His stories always have a gentle, but twisted, feel to them that I love. This original story is no exception. Enjoy.

Dreams of Memories Never Lived
Rob Vagle

DETAILS OF DOM'S entire life came spinning around him like crazy sideshow mirrors. Some things were familiar, yet many of the images were distorted, unfamiliar, some out of place.

Then they were gone and he stood at one end of a casket. The lid was open and the body inside looked like his younger self, back in the days when he had a thick mane of red hair. His long hair pooled against the white pillow, underneath his shoulders, dressed in a black suit. A green gem glittered in his left ear and Dom couldn't remember having a pierced ear. The young Dom in the casket couldn't be older than late twenties or maybe early thirties. In Dom's opinion, when you're in a coffin you don't look any particular age. The age you looked was dead.

The trouble was Dom had died at the age of sixty-four, which was still too soon. He had died in his own bed, heart attack. He still had the red hair, although cut short.

Then why was this young version of him inside the casket?

People were whispering around him and talking in hushed tones. One person was sobbing. He smelled lilacs and an old odor of pot.

Rows of chairs were lined up in the room, all cushioned with red velvet. Young Dom had dozens of mourners and almost nobody over the age of forty. His own mother was one exception. She sat in the front row wearing a navy blue dress, her red hair cut short and she held a tissue to her red nose. She had been the one sobbing.

This confused him like seeing the pierced ear. His mother had died when Dom was forty-two.

The ceiling vaulted twenty feet high with four chandeliers dangling, shedding light on the mourners. The wallpaper was a pastel blue. Huge bronze flower vases flanked the wide doorway. This place looked high-end expensive. He smelled money and he never had a lot of it. This place smelled wrong. Except for the old smell of pot—that was prevalent in his youth.

When he looked at the other mourners he didn't recognize anyone. They were strangers, many dressed in trench coats.

"Who are you people?" he asked.

Not a soul glanced up at him.

But he noticed his voice had sounded hollow and far away as if he called from inside a well.

He stepped away from the casket on a plush white carpet. He stood over his mother but she didn't notice him standing there, so he walked on by and down the aisle leading to the wide doorway. People were standing in the doorway and along the aisle. Dom raised a hand, ready to tap someone on the shoulder when he was distracted by the girl coming into the room.

She was a teenager with strawberry blond hair swishing across her shoulders at every turn of her head. She moved like a pinball from person to person, tapping them with one finger and the person shuddered as if someone had goosed them.

She used both hands, index finger pointed, unbending the elbow, lashing out, touching a shoulder, a back, even someone's derriere.

She moved through the crowd, wreaking havoc with the piston action of her arms, tapping, tapping, tapping. She laughed gleefully at every shudder she caused, laughed manically at every "Oh!" she elicited with her touch.

It was like a catchy yawn that moved through the room.

Anyone she touched looked around themselves, not seeing her.

She was invisible, like Dom was, yet she could make everyone feel her, like the touch of the dead.

She made her way down the aisle toward him. He stared at her face and willed her to make eye contact. If the two of them were invisible to everyone else here, he reasoned, then the two of them should be visible to each other.

When the girl finally faced Dom with a finger ready to strike like a poised snake, she took note of him, her face darkened, that bright smile snuffed out like a candle flame. She grew pale, her eyes as large as saucers. Her mouth hung open and a frightful moan escaped.

Dom was not prepared for what she said next.

"Dad."

She back-pedaled away and bumped into a man and a woman holding hands, eliciting squeals from the both of them. "Omigod, dad," she said again before tearing her attention away from him and fleeing the room.

He stood there stunned. Did he look like her father? Like the pierced ear, he couldn't remember having a daughter.

"Wait, young lady, come back!"

He weaved his way through the crowd, careful not to touch anyone. The poor souls had had enough shivers. He smelled Old Spice and perfume that smelled like lilies. He went through the doorway and into the hall, but the girl was long gone and no clue which direction she went. Apparently, when she fled, she had stopped sending shivers through people. And the hallway was filled with wandering men and women dressed in grays, blues, and blacks. Some entered doorways along the walls, while others exited them into the hallway. Sobbing came from many of the doorways.

In both directions, the hallway seemed to go on forever. Dom couldn't see an end. The carpet here was red, the baseboards a soothing blue. The wallpaper was beige with green chevrons.

He felt disoriented and lost in the hallway, uncertain which way to go. Once, when he was a teenager on a trip to Yosemite, he'd gotten separated from his friends. One moment, one wrong turn, and the forest closed in on him like it swallowed him up. He couldn't decipher which direction was the campsite and panic seized his throat, turning his mouth dry. That feeling returned in the hallway that seemed to stretch into infinity.

Two women wearing veils (did anyone really wear those anymore?) bore down on him and he pressed his back against the wall to let them pass.

A man with salt and pepper hair, mustache, and wearing a gray suit and fedora, stepped up to Dom and he realized the man could see him. The man had pale blue eyes and a blue handkerchief to match in his lapel pocket. Looking into the man's eyes, Dom thought he was looking at a dead ringer for young Frank Sinatra.

"You're one of the lost ones," the man said and he smiled with bright white teeth, but all they made Dom think of were a row of tombstones.

"You can see me," Dom said. "I just scared the bejeesus out of a girl when she noticed me."

The man frowned, sharp creases between his brow. Then his expression changed back to a smile and he waved his hand at the hallway. "Welcome to Infinity Funeral Home & Mortuary, where everybody who ever was comes to die."

Dom's lips moved as he silently repeated the name. *Infinity Funeral Home where everybody who ever was comes to die.*

Laughter carried from one of the nearby rooms, a break from the sobbing heard from most of the other doorways. The air smelled pungent with perfume and air freshener, almost a sterile and disinfectant smell one would find in a hospital, and he didn't know why that would be. When he glanced at the ceiling, it vaulted high like a Cathedral with the chandeliers hanging by chains.

"You're a ghost here," the man said. "One of the spirits who haunt these halls and rooms, lost until you find what you're looking for."

"What am I looking for? What am I doing here? Seriously, because I don't have a clue."

"You're looking for your daughter, of course," the man said.

Dom knew he wasn't dreaming. The pain in his chest and arm came rushing back to him like he was reliving it. His life had been a quiet one working as lead mechanic in the fleet department of facilities maintenance at the University of Oregon. He had been divorced from Juliet for ten years. They had no children. He liked to drink beer on the weekends and explore the Oregon coast. Again, there had been no children. He was sure of that, just as he was sure he'd never had a pierced ear and his mother was dead before he was forty-two.

"I can understand your confusion," the man said.

"Thanks for small miracles."

The man reached inside his lapel pocket and pulled out what looked like a Polaroid picture. "This will help me explain," the man said.

Dom held the picture in his hand but he couldn't believe what he was seeing. A younger Dom—just like the one in the casket in the room back there—held an infant in his arms. The infant had a tuft of fiery red hair just like the young Dom."

"Her hair changed color as she got older," the man said and Dom clenched his jaw, irritated by the way the man could read his thoughts.

"I don't have a daughter," Dom said. "This could be a picture of me holding someone else's child."

The man was undeterred. "That picture is of you and the girl you say you scared the bejeesus out of. Her name is Charity. Her mother is Cindy Swenson…"

Dom didn't hear the rest of what the man had to say. He remembered blond-haired Cindy who he dated for two years in his early thirties. She was a part-time student at the community college while working full time as a receptionist at Wayne's Garage. That's where he had met her. They had two wonderful years for the most part. He remembered he had been irritated by how busy she was and how it annoyed him.

"You married her," the man said. "A year later Charity was born."

None of this made sense to Dom. Why was he hearing this, all of the *what could have beens* and *might have beens*.

Dom shook the Polaroid. "Just tell me what the hell is going on here."

The man snatched the picture from his hand and it disappeared in his lapel pocket once again. "Charity needs your help, sir. She died in a car accident the morning after her senior prom."

"That's terrible," Dom said.

"She needs your help to move on."

***

CHARITY RAN DOWN an endless, carpeted hallway, her feet nothing but dull thumps like tiny fists against the floor. The hallway stretched on, full of light, much like the proverbial tunnel of light, which made her think about her death and she shook her head as she ran. She ran past women wearing burkas and a young man in a black leather jacket who fell to his knees, his sobbing wringing out the last drops of emotion from her heart.

She didn't think she could cry anymore, thought her eyes had all dried up. For a brief moment she had been having fun, learning she could make people squeal here with her touch. That's because they couldn't see her. Then she had seen her father. Her dead father. The father she hadn't known because he'd died when she wasn't even two. She only knew her father from pictures and the one who'd seen her (in a place where nobody else could) was him.

THE UNJUST, DUST, AND HOPE

The town of Dobson in the Arizona territory, February 5th, 1877.

Cleve Biddle begins not only his story, but also one of injustice.

Cleve sees a dark future for America already filled with lynchings and Black Laws. Otis, the clairvoyant, believes mankind will come to their better natures. These two men with memories of enslavement face the impossible in the desert and an uncertain future.

www.robvagle.com

Tears rolled down to her lips and she tasted salt. And before a sob broke from her throat, she jammed her right hand against her mouth.

She passed arched doorways, some made of wood, some of concrete, some of brass, some of adobe, every single one led into a room where the dead lay in a coffin.

She spotted a small stone doorway between two wider and more elegant doorways—there were Chinese characters on one, maybe Arabic on the other, whatever. She dashed through the stone doorway and down concrete stairs lit by bare bulbs dotting a brick wall. At the bottom, her feet slapped solidly on white linoleum, the room lit with bright fluorescent light. The room was lined with stainless steel counters and glass cabinets. It smelled of disinfectant and a harsh smell she couldn't place. And in the middle of the room was one stainless steel table with a body shrouded with a sheet. She backed away until she hit a brick wall and slid down to the floor and cowered next to a desk with metal drawers. At least the place was cool and dank, away from the lightness upstairs. Away from people sobbing.

A woman carrying a clipboard entered the room through a door at the back. She was tall and heavyset with thick black hair tied in a bun. She wore glasses and a long white coat.

She walked to the body shrouded on the table. When she put the clipboard down it snapped against the stainless steel surface. The woman pulled at the sheet and folded it back, revealing a face Charity recognized in the mirror.

Charity pushed herself up, her back sliding up the wall. Her body was on the table. Her doppelganger's face was pale.

The woman noticed her and said, "You again."

"Me again?" Charity said.

"You're dead, honey," the woman said. "Shouldn't you be upstairs?"

Charity bolted around the table, running straight for the door the woman had entered.

There had to be a way out of this place. If she didn't stay here, she wouldn't be dead. If she didn't stay here, she wouldn't be with the dead like her father.

"Stop!" The woman's voice was loud in the basement.

The door looked heavy duty, metal, like it was for a walk in freezer, painted black. Charity pulled at the door handle and air pungent with dead leaves wafted in her face.

"Don't go out there, honey," the woman said.

Charity ran, leaving the door open behind her. Ahead, there was a trail made of yellow sand. She ran. Her feet sank with every step but after a few strides, she was sprinting down that road, the yellow sand kicking off the soles of her shoes.

It was dark outside with a million pinpoints of light in the starry sky. She had never seen so many stars, so many of them close together, packed into the night sky to light up the sand she ran on.

Death would not have her. Not today.

So she ran.

***

"WHY ME?" DOM asked. Thinking about it all made his head hurt. "I'm the wrong father. I'm not the one who died after she was born, I'm the one who never got married to Cindy, never had a child, and died just short of my retirement."

"Because you're here," the man said. "You're who she bumped into. Like all intersections in your life they come at you. You have a choice where to turn. It's the same in death. You have the opportunity to save a daughter you never knew."

"You said I have a choice," Dom said. "It's one I don't understand in this place. I'd sooner go on my way, shed this mortal coil, so to speak."

"Your choice is this, sir. Save Charity and the two of you move on. Don't save her and you'll roam these hallways for eternity.

Those are the choices. Only one of them will result in moving on."

"You got me between a rock and hard place," Dom said.

"Don't be so melodramatic," the man said.

"I don't know where to find her," Dom said, hoping that might settle things.

"She's outside of this place now," the man said.

"Lucky her," Dom mumbled.

"It's not a good place to be. Shall I take you there?"

Dom looked down both ends of the hallway. No end in sight, this place was filled with one funeral after another. That could be his eternity. He wasn't sure what was next, but it sure in hell wouldn't be this.

"Alright," Dom said. "Take me there."

***

CHARITY STOPPED.

She grabbed her knees, bent at the waist, breathing hard and fast. When she looked back at the way she had come, the building with the dead was massive. It was taller than any skyscraper she'd ever seen. As she craned he neck up to look, she couldn't see an end, only floor after floor into the starry sky.

That was just the height of it. The building itself, like the hallways, went on forever in both directions.

"Well, duh," Charity whispered between breaths.

The building was dark brick with lighted windows and every single one was lit up. She wondered about the size of the building and if she could even call it one. It was more like a wall or something impossible to pin down. Something impossible to name.

Then there was the fact she had been running toward the same thing she'd been running from, for the sand road ended at what looked like the exact same building.

There were two sets of prints behind her. One trailing out and one trailing back to where she was standing. There was only one set of footprints coming from the door.

She straightened her back and looked at the same metal door she had run out of, the one that looked like something that belonged in a restaurant kitchen. Was it really the same one? Or an identical one? In this place it was impossible to be sure.

The same light was above the door, the one with the slanted shade. At least she thought she remembered it slanted. She remembered the way the edge of the light angled across the sand path.

As she stared at the light, the door swung open and her father came outside.

He saw her standing there, didn't seem surprised, and gave a small wave. "Can I talk to you?" he asked as if this was all totally normal.

She wanted to run again, could feel her leg muscles twitch. Instead, she crossed her arms and watched him walk to her through the sand.

She wanted to be wrong about this man being her father. Because if it was her dead father, it would just cement the idea more in her mind. She was dead, the morning after prom. She'd never kiss Justin again, never go off to college. She hadn't found out where that might be.

As she thought these things, she wondered why she was denying it. She was in a place for the dead. She was dead. Dead. Dead. Dead.

The evidence was everywhere.

"This is rather awkward," he said as he reached her.

He raised his arm as if he might touch her or put an arm around her shoulders, but she hunched her shoulders and stepped back.

"Don't touch me," she said.

He raised his hands as if to give up. "Sorry. Sorry."

Then they stood there in silence.

She wondered why her father was here. He'd been dead for over fifteen years. He should be long gone. He wouldn't look her in the face. Instead, he looked to the sky and marveled at the stars like she had.

"Why are you here?" she asked.

"I came here to find you."

"No," she said. "Why were you in this place? You've been dead a long time."

He laughed. It was a forced laugh, but the way his facial muscles twitched triggered a memory. She remembered her father laughing. She was looking up at him as he laughed at something someone—her mother?—said.

"I don't think I have to tell you things don't work the same here as it does in, well, life," he said. "I can't figure it out and I don't have an answer for you."

"Is there something you wanted to tell me? You came out here looking for me."

He glanced back at the door and turned back to her, leaning in. "Do I really look like your father?" he asked.

"Just like in the picture," she said.

"I feel young, I feel good. I didn't find a mirror inside so I couldn't check myself out."

"What are you talking about?"

He closed his lips, took a breath through his nose. "Charity, I'm not exactly your father."

"Not exactly? How does that work?"

"I am Dom, your father. DNA would prove it. But the way things work here? I come from a life where I died in bed from a heart attack at the age of sixty-four. In another life, I married your mother, Cindy, and you were born."

"You don't look old. You could be my older brother."

His face blushed at that. "Believe me, I'm older than dirt. Why you see me just the way I was in your life, I can't explain."

"That's the theme here," she said. "Nothing makes sense."

"Definitely."

"You didn't have to talk to me," she said.

"No. No I didn't," he said.

"Thank you for being honest," she said.

"You're too big for me to wrap my head around," he said.

"What?"

"You could have been my daughter if other choices were made. It's one thing to think it, but to have you standing in front of me is quite another."

This made her think about her death again. She was driving from Samantha's house where the whole gang had stayed up past dawn. She left after eleven in the morning and felt wide awake. She didn't have to leave, but she did.

She didn't see the van come around the curve until it struck the driver side.

She shook her head, not wanting to think about it.

"I had a Honda Civic," she said. "Mom said you loved those cars, that you liked to trick them out and detail them."

He beamed and that triggered that memory again of him smiling and laughing.

"Those are dependable cars. I was driving one when I was with your mother."

She nodded, excited. "A red one. You found some Radio Flyer decals and stuck one on each side of the car, on the doors."

"That's right. She told you," he said.

She felt giddy and on the verge of tears, yet she couldn't stop herself from talking.

"Mom got me a used Honda Civic for my sixteenth birthday," she said. "It was white but we got it painted red."

The tears were brimming in her eyes and she wiped at her face.

"That's sweet. Why are you crying?"

She replied with her hands covering her face. "We put on Radio Flyer decals," she said.

"Charity, are you okay?"

"I died in that car, dad."

She hid her tears behind her hands. She couldn't look at him and didn't know why she had told him that. It was punch in the forefront of her brain that she was dead. It just so happened that car was the embodiment of her father's memory.

The same man who stood in front of her.

"I'm sorry," she said.

"You have nothing to be sorry about," he said.

When she removed her hands from her face he was standing closer to her with a look of concern.

"What's going to happen to us?" she asked.

Her father looked back at the door to the building and said, "Daughter, first things first. We're going inside there and we're going to give everyone, and I do mean everyone, a good dose of the chills."

She laughed and the good humor sliced through her sorrow. She dropped her hands.

"That'll take eternity," she said.

"We better get started," he said.

He offered his arm by jutting out his elbow and Charity latched onto it.

They giggled as they walked back into the Infinity Funeral Home, their choices made.

They might as well laugh a little longer.

Death could wait.

—

Latest From Fiction River Presents

David H. Hendrickson sometimes leaves his award-winning mystery worlds and ventures over into fantasy. Really twisted and fun fantasy. Which is great for this magazine.

His short fiction has appeared in Best American Mystery Stories 2018, Ellery Queen's Mystery Magazine, Heart's Kiss, *and numerous anthologies, including over a half dozen issues of* Fiction River.

Dave has also, besides his wonderful novels and short stories, published over fifteen hundred works of nonfiction, most notably his first book for writers, How to Get Your Book into Schools and Double Your Income with Volume Sales, *and also* Travis Roy: Quadriplegia and a Life of Purpose. *He has been honored with the Joe Concannon Hockey East Media Award and the Murray Kramer Scarlet Quill Award.*

A Pathetic Excuse for a Dragon
David H. Hendrickson

A PATHETIC EXCUSE for a Dragon. That's me. Even my name, Dullah, is boring and pathetic. What dragon parents name their daughter Dullah? Perceptive ones, apparently.

You've heard all the stories about heroic and terrifying dragons, and most of them are true. Dragons like my beloved Phillippo fly through the air, flapping their mighty wings with such force that the air audibly cracks as it compresses beneath them. And when they bellow their fury, a blaze of fire shoots out of their fearsome, jagged-toothed mouths, turning everything in its path into charcoal.

The only fire that comes out of me is a day or two after I eat Szechuan.

I can't fly either. I know there are serpentine beasts in China, Japan, and throughout the Far East that are referred to as dragons yet have no wings, so they also can't fly. But I roam no further east than the Maine coastline, and I do have wings, but they are as useless as a human's umbrella in a tornado. Something in both wings broke either during my birth or shortly thereafter. Their bony supporting structure tilts at all the wrong angles. When I extend my wings, they form Vs, so instead of pushing the air beneath me as normal wings would do, they allow the air to rush uselessly past them, up both sides of the V. As one of my childhood tormentors once said, air goes through my wings, "like shit through a goose."

I will never know what it is like to fly, like the rest of my kind. Like my strong and powerful Phillippo. My twenty-foot-long, gray scaly form—the last six feet of which is my tail—will never soar high into the air, up above the rooftops in the cities and the treetops in the country. I will never celebrate that freedom. I will always be chained by gravity to the earth I walk on with padded feet.

And I will always be at risk of capture by humans, since I cannot escape by flying away. It is why the rest of my flock and family abandoned me. For the greater good, I was sacrificed. It was said that I have a good heart and a sharp mind, but a good heart is rarely a positive survival trait. And while a good mind has great advantages, mine is trapped in my Earth-bound, quite useless body.

I expected my parents' betrayal. They were humiliated by my ugly uselessness, at my inability to do what all others in our flock could do. My mother was the greatest flier of them all. She could climb effortlessly and soar with an unmatched grace. But in her eyes, my infirmity also diminished her. So when I grew to the point where they could no longer carry me where we needed to go, they rid themselves of me without hesitation.

What hurt more—infinitely more—was Phillippo leaving with the rest of the flock, and without even saying good-bye.

My Phillippo. Strong wings, a wide, muscular back, a thin nose, and gorgeous blood-red eyes. I had thought he looked my way with affection, and laughed heartily at my jokes.

But I was deluded. There is nothing funny about a fireless dragon who cannot fly. No reason to show affection to the most pathetic excuse for a dragon ever. I had mistaken affection for pity.

As winter fell and the flock abandoned me, it apparently assumed that I would quickly die of hunger or be captured. But I made my lair in a cave cut into a secluded hillside, and I learned to forage in the dead of night, mostly from the dumpsters

of three trendy, eccentric restaurants, all tucked away within a half mile of each other along an otherwise wooded stretch of a small two-lane road that meanders up from Massachusetts, through New Hampshire, and into Maine. Young people, thinking themselves hip to have found such out-of-the way treasures, keep these places in business, and allow me to fill my belly with their refuse.

It's garbage, but hey, at least it ain't McDonald's.

***

It's a lonely existence. I avoid human detection at all costs, of course, and most of the birds that once filled the now-gnarled and barren branches of the oaks and white birches that dot the hillside have flown south to warmer climes. Even the black bears that roam the surrounding forest have hibernated, some in caves much like my own except for their smaller size.

I still smell the scent of the pine trees, and a few birds and an occasional wolf still remain, but as I make my way back to my lair from a night of foraging, the snow crunching beneath my weight, I'm struck by an overwhelming loneliness and a need to be with others of my kind.

Be with Phillippo. My Phillippo, who was never really my Phillippo at all. Because I am Dullah, a pathetic excuse for a dragon, no more magical than a giant wild boar, and my fate is to live out my days alone.

I try to cheer myself with pleasant lies of how I enjoy my solitude—I relish it!—and how it offers me a freedom I would have to sacrifice to be part of a flock. But the very thought of swallowing those lies, like a fish gulping down a tasty worm that covers a sharp hook that will tear it apart, saddens me to the point of tears.

I hate being alone. I hate that I cannot fly or belch gusts of fire like any true,

self-respecting dragon. I hate that I am the most pathetic excuse for a dragon ever.

I hate being me.

***

As if in answer to my anguished plea—or if I'm honest, to my wallowing in self-pity—Phillippo appears at dusk the next evening. He is waiting for me when I awake, with a freshly killed gray wolf.

When I smell the blood, the heavy lids of my eyes shoot wide open. I am on instant alert, only one step removed from panic.

And then I see him. *Phillippo.* Strong, leathery wings. Muscular back. Thin nose and gorgeous blood-red eyes.

My Phillippo. Even though he wasn't mine.

"What are you doing here?" I ask.

"Isn't it obvious?" he says, a smile forming at both sides of his mouth. "I had thought you were the most intelligent of our flock. That question makes me think I must have been mistaken."

"But…"

"I am here for you," he says. He looks about. "There is hardly another living thing in sight, so of course, I am here for you."

My heart beats faster. "But why?" I ask, and instantly regret the words. Phillippo and his gorgeous blood-red eyes have returned for me. *For me.* Why question what Providence has brought back to my doorstep? But he answers my question anyway, and in the most amazing way possible.

"Because I never wanted to leave you," he says, and looks away guiltily. "My parents forced me to continue with the flock. I was of the age where I could not defy them. So I put this location into my heart, and knew I would return, hoping only that I would find you and that you would be well."

"But I cannot fly," I said, dumbfounded. "I can breathe no flames of fire. I am the—"

I am about to say that I am the most pathetic dragon ever, so useless that the rest of the flock left me to die. As if he has forgotten. But he doesn't allow me to say the words.

"You are beautiful even though you cannot fly, and even though you breathe no flames. Your intelligence and quick wit make you beautiful in ways that others with their perfect wings are not."

"*Me? Beautiful?*"

His smile broadens from pointed ear to pointed ear, exposing his razor-sharp teeth. "Yes, although if you keep insisting on how unworthy you are, I just might begin to believe you."

"No, no, no, no!" I say, finally getting my wits about me. "I had just given up hope that you cared for me. I had given up hope that *anyone* cared for me, but especially you. I have been alone for what feels like such a very long time."

"You will be alone no more," Phillippo says, and bows his head meekly. "I love you, Dullah." And when he says my name, he makes it sound exotic. "If you will have me."

"Of course, I will have you, Phillippo. Yes, yes, yes."

"Then let us eat." He looks to the side, at the gray wolf, and breathes out hot fire, as if warming up. "How do you like your wolf?"

After what has felt like an eternity of foraging food from dumpsters, it takes me no time to reply.

"Extra crispy and crunchy on the outside. Pink in the middle."

~

Jason A. Adams makes his debut in these pages with a powerful look at one of the great moments in history, when the Moulin Rouge opened in Las Vegas.

Jason makes that opening night come alive, and he gives the entire story heart, as well as a sense of history.

Might want to look up the Moulin Rouge after reading this story and learn about its amazing and very short history and how that history and memory was kept alive through the decades. Jason got it right, every detail. Amazing story, just amazing.

Moulin Rouge
Jason A. Adams

SOME THINGS ONLY make sense in Las Vegas.

Johnny Bianchi walked through the huge crowd milling through the ruins of the Moulin Rouge, one of Vegas' most famous casinos. Famous even though it had closed six months after opening, way back in 1955.

All around him the huge Gaming Night party roared, a whirl of lights, colors, and noise. The Rouge still kept its gambling license all these years later, although not much of the original buildings remained. The Nevada Gaming Commission allowed it so long as the establishment "conducted routine gaming business not less than once every two calendar years."

Thus, the party. Tonight, a large flatbed truck sat parked amid the charred embers and toppled masonry of the old casino, which finally succumbed to repeated arsons back in 2003. Inside the shipping container the truck carried a miniature casino. A row of sixteen video poker machines, but more gambling action than the place had seen for, well, two years.

Kiddie machines which most residents left to the tourists, but the gambling wasn't the point at all.

Johnny had been sent by the Las Vegas Sun to write a byline about the event, something upbeat to counter all the depressing shit coming from the other side of the country. This would be his third assignment to cover the Moulin Rouge Gaming Night extravaganza, but he'd come even if it weren't his job. He loved it.

Cool breezes rolled down from the surrounding mountains, carrying the resinous scent of desert creosote and competing with the heat radiating up from the sun-baked pavement. Johnny, like most locals, wore tough leather sandals on his feet and a windbreaker jacket. New arrivals were often shocked by the thirty or forty degree drop in temperature that hit pretty much as soon as the sun fell behind Mount Charleston to the west of the city, but the streets and sidewalks spent the night paying out stored-up energy, like an oven underfoot.

Amazing how eighty degrees can feel chilly.

Most of the people here were either locals or out-of-town history buffs. The glut of visitors to the Strip or the classic old casinos downtown didn't know the Rouge existed. But it was a legend among people in the know.

Even the original funky deco sign had been trucked in from the Neon Graveyard. Johnny had loved that sign as a kid. The swooping Modernist letters could be seen where I-95 crossed over Bonanza back then, and he never failed to ask his dad about them on the days the family drove to Nellis from their cheap, dusty split-level out toward Red Rock Canyon. Now the sign blazed again for this one night, a thousand tiny yellow incandescent bulbs competing with the glow of neon and giant LED boards on the downtown casinos built by Benny Binion, and further off, the gambling cathedrals on the Strip built by Bugsy Siegel and his pals.

Maybe five thousand people milled around the trucks. Not many fed coins into the machines; most were here for the party.

White people, black people, people with Asian faces, Chicanos…everyone rubbed shoulders at the bar, the water stations, and the church-feed style dining tables loaded with tart-sweet apple fritters and other Las Vegas comfort foods. They laughed together, shouted encouragements and toasts, celebrated community. Some danced to the music thundering out from the giant sound system provided by KOMP, loud enough to drown out the freeway noise and the occasional fighter jet roaring overhead.

They all mingled together with no notice of accent or skin tone.

That is what the Moulin Rouge means to the citizens of this odd city out in the middle of the heat-blasted Mojave Desert. The Rouge was the first casino in town that hired everyone, let everyone in, and it did so from the very start. Because of this one casino and the bravery of its owners, employees, and clientele, Vegas had become a pioneer in rupturing the race barriers.

He pushed through a crowd of drunken college kids in UNLV football jackets, all busy mangling *Low Rider,* the old War song. Johnny was impressed. It took a legendary amount of alcohol to screw up those lyrics.

And he finally saw her, the woman he'd come to interview.

She stood close to the northern edge of the lot, almost under the rumbling freeway traffic. An elderly woman with skin of sunburnt mahogany and snow-white hair, carefully styled into a matronly bun. She wore a simple green dress and low heels to match, and a yellow feather, just one, over her left ear. Her movements were stiff, but Johnny could see the grace that still lived inside her slender body. Though one age-gnarled hand gripped the polished silver head of a stout cane, she stood ramrod straight, staring at the edge of the lot where a stage once held the likes of Sammy Davis Jr., Louis Armstrong, Frank Sinatra, and other great names of the 50s nightclub scene.

Staring, but not seeing.

Johnny wanted her story. Very badly.

The old woman didn't show any sign she'd heard him coming, but just as Johnny cleared his throat, she turned and gave him a smile. A smile that melted decades from her eyes.

"Mr. Bianchi?" she said in a rich, throaty voice, switching the cane to her left hand and extending her right.

"Yes, ma'am," Johnny said, taking her hand. "I'm very glad you agreed to speak with me, Ms. Monroe. Please, call me Johnny." Her grip on his hand confirmed his first impression. If age had taken any toll, it sure wasn't much.

"My pleasure, young man. And do call me Annalee. Ms. Monroe is my maiden and stage name, and I haven't needed it since Methuselah wore diapers. My real name is Mrs. Annalee Macintyre, but that's neither here nor there. I understand you want to know about my time as a dancer at the Rouge. Walk with me a little, let's get on down some from all this racket."

She took her cane again, placed her left hand through Jonny's offered arm, and they moseyed away from the party over toward the remains of one hotel wing. The whole time, Johnny watched Annalee Monroe's face.

Her eyes never stopped moving. She looked at everything around them, from the rubble pushed against the few remaining walls to the boarded-up windows.

It was the way she focused on different things that told Johnny she was looking well into the past. Just like when she was looking at the stage that wasn't there anymore. He wondered what she saw that he didn't.

He'd seen all the photographs and sketches, of course. He'd been a student of the Rouge since his first assignment four years ago. He'd spoken with several people who'd stayed at the hotel or frequented the nightclub, but this was his first chance to talk to a bona-fide Moulin Rouge showgirl. He'd run a notice for three weeks and had nearly given up, when he'd gotten Annalee's email. Yes, she'd danced at the Moulin Rouge. Yes, she'd been there on opening night, and until the doors closed in December. Yes, she'd be willing to be interviewed about it.

There aren't many real jackpots in Vegas, in spite of all the ads. Johnny wouldn't turn one down.

They came to a low block wall, surprisingly intact considering what the rest of the hotel looked like.

"Let's sit a spell," she said, easing down with a sigh and planting her cane between her feet. "Bricks feel good 'n warm on my old hips." She patted the space beside her. "Sit, honey. I don't bite." She gave him another of those age-blasting smiles, a wicked twinkle in her eye. "Well, not so much as I used to."

Johnny laughed and sat beside her.

"Ms. Mon…Annalee, I mean, if you just happen to bite, I'll take it as a compliment."

She laughed at that. Threw her head back and guffawed.

"I like you, Johnny Bianchi," she said, wiping her eyes. "If I was twenty years younger, I swear."

She caught her breath, fanning her face with one hand. Johnny took the time to fix her in his mind. For her description in the story, of course.

If she'd been twenty when the Rouge opened, she'd have to be eighty-two or three now. She looked maybe sixty at most. She had gray hair, sure, but his own dad went gray in his thirties. Her face bore the lines and creases of life, but nowhere near as deep as his mother's, and Ma was seventy-one.

"Are you giving me the eyeball, young man?" Annalee said, and gave him a wink.

Johnny snapped his face forward, heat climbing up from his collar. "No, ma'am. Annalee, I mean. I was just, you know, your description for the article…"

She let out that handsome, youthful laugh again.

"Lord God, child," she said. "My, if you aren't the cutest thing. And you even blushed for me. Does an old woman's heart good."

He had to laugh with her. Feisty. That was the word for Annalee Macintyre.

"So, about the interview," Johnny said.

"You need to get your notebook or recorder?"

"No ma'am. Annalee. I have a phonographic memory," Johnny grinned. "I remember everything I hear, so if you're going to tell me any juicy bits, I'll have 'em forever."

"I like you, Johnny," she said. "I think we'll get along just fine. But just you sit there and be quiet, and let an old lady talk awhile without you asking questions."

Annalee went quiet then, tapping her cane on the pavement, looking far off into space or far back into the past. Johnny waited. Patience was something any good interviewer learned early on. Let people tell their own story in their own time.

"The Moulin Rouge Hotel and Casino," she said, her voice nearly a whisper. "Such a time. Nothing like it before or since, especially not for us colored folks. Let me tell you how I got to be part of it, Johnny. Why I'm still a part of it. Why I come here time after time, back to this place. The Rouge is dead, but its ghost runs through this whole city."

***

I DON'T KNOW all of it, but I'll tell you what I can. My part starts in a little bitty coal town called West Dante in Virginia. At least that was the name on the post office. We called it Colortown. Other folks called it… well, you know.

I wasn't but nineteen when I left, back in 1954. Didn't want to marry a local boy who'd die down in the mines before he got a gray hair. Besides, I was tall, and I loved to dance.

I spent two summers grubbing the mountain for ginseng, bloodroot, anything I might could sell. Finally made enough to buy a ticket on the Norfolk and Western to New York.

When I got there, I didn't know what all to do, except I'd read about the Cotton Club and a few other places up in Harlem that might hire entertainers. I didn't know nothin' about nothin', I swear. Just picked up my bag and walked all the way from Penn Station up to 142nd Street. That's the first I knew the Cotton Club and the Café Society had been gone for years.

I don't mind telling you I was discouraged. In fact, I sat down on my suitcase and had myself a good long cry. Nobody stopped or offered to help, just walked on by carrying their own problems and ignoring mine.

I finally got myself together, found a phone booth, and asked the operator for a talent booking agent anywhere near where

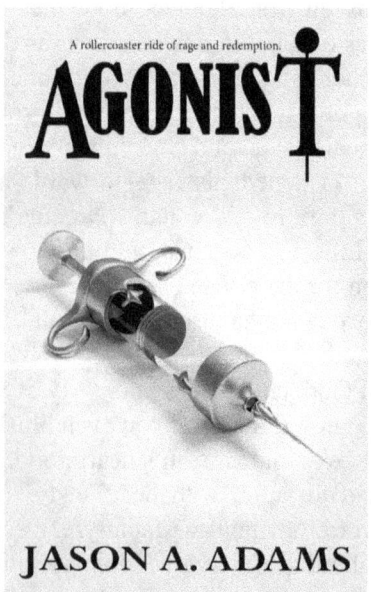

I was. The operator connected me to Gus Blumenthal's Revue Talent. I got myself over there and signed up.

Gus was a good man. Didn't want any extra favors from his girls, just his cut of our pay. He helped me get a room in a colored boarding house, a job making beds at the Roosevelt Hotel, and even a few jobs dancing in nightclubs around town. Wasn't what I expected, but I was making my own way, and that suited me just fine.

This all went on for a few months. Weather was still pretty cold but the slush was melting, so I guess it was late February, maybe early March. I was working a chorus line at a tiny club called The Ink Spot. We'd just finished our last number when the boss, big guy named Henry, called me over to the bar.

"Annalee, this here's Mr. Schwarz," Hank said. "He wants a word with you."

"Miss Annalee, I'm pleased to meet you," the new guy said, sticking his hand out like I was folks.

I didn't much know what to do. Hank told me to be polite to the man, and he sounded so much like my daddy that I shook that white man's hand and asked how I could help him. Me standing there in my not-quite-there dancing outfit.

"Miss Annalee," he said again. "Or is it Ms. Monroe? I represent the talent acquisition office of the Moulin Rouge. Not the one in Paris, the new casino and hotel opening in Las Vegas this summer."

"Las Vegas?" I said. "Where they test the A-Bombs?" Like I said, I didn't know nothin' about nothin' back then.

Well, Mr. Schwarz, he laughed and told me he wanted me to come join their dance troupe. $135 a week, and a chance to work in the first integrated hotel in Nevada. Not just the entertainers, mind, but the whole place. He told me they'd even made Joe Louis a part owner, and that he'd be greeting everybody at the door, no matter how deep their tan was.

Then Mr. Schwarz gave me his card, an envelope with five ten-dollar bills, and a ticket. I didn't know if I was ready to hop a Gray Dog across the country on this fellow's word, but I looked at the ticket and it was for an airplane. I would fly to Vegas on a TWA airliner, can you imagine?

I showed everything to Hank. His eyes went big as saucers, then down to little ol' slits.

"This on the level, Schwarz?" he said. He had a quiet voice, Hank did, but folks always listened close. He just had that air about him. People knew they didn't want to really piss him off.

"Absolutely, Henry," Mr. Schwarz said. "This lovely lady is gonna be a part of history! Once The Boys see her, they're gonna love her!"

You could hear the capital letters in the way he said The Boys. I wasn't sure what that meant. Not then, anyhow.

So two weeks later, after I'd hugged and said goodbye to everyone I knew—I near hugged poor Hank to death—I hopped the subway and then a bus out to the airport, walked right on to that plane with my head held high though my knees were shaky, and did my best not to faint when the propellers started turning. I've been on a lot of planes since then, even a Concorde once, but nothing like that very first ride. Back then, most folks went by train or by bus. Nobody I knew ever flew, unless they fell out a window.

A few hours later, I felt us start to drop down. I'd stared out the window the whole trip and watched the land go from trees to grass to brown and red dirt. We landed at McCarran Field, which wasn't much more than a couple of macadam strips and a wooden building.

Soon as I stepped out on the tarmac, I started sweating. I was dressed for New York winter, not Vegas winter. It was already dark, probably seven in the evening, but it had to be on up in the sixties still.

I shucked my winter coat, hat, and gloves, then walked over to the terminal. On the way, a colored boy in coveralls grabbed my arm. He didn't look mean or angry, he looked scared.

"This way, lady," he whispered, tugging at my arm like I was a fish on his line. "You got to go through this here door."

I was surprised, and not. The white folks on the plane had mostly ignored me. Nat King Cole and Lena Horne flew around, so wasn't like I was the only pepper in the biscuit. But I was kind of disappointed. Still, I followed him through the maintenance halls until we got to the front of the terminal.

I don't know what I expected, but it sure wasn't a limousine. But there it was, long and pretty. A big fellow in a tuxedo stood beside it, holding a sign with my name on it and four others. All women's names. The driver was white, but he opened the door and held it for me. I got in, and he shut the door and put my suitcase in the trunk.

I wasn't alone in the limo. Four women were already in there, I guessed the ones whose names were on the sign. See how clever I was for country?

We introduced ourselves. There was me, Dee Dee Jasmin, Anna Bailey, Janie Walker, and Beth Goode. We'd all been hired by Schwarz. Me and Anna from New York, Dee Dee and Janie from LA, and Beth from Chicago. We chattered like magpies, all of us excited and scared and someplace new. But one thing about folks in the entertainment business, we all get to be friends awfully fast. You got to, you know. Want to know folks got your back up there on stage. Sometimes off stage too.

We rolled down the Strip, then through downtown. Glitter Gulch. I'd been to Times Square, but that was like a match compared to the bonfire of lights I saw that night. But we kept on going, over the railroad tracks, past shabbier buildings, on in toward the West Side. I didn't have a map, and I didn't know a thing about Vegas, but I didn't need a college degree to see we were heading toward Vegas's version of Colortown.

We went quiet, I guess scared of where we might be going, but then we saw it. This gorgeous white building with red awnings,

like something from Spain or the French Riviera. A big tall tower all lit up, and that sign! I fell in love right then.

I expected the car to pull around back, but the driver stopped right in front of the main door and helped us all out. Called us all by name and took us by the hand. I still remember his deep, deep voice saying, "Miss Monroe, watch your step."

And right there in the doorway was the Brown Bomber himself. Joe Louis. My! He was handsome. And so charming. He came over and shook all our hands and asked us to come inside.

There was plenty of construction still going on, but the place was still beautiful. Paintings on the wall styled after Toulouse Lautrec's playbills. Mahogany everywhere. On the walls and in the clothes. It was gorgeous. We could hear the orchestra practicing from the big double-doors that led to the showroom.

Mr. Louis turned us all over to Clarence Robinson, the show producer. He checked us all over, took us through the double doors to introduce us to the other girls and menfolk who'd be dancing in the show. Then we met the band.

It was the first time I'd seen black and white musicians in the same orchestra pit. I mean, I knew we'd been told the place was integrated, but I think that was when it really sank in for me. All those players, and all of them damn good at what they did. They'd all be playing music for me and the others to dance to. I wish I could explain how that felt.

I met all of them. Tommy Hornblower played trumpet. I'm sure I knew his real name once upon a time, but everybody called him Tommy Hornblower. Showfolk don't always have good imaginations. Then there was Sully Warwick on sax, Jack Malone on drums, Miguel Castillo on guitar, Larry Havers on bass fiddle.

And on piano? That would be Hutch Macintyre. Hutch was a boy from South Carolina, little place called Lane. The other guys in the band were plenty good, but Hutch? He made that piano sit up and *talk!* And good looking? I don't mind telling you that seeing him in that white shirt, garters on his sleeves and a shiny bowler hat on his head, I had me some thoughts I wouldn't tell my mamma or my preacher.

Anyway, we didn't have much time to make eyes at the band. First thing we did was get settled in our rooms. Back then, most places in Vegas would hire colored folks as entertainers, even the great ones like Lena and Cab Calloway, but turn them away from the rooms, casinos, restaurants, and so on. Louis Armstrong would get a standing ovation at nine, and go sleep in a colored boarding house on the west side come midnight.

But not us. We had nice double rooms in the staff wing of the hotel. They weren't big, but they were clean, comfortable, and ours so long as we wanted them.

Once we dropped our bags and changed out of our traveling clothes, we got a big supper in the lounge. I'd never seen so many different shades of skin in one room before. And everyone getting along, sitting at the same tables, laughing and carrying on. I can't tell you what that was like for me.

We sat up late, and I maybe had one or two more drinks than I should. Next thing I knew the sun was blazing through my window. Anna was shaking my shoulder and hollering, "Get up! Get up, girl! We got to go downstairs for rehearsal. Get a wiggle on!"

I try to be a lady, but I may have used some language. But I got up, washed the worst of the night before off my tongue and skin, then dressed in my practice leotard and chased down the hall after Anna.

We got to the stage ahead of the last stragglers, which was something. Clarence looked us over through eyes the color of Red Rock Canyon. His face looked like a candle that sat out in the sun too long. But I suppose he looked like most of us felt that first morning.

Clarence looked bad, but he got us right to work. First we split up, men in one room, women in the other. We stripped down to our drawers while Asami and Kyoko, two Japanese seamstresses, measured us up one side and down the other. One by one, they took us behind a screen and made us strip down completely, then measured us all over again.

Once that was done, Clarence started us on the dances we had to know for opening

---

night. The mambo I already knew, but the Watusi was something else. The music was heavy on the drums, and Clarence said we'd be in grass skirts, playing wild men and women from darkest Africa.

The fun one though, that was the Tropi Can Can. It was based on the Cancan from the real Moulin Rouge, but done to a Cuban beat. Fun, but wore me plumb out. I guess it'd kill me these days.

We worked ten hours a day, getting ready for the grand opening. When we weren't dancing, most of us slept like corpses. Dancing like that is plenty hard work. But we had plenty of good times, too. The musicians and dancers in any club are like a big family, and that was even more true at the Rouge. We all felt like we were part of something. Besides, we didn't get out much. We were part of something, part of a group trying to make a difference, but there was still plenty of ugly to go around out in the other parts of town.

We had our first dress rehearsal on the first of May. The costumes took my breath. Grass skirts and leopard-print bras for the Watusi. French dancing-girl skirts and petticoats for the Tropi Can Can. But the outfits for the mambo? My, my. They were all green and bright yellow. The body was just a regular leotard, only leopard print. The headpiece and tails were long plumes, a yard or more. All green and yellow feathers. The Cancan is what folks remember, but I remember the mambo.

That was the first number. When we all came out on the stage looking like tropical birds that lost their buttons, I felt…I don't know. Powerful. More like a woman than I ever had before. Like a goddess.

I felt something that gave me goosebumps. I peeked around between takes, and saw Hutch down in the orchestra pit. All the musicians were laughing, slapping hands, blowing spit out their horns. But not Hutch. He was looking straight at me. He saw me looking back, and that man blew me a kiss.

If you'd been there that day, you'd've seen a black woman blush.

Anna came over then. "What's wrong, Annalee?" she said. "You look like something hot stuck you in the behind."

She saw where I was looking then, and gave me a big tomcat-with-a-canary grin. "Uh oh. I think maybe you might be throwing sparks for the good-lookin' man on the keys."

"No I am not," I said. Maybe a little snappish. "I'm not looking at nobody." I turned away and hustled back to the other girls. I heard somebody laugh behind me, but it wasn't a mean laugh. It was a good laugh. And a warm laugh. Sure did warm me up, anyhow.

The next three weeks were all rehearsing, eating, rehearsing, sleeping, and more rehearsing. We worked as long as we could keep moving, and sometimes longer than that. Every now and then I'd catch Hutch looking at me, and sometimes I believe he caught me looking his way. I'd see Anna, Dee Dee, and the others whispering behind their hands and giggling my way whenever they caught me with my eyes all full of Pianoman, but they didn't tease me too bad.

Finally the big night came. May 24, 1955. We were all nervous as could be. Clarence was all over everybody, adjusting costumes, checking our makeup, making sure everything was perfect.

We all lined up in the wings in our green and yellow feathers, waiting to go on. I could barely breathe. Anna squeezed one of my hands, and Dee Dee caught the other. We all told each other how great we were going to be.

Then Jack Malone rolled on his drums, the horns blew a crescendo, and I heard the prettiest Latin piano ever cutting through it all. Beside me, Anna squeezed my hand again.

"He's playing that just for you, Annalee," she said, smiling like a sunrise.

I wanted to say something pert, but Clarence was waving us onto the stage. I swallowed hard, hoisted on my own smile, and sashayed out into the lights.

When the music really got going and we flashed our legs and tail feathers through the first Mambo City number, all my nervous fell off. The lights were plenty bright, but I could see enough. The house was packed like a sardine tin. It wasn't just white folks, and it wasn't whites up front and colored behind. Everybody was all mixed in together. And they were all having a blast. Cheers, whoops, applause, all the noises an audience can make. And all for us. Twenty-four black women and a dozen black men had that whole crowd on their feet after every number.

We didn't have time to think much. After each act we rushed back to the dressing rooms to change into the next outfit, then right back to the stage. Belafonte was there, singing between our numbers. His dressing room was on the other side. I didn't even know he was there until later. When he wasn't singing the little Hines boys, eleven years old and nine, would tap dance and tell jokes. I didn't know it then, but I was seeing some of Gregory's earliest work. We even had The Platters doing "Only You." That song still makes my eyes wet.

We did the Watusi next, shakin' our goodies all over the place. And finally we closed the night with the Tropi Can Can. Tommy Hornblower and the other brass players really worked the music, and we couldn't hear anything over it all. Except I still picked out the piano bits. I had quite the ear for Hutch's playing for some reason.

It seemed like somewhere between forever and no time at all when the curtain finally dropped and the music died off. We'd danced off the stage, but came back on for the curtain call. I was scared as anything again, because I couldn't hear any noise from the audience. Oh, maybe a low buzz, like a crowd all muttering, but that's all.

Then the curtain rose and the house lights lit us all up.

And the place exploded.

Everybody in the audience was on their feet. They clapped, whistled, hollered, jumped up and down.

Bob Bailey, the emcee, beamed at us all and gave us a bow. "That show was a popper!" he said.

I looked down in the orchestra pit. All the musicians were slapping each other on the back and waving to us and the crowd.

Except Hutch. He was clapping, sure, but I would have sworn he didn't look at anybody but me. I couldn't help it. I smiled back down at him while tears rolled down my cheeks. I've never been as proud of anything as I was of all of us that night. That moment.

The second show of the night went off as well as the first. Afterward, we should have gotten in bed, but none of us could even think about Old Man Sleep. We got dressed in our regular clothes and went up to the lounge. Seemed like nobody wanted to go home. There wasn't room in there to change your mind, let alone do much else.

Anna pulled me over to the bar. She was a tough girl, but right then she was stammering and stuttering fit to split. Finally, she tapped a black man in a tuxedo on the shoulder.

"Mr. Davis, sir? This here is Annalee Monroe that I told you about."

The man turned around, and it was Sammy Davis his own self. I nearly died, but he wouldn't let me.

"Miss Monroe," he said in that voice of his. "I'm so delighted to meet you. If I may say, I can't choose between you and Miss Bailey here for Belle of the Ball." Then he took my hand and kissed it, like I was royalty.

"I...uh...that is to say...thank you, Mr. Davis." That was all I could get out.

"Madam, please call me Sammy. If you'll still be dancing here this weekend, I'd like to bring Dean and Frank to the show. I know they'll love it. And you." He smiled that Sammy smile and I about turned to rubber. Anna wasn't much better.

"You trying to steal my date, Sammy?" said a smooth, southern voice from behind us. "I might have to ask you out to the woodshed."

Sammy looked past my left shoulder and smiled even wider.

"I wouldn't think of it, Harlan," he said. "In fact, I believe I saw the young lady looking down into the pit instead of at the audience."

I turned around, and saw a slim young man. Tall, neatly dressed in a green suit with a yellow necktie. He looked familiar, then I saw the bowler in his hand. It was Hutch, the piano player. Talking back at Sammy Davis, Jr.

"H-Hutch?" I said. You can tell I was always good with words.

"Miss Monroe, Anna," he said, sparing my best friend a glance. "I wonder if you would join me for dinner in yonder dining establishment." He gestured toward the restaurant, which looked full.

"I don't think we'll get a seat," I said, hating all those people in there.

Sammy looked at us, or I suppose he did. Then he spoke up again.

"I could use some food," he said. "If you two will allow me, and Miss Bailey will agree to be my date, I'm sure we can find a table. Come on."

Anna said something, I don't know what. All I could see was a beautiful young man from South Carolina. He took my hand in his and we followed Sammy and Anna. The staff found us a table with no problem, and we stayed until the cleaning crew shooed us out.

***

"THERE'S NOT MUCH more to tell than that," Annalee said. "You know all the rest. How the Rouge went bust, or got railroaded out of business, depending on who you believe. Hutch and I barely noticed. Hutch got a chance to play with Cab Calloway's orchestra, and I followed him everywhere he went. Danced when I could, watched him work that piano whether I could or couldn't."

"What about the showgirl life?" Johnny asked. "Were you sad to leave that behind?"

"Oh sure," she said. "At least until 1960, when the west side got organized enough to make the rest of the casinos integrate. I thought I'd be first in line for a job, but Anna Bailey beat me to it. Most all the girls got to dance after that, one place or another."

She sighed, gripping her cane.

"Those were my best friends I ever had," she said, "Anna, Dee Dee, and the rest. Except for Hutch, of course. We married in 1956 and

rode the good times and bad until he passed five years ago. Most all of them are gone now. No one left but one old woman with old memories. Old memories and one old feather." She touched the yellow feather over her left ear. "This is all I have left from that time. We moved around so much, most everything got lost or left behind along the way."

Johnny couldn't think of anything to say. His head was full of images. Dark-skinned dancers, yellow and green feathers, black and white faces.

He jumped when she slapped his hand.

"Don't look so down in the dumps," she said, that age-defying smile on her face. "Just look out yonder at those people. They aren't grieving the past tonight, they're celebrating. In fact, we should go join them, don't you think? That is, if you don't mind dancing with a dried-up old apple like me."

Annalee stood, and Johnny stood beside her, taking her hand in his arm.

"Now let's go show 'em how it's done," she said. "If you're lucky, you might find out the old apple has a little juice left after all."

They laughed all the way back to the party, where she nearly danced him to death.

It was the best night of Johnny's life.

"I say we skip the reception, sneak to the car, and head straight to Fiji"

C. A. Rowland's first appearance in these pages is a great one. A story of love, trust, relationships, and magic. A perfect Pulphouse *story.*

C. A. says in real life she is a recovering lawyer. But as a writer, she is doing great, having published stories in numbers of places, including in two different volumes of Fiction River. *After this first fantastic story, I hope to have many more from her in the future.*

Maddie Sue's Locket
C.A. Rowland

I WHISPERED IN Jimmy Don's ear, just as I had the last thirty nights.

"Get the locket."

Thirty nights of returning to the century-old log cabin where the wind blew relentlessly. Caulked each year to keep the wood water-tight, the two rooms were like living in an icebox in the winter and over a pot of boiling water in the summer. Life in the Virginia mountains.

My life.

Where the tree trunks were dressed in greens during the warm seasons, before shedding their brown coats to stand naked during the winter snows.

There's those that would try to tell the story of the locket. But they're only fooling. Anyone who says they know the true story is a liar.

But I wander. It's a habit of mine. Follow a dirt trail in the woods, only to find something else to see. I've lived in this place my whole life. I know my way home—even in the dark, I am never lost.

"Get my locket," I whisper again as I rise at the five-foot-nine twenty-year old's stirring. In his sleep, I know he has heard me. He brushed a hand against his freckled face as if trying to push me away, but I was not easily removed. Now, he just needed to get doing what I tell him.

It is a small thing in and of itself. But a vital one to me. For the locket is mine, given to me by my mama when I married Carl. Bound us together, through good times and those not so good, and then beyond.

I'd loved Carl from when we were young children. His dark wavy hair crept down his strong lean back. His dark eyes flashed with anger and humor. He'd grown into a man whose arms could sweep me up in them and hold me a foot off the ground. Six feet of a working man, only comfortable in blue jeans and a cotton plaid shirt. Plain-spoken like the rest of us, but treasuring what was special to us. A good man with a huge heart for his family.

Like my locket. Heart-shaped. The kind that opened with pictures on either side. One of me, Maddie Sue, and one of Carl. Blessed by my mama who was a healer of sorts, for us to have a long and happy life together. She'd asked me three times before she'd agreed to give me the locket with her blessing. Just as her mama had passed it on to her before she married my daddy.

My mama had the Halley women's gifts of foresight. And other gifts we don't talk much about since people get the wrong idea. Those abilities pass to each new generation of women, without fail.

Carl's and my happy life together turned out to be seven years. Before I gave birth to our daughter, Sarah Jean.

Carl had been so proud I'd finally gotten pregnant. Proud that he was going to be a papa. Proud until Sarah Jean showed up with yellow hair to two dark-haired parents.

I'm sure the rumors started from Carl's mama, who'd never liked me. Called me Mad Sue, as if I was crazy or something. Resented her son being out from under her thumb. Her

being all alone since her husband had passed hadn't helped, but I figured her husband had likely wanted to be free of her too.

"Maddie Sue's been catin' around," his mama had told Carl any time she thought I wasn't listening. "Probably that Jacob Satter. He's always admired Maddie Sue."

Me and Carl, we'd sit on the porch each evening, me in one wooden rocker and Carl in the other, both hand-made by my daddy. Not like when we first married, and we cuddled up in one as we talked of the family we'd have. Carl denied his mama said anything, but I knew better.

"My great-great-granddaddy, Samuel, married a yellow-haired girl from over in Prater. They had four sons, all dark-haired. Haven't had a child with yellow-hair since but it's possible."

Carl would just nod at my words, staring out at the woodpile like he was contemplating whether he'd chopped enough for the coming winter.

"I swear on my marriage locket, what I say is true."

He'd nod again.

We'd sit, staring out at the trees, watching the dirt dust up in the breeze, until the moon rose. Head to bed where I'd reach for him, knowing he thought I'd betrayed him. Wanting him more than anything to touch me as he had before Sarah Jean had been born. Finding cold comfort in the fact his body betrayed him even as his heart was walled off to me. Many a night I lay still in the sheets, a patchwork quilt pulled up around my neck, wishing things were different.

Sarah Jean though. She saved me. I loved her from the moment she stirred in my tummy. Small boned, with a melodic voice commanding my attention, she was thin from birth, almost fragile in appearance. I was born to be a mama, and my one regret is I had no other children. No matter how hard I tried each night with Carl.

From her first days, Sarah Jean went everywhere with me. I knew she'd gotten my instincts for directions the day I stopped, looked around to see where to go next and Sarah Jean had pointed us home. I'd wondered what else she'd inherited, and it wasn't long before I knew that included the stubbornness of the Halley women.

The trouble started when Sarah Jean was twelve and Carl got wind she'd been seen with Jacob Satter's son, Jimmy Don.

Before Sarah Jean had been born and Carl's mama had planted the seeds of distrust in his ears, Jacob and Carl had been good friends.

No more.

Carl stayed up two days chopping wood before he laid the law down. "Sarah Jean, I don't wanna see that Satter's spawn on my property. Nor you on theirs. Or anywhere near that boy, Jimmy Don."

"We go to school together. I can't not see him."

"Find a way, or you won't be going to school neither," Carl said.

Sarah Jean crossed her arms and stood firm. Carl stared at her for a minute before he turned away mumbling something about "Halley women."

Sarah Jean went to school, but I walked her there and back. There were some taunts but always in the background was Carl's mama, "Watch out for Sarah Jean. She's just like her mama. Only thing worse would be incest with her half-brother."

I'd watch Carl's deep blue eyes turn black with rage, but he'd never laid a hand on either Sarah Jean or me. I'll give him credit for that. Nor did he ever treat Sarah Jean as anything but his own. But I knew the questions festered inside him.

I cooked and cleaned, making sure he always knew where Sarah Jean and I were or had been. He'd grunt an acknowledgment before he sat on the porch, stewing even while supper stewed on the stove. Even laughed at times as Sarah Jean and I talked and argued with each other.

But then, he'd be back on the porch once supper was done, while Sarah Jean and I washed the dishes and prepared for the next day.

Life continued.

Until Carl came home several years later, his freckled tan face, struggling to hold in his rage.

"Mama says Sarah Jean was with that Satter boy, wanderin' in the woods on the east side of the mountain."

"I know. I was there."

"You know I don't allow that."

"Was homework for school. I was watching over Sarah Jean."

Carl scoffed. "Time for that girl to learn how to cook and clean. She stays home now."

"That's not fair to her."

"Neither is what's been done before."

I sucked in a breath and stood my ground. That was the closest Carl ever came to accusing me of being with another man. Before I could come up with a response, Carl whirled around, stormed out of the cabin and slammed the door. I could hear the ax meeting the logs of wood as he worked out his anger. The sound of the blade against each piece of timber rang through the cabin and my body as if he was cutting his rage out one swing at a time.

Chop.

Chop.

Chop.

Rhythmic and unrelenting.

All night. A full moon lit the area so the shadows of our love and the perceived deceit could dance, break away and dance again.

Tears washed over my cheeks as I realized I'd never be able to convince Carl I hadn't cheated on him. Waves of anguish, held in for years, convulsed in my stomach. I curled up in a ball, letting all the hurt, anger and frustration come out as the chopping continued.

In the morning, Carl said nothing about my red eyes. I said nothing about the way his arms and body dragged from the lack of energy after cutting wood all night. Sarah Jean looked at each of us and then lowered her head as she shoved the freshly made biscuit from my cast iron skillet drenched in churned butter into her mouth.

I silently cursed Carl for hurting her for something she'd had no part in.

Carl downed four biscuits. "I'm going to town." No asking if we needed anything. Just that he was going.

Only later would I learn what happened.

Carl didn't come home that night. Folks are usually good about spreading the bad news like wildfire, but I guess Carl's mama clamped down on that. Only after I walked Carl's route the next day did I find out a broken axle had caused Carl's death.

Carl's mama blamed me.

No matter I wasn't anywhere near the wagon. Seemed Carl was lifting the wagon to slip the wheel off to repair it, when the wagon slipped, fell and pinned him to the ground.

"Cursed, my boy was after he married that tramp," Carl's mama told everyone who would listen. "Her and Jacob Satter did him in so they could be together."

Seemed Jacob had come along and found Carl. Jacob managed to lift the wagon and get Carl out, then bring him to the next cabin where they tried to help him.

Jacob said Carl's last words were, "If I die, tell Maddie Sue I want to be buried with the marriage locket."

Truth be told, I was horrified at the thought but could figure no way out. The marriage locket bound us, and he knew that. Seems in death, he thought he could keep me from doing what he feared most and what I had always believed he thought I'd already done. If only I had been there, I could've told him how much I loved him.

Carl's mama insisted I abide by the dying wish of her son. I could find no way to do otherwise since she kept checking his body until he was safely in the ground.

I could have told her what she'd condemned her son to, but it was unlikely she'd believe me and if she did, that would simply confirm what she'd thought all along—I was not fit to be Carl's wife.

So I allowed my locket to be placed in the chest pocket of his favorite blue plaid shirt.

And there it lay for the ten years, knowing in death he was still bound to me through the blessing.

Ten years of watching over Sarah Jean, making sure she knew all I'd learned from my mama.

Ten years until the snows came and I walked out to wait for death.

I'd known the time had come when I could leave Sarah Jean alone to live her life.

TETHERING THE SUN
from
FANTASY PORTALS, AN ANTHOLOGY

Ruthie Jackson traveled to Machu Picchu, a place of power, only to feel nothing. Can an old legend of stone reconnect her deep empathy with places? And if not, does this place have other plans for her?

www.carowland.com

"Mama, don't go. I need you."

"Your daddy needs me more. I can't leave it any longer. We need to settle things. You know that."

Sarah Jean had nodded, her eyes filled with tears. I hugged her hard until she pulled away and ran to her bed in the corner of our cabin. Flung herself down and cried into her pillow as I pulled my old blue crocheted shawl over my head. With my wool coat on, I opened the door and walked out, never looking back.

The family plot was only a couple of hundred yards away. I trudged through the snow and sat beside where he lay.

I shivered with cold, letting it fill my body just as my mama had told me my grandma had done when her time had come. Feeling the numbness begin in my fingers and my feet.

Feeling the lightness in my head as I began to nod off. Slipping off into the sweet slumber of death. That's what my mama had said it would be like.

She'd lied.

I was miserable sitting out in the snow, feeling wet as an old dog, wanting to shake the moisture off me.

Instead, I steeled myself against the pain of the cold until the numbness wiped away the pain. And sleep finally came.

I wasn't sure how long it took to die, but I felt my spirit rise up from my body. I looked down and could see what remained of my human form, sitting near Carl's grave.

Sarah Jean would find my body there. She'd known where I was going. Just like she'd known all the things I'd told her before I left the cabin.

I'd told her the story of the locket—even the part about needing Jimmy Don to get it back. Since the locket would go to Sarah Jean next, she couldn't retrieve it. A stupid rule but one I knew in my gut had to be obeyed.

So, I'd begun trying to influence Jimmy Don as soon as I died—a nudge here and there to be ready for the real task. Once the weather broke, I'd set about talking to him each night.

Thirty nights later, it seemed I had worked through his subconscious so he rose from his bed and headed to what was now Sarah Jean's cabin.

I'm not a praying woman, but I prayed he knew to be careful not to be seen.

Jimmy Don slipped across the valley on the moonlit night. Still in a light coat and jeans, he blended in with the shadows of the trees as he walked a trail lit only by a half moon.

Sarah Jean was on the porch. Rocking. Waiting. Halley women knew when things were stirring in the night.

"Sarah Jean? What are you doing out here?" Jimmy Don asked.

"Waiting on you."

"But how'd you know I was coming?"

"You been dreaming about my mama?" Sarah Jean asked.

"Yes."

"What did she tell you?"

"I have to get her locket. Guess that means I have to dig up your daddy."

"Yes. That's about the size of it. We need to finish before daylight so no one knows."

I watched Jimmy Don peer onto the porch beside Sarah Jean. "You got the shovel already?"

"Yes. Thought you'd need it if you didn't bring one."

Jimmy Don nodded again and retrieved the shovel. The two walked across the front of the cabin, turned right and headed to the family plot.

I'd waited to tell Jimmy Don to get the locket until the ground was softer with snow-melt and no longer frozen. I hoped that meant the digging would be easier.

"Isn't it a crime to take something from a grave?"

"I think so. But you're getting it for me… and my mama, so it's not like you're stealing anything. Besides, I'll never tell on you," Sarah Jean said as she checked Jimmy Don's progress. "Want me to take a turn at digging?"

"No, I don't think this will take too much longer," Jimmy Don said as he wiped the sweat from his brow and removed his wool jacket.

A dog howled, and I checked the area. No humans. A wind rustled the brush as Jimmy Don sunk the shovel in the ground.

Swoosh. Lift the soil.

Plunk. The mound of soil grew as Jimmy Don tossed what he dug on to the growing pile.

Swoosh. Plunk.

Crunch. The shovel hit the wooden coffin.

Jimmy Don sank the shovel in several places, hitting the coffin each time.

"Clear the dirt so you can open it," Sarah Jean said.

Jimmy Don made a few shallow passes over the wooden box to clear as much dirt as possible.

He turned the shovel to use as a lever on the wood, loosening the top. As I watched, Jimmy Don forced the casket open a crack. Then a bit wider.

"Whew. That smells something awful."

"I think it's open enough. Mama said the locket is in his chest pocket."

Jimmy Don reached inside, his face grimacing as he held his breath and he ran his hand along the chest of my dead husband. Wiggling around, he gave a soft pull and brought his hand out, the golden locket glistening in the moonlight.

"Here you go. It's all yours," Jimmy Don said.

Sarah Jean smiled. "Mama, I know you're here. It's done. Call papa."

"Carl. Carl, are you there?" I called.

I listened as the wind rose and fell. Heard the small rodents rustling in the underbrush.

Jimmy Don pushed the top of the coffin back down and began to shovel the dirt back on top.

Filling in the grave moved much faster than the digging. Soon, Jimmy Don patted it down and used some branches to cover the site.

"That's good enough," Sarah Jean said. "We should go. You need to get back home before daylight."

"I know. But what was this all about?" Jimmy Don asked.

"Peace for my mama and daddy. Thank you for doing this for us," Sarah Jean said as she turned toward the cabin. "Come on. I'll get you a cool drink of water before you head home."

Jimmy Don followed Sarah Jean as I settled in to wait. "Carl, they're gone. Carl? Are you here?"

The moon moved across the sky and as the first fingers of light began to appear, I saw Carl. A grayish shape, indistinct but I'd know Carl anywhere.

"Took you long enough to die, Maddie Sue."

"I had our daughter to raise and protect. You know that."

"That is the question, isn't it? Or am I here for some other reason?"

"You're here because we were bound by my mother's blessing on the marriage locket that was just retrieved for Sarah Jean."

"By that Satter boy?" Carl asked as he shifted to move closer, his color shifting to a darker gray.

"Yes."

"Do I have a choice in the matter?"

"You always had a choice. But once made, it was forever unless we both choose to unbind ourselves," I said as I floated over to Carl. "I always loved you and always will."

"Then tell me the truth. Was Sarah Jean my daughter?"

"She is your daughter. Always will be. But no, you didn't father her."

Carl began to float away.

"Please hear me out. It's not what you think."

Carl turned. I could see no expression, but at least he wasn't moving away.

I continued. "You wanted a child so bad. And I couldn't get pregnant. I had my mama divine if there would be a child and she said no. I checked with the healer woman in the next valley. She said there'd be no child. I didn't know what to do and didn't want to disappoint you."

I paused and saw Carl was listening. "So I approached Jacob, your best friend. Someone I knew we could trust with the truth. Took some convincing, well pestering really, but he eventually agreed because he knew how much you wanted a child. And how much I loved you."

"You're saying you laid with Jacob to give me a child?"

"Yes. You might not believe it but it's true. Don't be mad at Jacob. It was my idea. Jacob may have gotten me pregnant, but Sarah Jean was always yours. No matter how she came to be."

"I've considered this the past ten years I've been bound to that damn locket. Watched you with Jacob. Watched you with Sarah Jean. You and Jacob never talked or met. This hair-brained idea is just crazy enough for me to believe you would do that," Carl said as the top of the hazy figure shook.

"That was our agreement. Jacob would live his life—marry, have children. We'd live ours. Carl, I never meant to hurt you, only give you what you longed for. I can prove it to you. The bond can be broken. You can be free of me. All you have to do is say the word, and I'll break the bond with you. I love you and want you to be happy. If that's what it takes I will do it."

I could barely say the words without my voice and heart cracking.

In the silence that followed, I almost broke down but knew I had to be strong.

"I never wanted anyone but you," Carl said. "But what about Sarah Jean? That makes Jimmy Don her half-brother. I know she cares for the boy."

"Of course she does. She's a Halley woman. She recognizes a blood relative when she's near one, just as I always did. She'll watch over him as if he is the brother that he is. Sarah Jean and I talked about all this before I moved on."

"And the marriage locket?"

"I'll know when it's time. I can bless any marriage union she wishes to make from this side of life."

The figure that was Carl began to shake with laughter. "You are never dull, Maddie Sue. My mama was right when she said you were crazy. But it's my kind of crazy. This is just wild enough to be true."

"What are you saying?" I asked.

"I think we give this another chance. See where it takes us. Forever is a long time without a little bit of crazy involved."

"It's a long time without love as well. I wouldn't want to spend it with anyone but you," I said as I floated the distance between us. I shivered as our shapes melded together. It had been a long time since we'd touched in any form.

~

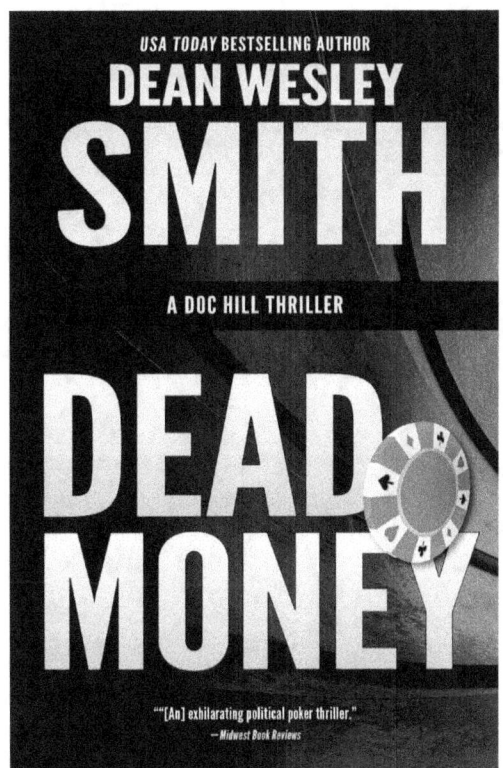

New York Times *bestselling writers Kevin J. Anderson and Rebecca Moesta team up for this powerful story. I'll let Kevin tell you about why he wrote it.*

"When my professional writing career was just getting under way, I was eagerly pursuing book contracts, building my name, selling stories to the major magazines, clawing myself up one step at a time. A hot new author exploded on the scene with a universally celebrated first novel, which won a bunch of awards; everybody read it, everybody talked about it.

"And we never heard from him again. No second novel that I knew of, no short story publications. The guy had achieved the pinnacle of success that so many of us longed for...and then he just disappeared. Why would anyone do that? The question obsessed me, and I still don't know the answer."

Rough Draft
Kevin J. Anderson
(written with Rebecca Moesta)

AFTER A DECADE during which he wrote and published nothing new, the fan letters dwindled to a few a year.

"Dear Mr. Coren, You're the best science fiction writer ever!"

"Dear Mr. Coren, Your book *Divergent Lines* changed my life. I felt as if you were speaking directly to me, and you helped me work through some major issues."

The entire experience, though great for the ego, had ultimately proved meaningless. Eventually he'd been forced to return the money for the second book advance, because he simply couldn't do it again. After enjoying a pleasant day in the sun, Mitchell Coren had retreated to his small apartment to live a normal life. The gleaming Nebula Award and the silver Hugo—both dusty now—were little more than knickknacks on the mantle of a fireplace that he never used.

Having convinced himself of the wisdom of J.D. Salinger's approach to authorial fame, Mitchell had squelched all thoughts of returning to writing. He immersed himself in a normal life with all its petty concerns.

Today, with an indifference born of long practice, Mitchell opened his bills and junk mail before finally tearing open the padded envelope that obviously contained a book. Another intrusion, no doubt. An annoying reminder of his old life. He still received advance reading copies from editors trying to wheedle a rare cover quote from him, rough draft manuscripts from aspiring authors who begged for comments or critiques, and books presented to him by new authors who had been inspired by his lone published novel.

Inside this envelope, however, he found his own name on the dust jacket of a novel he had never written.

INFERNITIES
Mitchell Coren
Multiple Award-winning Author of *Divergent Lines*

Whirling flakes of confusion compacted into a hard snowball in the pit of his stomach. "What the hell?"

His initial, and obvious, thought was that someone had stolen his name. But that didn't make sense. Though many editorial positions had changed in the decade since he'd published *Divergent Lines*, Mitchell was still well enough known in the insular science fiction community that somebody in the field would have noticed an imposter. Besides, how much could his byline be worth after all this time? It wasn't worth stealing.

Someone had tucked a folded sheet of paper between the book's front cover and the endpaper. He read it warily.

Dear Mr. Coren,

As a longtime fan of yours, I thought you'd appreciate seeing this novel I came across in a parallel universe.

I'm a timeline hunter by profession. Perhaps you've heard of Alternitech? Our company uses a proprietary technology to open gateways into alternate realities. My colleagues and I explore these parallel universes for breakthroughs or useful discrepancies that Alternitech can profitably exploit: medical and scientific advances, historical discoveries, artistic variations. My specialty is the creative arts.

I stumbled upon this book in an alternate timeline while searching for a new Mario Puzo. Since the science fiction market isn't nearly as large or profitable as the mainstream, I couldn't spend much time checking out its background, but a brief search showed that the 'alternate' Mitchell Coren published a dozen or so short stories after Divergent Lines, *then produced this second novel. I'm hoping Alternitech will want to arrange for its publication, but naturally I felt you should see it first.*

With deepest respect,
Jeremy Cardiff

Mitchell stared at the letter with mistrust and growing irritation. He had heard of this company that searched alternate realities for everything from new Beatles records, to evidence of UFOs or Kennedy assassination

conspiracies, to cures for obscure diseases. He could understand the more humanitarian objectives, but why *fiction*? What gave Alternitech the right to infringe on his life like this?

He opened to the dust jacket photo and saw that the picture did resemble him, though this other Mitchell Coren wore a different hairstyle and a cocky, self-assured grin. The bio mentioned that after completing *Infernities* he was "already at work on his next novel."

Oddly unsettled, Mitchell pushed the book away. Its very existence raised too many disturbing questions.

***

THREE INCREASINGLY URGENT phone calls to his former agent went unreturned. Since Mitchell had neither delivered anything new nor generated much income, his agent wasn't in a great hurry to attend to his so-called emergency. Even in the days when he'd briefly been a hot client, Mitchell had been relatively high-maintenance, needing encouragement and constant contact.

He decided to contact his entertainment attorney instead. After all, Sheldon Freiburg charged by the hour and therefore had an incentive to get right on the matter.

"Mitch Coren! I haven't heard from you since the last ice age." Freiburg's voice was bluff and hearty on the telephone. "What on earth have you been doing? You dropped off the map."

"I've been working a real-world job, Sheldon. You know, regular paycheck, benefits…security?"

"Yeah, I've heard of those. Hopped off the old fame-and-fortune bandwagon, eh?"

"A modicum of fame, not a whole lot of fortune—as you well know."

Freiburg had handled the entertainment contracts for the two movie options on *Divergent Lines*. Mitchell had been young and naïve then, believing the Hollywood hype and enthusiasm. He'd been surrounded by smiling fast-talkers whose eager assertions of certain box office appeal and guaranteed

studio support were built on a foundation as strong as a soap bubble. After the attorney's fees and the agent's commission, the option money had been just enough to pay off his car, which was now ten years old.

"So, Mitchell," Freiburg said now, "people don't call me unless they have a situation—either good or bad—so let's hear it."

"Someone's trying to publish an unauthorized Mitchell Coren novel."

"You've actually done other work?" The lawyer sounded surprised. "Something new? I thought you'd turned hermit on us. Did somebody steal your manuscript?"

"This is trickier than that. It isn't exactly a matter of stealing. This is a novel from a parallel universe, and Alternitech wants to get it published here." He explained the situation in full.

"Oh, that *is* tricky—but not unheard of. Listen, since it's Tuesday, I'll give you a special deal, a quick and inexpensive answer."

"Inexpensive? You've changed in the last ten years, Sheldon."

The lawyer chuckled. "How could I help it? The whole world has changed. But you're not going to like what I have to say."

Mitchell braced himself, clutching the receiver; thankfully, Freiburg could not see his tense expression.

"Precedents have been set in this area. In every dispute about the use of materials from alternate universes, Alternitech has come out the winner. I'm convinced the company spends as much money each year on their team of lawyers as they did developing their parallel universe gateway. You'd be wasting your money to try and block the publication. Compared to the rest of the entertainment industry, authors and books are minnows in an ocean. Even the Big Fish in the music and film industries haven't won a single case.

"Alternitech's timeline hunters bring back intellectual property that might conceivably belong to a counterpart in this universe. The first big case was when one of their music specialists, a guy named Jeremy Cardiff—"

"That's who sent me the novel."

"Great," Freiburg said, then continued, ignoring the interruption. "In Alternitech v the Carpenter Estate, Cardiff found several new albums by the Carpenters, in an alternate reality where Karen Carpenter never died of anorexia. The CDs sounded like the same old shit to me, but don't underestimate the huge amount of money generated by piped-in background music. The Carpenter Estate sued, citing copyright infringement and unlawful exploitation of a creative work.

"Alternitech countered that since Karen Carpenter was dead in this universe, she could not 'create' new works after the date of her death. They also argued using an old favorite of the pharmaceutical companies, that since Alternitech had made such a substantial investment developing their technology, they deserved to reap the benefits of its commercial exploitation.

"The ruling sided with the Carpenter Estate insofar as establishing a 'fair percentage' of profits that should go to the creator's counterpart in this reality—fifteen percent, I think it was. But since Alternitech's timeline hunters did all the work to obtain the property, kind of like salvage hunters on the high seas, they were granted full control of its use. Similar lawsuits have been raised by individual movie producers, screenwriters, directors, and even actors who resent the release of 'new films' starring them for which they never got paid. Like I said, in every case, they lose."

Mitchell remembered that one of the alternate Mel Gibson films had caused something of a stir, because the parallel-universe version of the actor had received an Academy Award for a role that this timeline's Gibson had turned down.

Freiburg continued. "When you get right down to it, Mitch, record companies and movie studios don't *want* the individual artists to win. Alternitech provides them with completely finished new work for a fraction of the cost or effort of making it themselves. Much less hassle, too. They just distribute the work through their normal channels and pay a standard percentage of artist's royalties directly to Alternitech. Then, if and only if the court orders it, Alternitech cuts a teeny weeny check to our own world's parallel artist or company or estate, and everyone is happy. Well, almost everyone."

"So you're saying I shouldn't even try, Sheldon? It's not...not *right*!"

"Mitch, if Paul McCartney can't win, then a mere sci-fi novelist doesn't stand a snowball's chance." He paused as if reconsidering. "On the other hand, Mitch my friend, I just thought of a factor that's ironically in your favor, if you really want to stop publication. There's a very real chance that Alternitech won't even bother with your little book. Look at your royalty statements. You're a science fiction writer ten years out of the public eye. Oh sure, there'd be a limited audience for a 'lost unpublished work' by Mitchell Coren... but it isn't exactly a Margaret Mitchell sequel to *Gone with the Wind*. If this Cardiff guy is a fan of yours, contact him and tell him how you feel. Who knows, he might do you a favor and pretend he never found it."

Mitchell didn't know whether to feel stung or take heart from the possibility...

***

DISTRACTED AND FRETTING, he polished the two awards on his mantel—something he hadn't done for the better part of a year. They looked quite impressive, he had to admit, and certainly gave him bragging rights. His occasional visitors asked about them, and he answered with feigned modesty. The awards seemed so irrelevant to his current life.

These days, Mitchell used his skills as a wordsmith in the unglamorous but stable profession of technical writing, producing essential documentation and annual reports for a manufacturing firm. Although it was a challenge to write compelling prose about new cereal box designs or recyclable plastic bottles, he was a master at slanting his text toward investors or consumers or environmental agencies, as needed.

Many of his coworkers—what the science fiction world called "mundanes"—were aspiring writers who never managed to finish or submit stories. Few of them knew about his past, however, since Mitchell rarely mentioned his novel.

As he rubbed a fingerprint off the Nebula's clear Lucite surface, looking at the suspended bits of metal shavings and semi-precious stones that formed a sparkling galaxy, he thought back to those brief, heady days. They were just memories now, but he wouldn't trade them for anything.

Divergent Lines had appeared with a splash like a giant water balloon. An excerpt of the novel had been published in *Analog* as the cover story and won that month's readers' poll. The novel itself had generated rave reviews and was immediately dubbed "a new classic" by critics and his fellow SF authors.

He had been welcomed as a hero at the World Science Fiction Convention. He'd always read science fiction, but had never attended a con before. The fans surprised him at panels, listening to everything he said. They lined up for his book signings in the autograph hall or followed him and asked embarrassingly earnest questions about details he himself had never considered.

When Mitchell went to the Hugo Awards ceremony, he found himself plunged into a sea of unreality as the emcee announced his name as the winner. Astonished and grinning, he stumbled up to the podium and held up his silver rocket ship with mixed feelings of shock and giddy triumph.

The following spring, thanks to the continued buzz, *Divergent Lines* had been a shoe-in for the final Nebula ballot. New to the entire experience, Mitchell stood like a lost puppy in the lobby and the bar, surrounded by luminaries of the genre. He recognized their names from the covers of well-loved books, famous writers ranging from Grand Masters to prolific hacks, all of them legendary and, for the most part, *personable*.

He'd been in a daze. These Titans of science fiction talked to him as a peer, praised his novel. Mitchell found it unnerving, and he began to wonder how he could ever live up to their expectations. Did he deserve so much praise and success? What if his next work didn't measure up to their expectations?

Would he be exposed as a fraud and cast out of this distinguished circle of authors? How would he bear the humiliation?

His publisher paid for his Nebula banquet ticket, and Mitchell was treated as a celebrity at their table. With his stomach tied in knots, he could summon no appetite at all. In an agony of anticipation, he endured the drawn-out meal, the mandatory chit-chat, the interminable banquet speaker. By the time the awards finally began, plodding through each category as if in a calculated effort to increase his anxiety, Mitchell had convinced himself that he had no chance of winning. He was a newcomer. He had no track record. He had never played the politics of exchanging recommendations. He had not campaigned for the award. These writers couldn't possibly consider him a friend and certainly didn't owe him any favors.

And yet the name in the presenter's envelope said *Divergent Lines*. The Nebula seemed even more amazing than the Hugo, because this honor came from his *peers*, fellow professionals who supposedly knew good writing when they saw it. As Mitchell stood clutching the award, he imagined that someday, when he stood at the Pearly Gates and looked back on his entire life, this would be the high point.

After that night, though, Mitchell Coren never wrote another word of fiction. He had left the science fiction community behind and let *Divergent Lines* stand as his sole legacy.

***

EVEN IN HIS heyday, Mitchell had not spent much time with die-hard science fiction fans. Not because he didn't like them—he appreciated anyone who bought and loved his novel. But he didn't understand their intensity or their passions and usually ended up feeling outclassed when they wanted to talk shop.

He met Jeremy Cardiff at a quiet place called Mrs. Coffee, a small bistro with shaded outside tables where they could have a conversation in a pleasant atmosphere. Mitchell didn't know which of them was more nervous. He could see in the timeline hunter's eyes that Jeremy was a bona fide fan.

"This is really an honor, Mr. Coren. I've always been an admirer of *Divergent Lines*, and now that I've read *Infernities*, there's no doubt in my mind that you're one of my all-time favorite authors. I felt so surprised and fortunate to have found the book." Jeremy, a youngish man with a thin face, long hair, and a neatly-trimmed brown beard, looked like a waif hoping for a pat on the head. His blue eyes were wide, his smile tentative.

Mitchell took a drink of coffee, then cleared his throat. "Well, Mr. Cardiff, that's what I'm here to talk to you about."

"Please, call me Jeremy." Then the younger man's face fell as he interpreted Mitchell's reluctant tone.

Mitchell chose his words as carefully as he would have in preparing a viewgraph presentation for the board of the manufacturing company. He wasn't sure his reasons would make sense to anyone but himself. Though he knew he didn't exactly have a legal case, he might be able to play the celebrity card. Perhaps by asking a special favor from his number one fan, he could get what he needed. "I think you're perceptive enough to understand why I don't want the novel published here. It's not *my* book. Somebody else wrote it."

"No, Mr. Coren. You wrote it. Another version of you, maybe, but it was still your talent, your creativity. When I was in college I read and reread *Divergent Lines* until my copy fell apart, and I've been waiting ten years for a new novel by the same author. When I found *Infernities*, I sent you the physical book I brought back through the portal, but I made a photocopy. I'm already on my second time through it. It's brilliant—full of intricate layers and nuances."

Mitchell desperately wanted to ask which book he thought was better. Dedicated readers like Jeremy were generally his toughest customers and his harshest critics and, because Mitchell didn't think a new novel could ever live up to their expectations, he had decided not to try.

"That man may have the same name and the same genetics as I do, but he grew up in a parallel universe with a different set of circumstances. He's not me. He obviously reached a different decision about his career. But I didn't write *Infernities*, and if you published it here in our universe, people would see it as my own work, no matter how many disclaimers you put on it."

"But it's good, sir. Have you read it?"

"No, I don't dare. It would seem almost… plagiaristic ."

As if clinging to hope, Jeremy said, "So… are you writing something of your own? Maybe a book that's similar to *Infernities*?"

"No. I'm not writing anything."

The young man looked at his coffee as if it were poison. He didn't seem angry at Mitchell's attitude, just deeply disappointed. "Then I don't understand. What made you stop writing? I mean, you got the royal treatment. People were lined up waiting for your next book. You had a contract to fulfull, didn't you?"

"Yes. And I…decided to return the advance."

"But why? It just doesn't make sense."

"Why? I'd already won the highest accolades in my field." Mitchell spoke softly, but his voice grew more intense. "Whether through brilliance or sheer dumb luck I muddled my way to the pinnacle of success my first time out of the starting gate. *Divergent Lines* was hailed as the best book of the year, won all the awards, got spectacular reviews in every periodical from *Publishers Weekly* and *Kirkus* to *Locus* and *Chronicle*. *Library Journal* called it an instant classic."

Mitchell sighed. "Don't you see? The weight of it all gets oppressive. Where could I possibly go from there? There's no place but down." An edge of bitterness sharpened his tone. "It's a very long way down. No matter how good it was, my second book—*Infernities* or whatever I might've called it—would never

be good enough. The fans and the critics certainly aren't kind unless your sophomore effort is unbelievably spectacular.

"As it stands right now, I'll go down in history as the author of a great novel. But if I published twenty other books, regardless of how well-written they might be, I can tell you some of the review quotes already: 'A solid novel, but not as inspired as *Divergent Lines*.' Or 'A fine effort, though it doesn't live up to the promise of its predecessor.' Or, worse yet, 'A disappointing follow-on to the author's first novel.'"

Jeremy frowned at what Mitchell was saying. "I think you're too hard on your fans, sir. We would have followed you. Even after ten years, most of us still want to read whatever you have to say."

"Maybe I don't have anything else to say," Mitchell said. "I can name author after author who falls into that category. Being successful is a Catch-22. If your first novel is a smash hit, an award winner and a critical success, it might mean your career has momentum and you're launched. On the other hand, it could mean your writing will never be good enough again. What should I have done—expanded *Divergent Lines* and written a couple of unnecessary sequels, so I could call it a trilogy? I could have licensed my universe, farmed it out to other authors, but that just didn't seem right to me. Either way, I would have been crucified by the fans and the critics."

"Just by the snobs," Jeremy said, "not by the *fans*. But you disappeared from fandom altogether. When's the last time you went to a science fiction convention?"

"The WorldCon where I got my Hugo was the first and last. I stopped reading *Locus* and *Chronicle* and *Ansible* after one of them ran an editorial about one-hit wonders that led off with 'What ever happened to Mitchell Coren?'" He looked at his coffee. "I didn't stand a chance of keeping up the momentum in my career. Fans and critics are too unpredictable. So I controlled the only part of the equation that I *could* control: I stopped writing fiction. My life is stable now that I've accepted the wisdom of anonymity. But if Alternitech publishes this apocryphal second novel that I didn't really write, then I'll be at the mercy of the public's expectations again. Please, don't do it."

Disappointment and resignation filled Jeremy's eyes as he unzipped his backpack and reached inside to withdraw a thick stack of photocopied pages. "Look, this is my only copy. What happens to it is not really supposed to be my decision. Alternitech owns proprietary rights to whatever I bring back through parallel universes. Still, no matter how much *I* loved this novel, I have to admit that this doesn't have the equivalent value to Alternitech of, say, an unknown collection of Sherlock Holmes stories by Arthur Conan Doyle or the Dean Koontz/Stephen King collaboration I uncovered once. I think people deserve to read it. I was going to have you autograph this for me." Jeremy slid the stack of papers across the table. "But now I guess you'd better keep it, so you'll know there aren't any other copies in existence. You decide what to do. It's your call, Mr. Coren. It's your book."

"I—" Mitchell started to speak, but found his voice choked with emotion. He took a long drink of his now-tepid coffee and started again. "Well...don't you want to keep it? You said you were reading it."

Jeremy shook his head. "If you know I have a copy, you'd always worry that someday I'd be tempted to post it on the Internet. It's better if you keep it."

The papers felt warm in Mitchell's hands. His vision blurred, and he took a moment to compose himself. "I...didn't expect this."

"I'm a musician myself, Mr. Coren. I write and record songs, but I haven't had much success so far. It was a minor consolation when I found that I did have a hit record in an alternate universe, but nothing here yet. I was the one who brought back the new music for that whole Karen Carpenter debacle, and

I don't feel very good about it. As a musician, I thought Carpenter or her estate should have had some control over her own creative work, no matter which incarnation made the album. The same goes for you, sir. If you're uncomfortable about having *Infernities* published, then..." He shrugged.

"I can't tell you how much this means to me."

"I think I understand." Jeremy slurped his decaf cappuccino. "Besides, I'm your fan. I can't think of anything cooler than to know I am the only person in this entire universe who's read your new novel."

***

DOZENS OF THE loose photocopy sheets wadded up under the fireplace grate made for good kindling. Mitchell rolled the remaining loose pages of twenty-pound bond into plump literary logs, rubber-banded them, and set them on the log holder above the crumpled pages. Then he fanned out the hardcover book and flattened it across the white paper logs. He stood back to observe the diminutive funeral pyre with a sense of uneasiness.

He should have felt relieved.

This potential source of humiliation or disruption would soon be dealt with. The book would no longer be in his life, could no longer irritate or goad him by its very existence. No fans would have a chance to either criticize or clamor for more. The chapter would be closed.

Yes, Mitchell was definitely relieved.

After he lit the match, he hesitated for a long, indecisive moment before finally touching the flame to the edge of one of the loose sheets. There. A burnt offering to a cruel muse.

As the fire caught, guilt gnawed at the ragged edges of his mind. There was something intrinsically criminal about burning a book, especially the only copies of a book. While this event would not go down in history with the sacking of the Library of Alexandria, it was still a loss to at least some tiny backwater of the literary sea—especially to the hopeful fans who had waited so long for any work by Mitchell Coren.

The flames grew higher, devouring the loose pages and curling the glossy dust jacket of *Infernities*. An interesting play on words, he thought. Infinity, Alternative, and Eternity all rolled together. Now he could add "Inferno" to the quadruple entendre. He wondered how it related to the story.

Didn't he owe it to himself at least to read his own work, to see what he could have done with his talent? *Infernities* was tangible proof that in some other reality his author-self had overcome the pressure and the expectations. But how? Didn't that mean that he, too, could do it?

No. He'd made the right decision. He thought with some satisfaction of the author photo blackening and blistering, cremating his cocksure successful doppelganger. The man had dared to risk his reputation, his spotless literary legacy, to write this second novel and offer it to an unpredictable reading public. He had dared. Had risked…

With a groan of annoyance and frustration Mitchell snatched the hardcover from the fire, dropped it to the floor, and stamped on it to put out the flames at the edges. He bent and picked up the singed novel that had disrupted his calm life.

As he picked up the blackened book, Mitchell's lips flickered in a smile. Though he still had no intention of publishing the novel, he would hold onto the book as a goad. Just to keep him honest. To remind himself of what could be.

He had his own ideas for new stories and novels, of course. Every writer did. The ideas had never stopped coming, and he had jotted down notes during lunch hours at his tech-writing job. Some of the outlines were damn good, but he had been too afraid of failure to write the books, believing it better to let readers live with his mysterious seclusion than to risk them shaking their heads in disappointment.

Yet his alternate self had somehow shaken off the fear of failure. Therefore, it could be done. And that sincere, appreciative look he had seen in Jeremy Cardiff's eyes told Mitchell he still had an audience, no matter how small.…

Some authors were motivated to write strictly for the critics, for the kudos and awards. Others wanted the money and name recognition of sales, with big print runs and splashy publicity. Some wrote only for themselves, giving the finger to anyone else's expectations. But why had *he* become a writer?

Now there was a group to whom he owed something: his fans—the readers who understood what he was trying to do and who saw him as a human being with a talent that should not simply be thrown away. *Those* fans would enjoy whatever he wrote.

Certainly, a few of them went to the crazy fringe, seeing him as a guru with unparalleled insight into their particular problems. But most were just regular people. If he struck the right note, his pool of fans would be large; if he chose a path that was too esoteric, the numbers might dwindle. In either case, the readers still deserved his respect.

Mitchell looked at the charred copy of *Infernities* he held. He realized now that burning the novel was selfish. There were thousands (or maybe only dozens) of people like Jeremy Cardiff, who would have enjoyed this book if he allowed it to be published.

Setting the burned hardcover down, he opened the bottom file drawer of his desk where he kept the folder of notes and ideas that were just too good to throw away. If he was going to bury this cuckoo's egg of a book, then he was obligated to give the readers something in exchange.

Mitchell skimmed his outlines. He had forgotten how clever or thought-provoking many of them were. Had he intended to be an Emily Dickinson, locking his notes away in a box for someone else to find after he died? Not long ago, he had been tempted to burn these, too.

Now he would write some of them.

As he flipped through his notes, the ideas reached a critical mass, and Mitchell saw how he could combine concepts and characters. What might have been simple short story ideas now became enough material for a multi-layered novel. It wouldn't be just like *Divergent Lines*, but so what? It would still be good, still be worth writing.

He spread the papers out on his desk. He had an old, outdated laptop computer and plenty of time during his lunch hours. Some of the greatest works of literature had been completed a few pages at a time during lunch breaks....

Mitchell glanced at the fireplace, where the fire had now died to a pile of orange embers. The photocopied novel was now nothing but ash.

On the mantel above, his Hugo and Nebula awards reflected the dull glow. He turned away from them and focused on his desk. *Divergent Lines* had been an unnecessary ball-and-chain to his creativity, along with all the other excuses he had made up over the past ten years. That was enough procrastination.

He looked at the charred but still readable hardcover of *Infernities*. First, before he started on any new book or short story, he had to write a letter.

"Dear Mr. Cardiff, let me make you a bargain." He proposed that if he had not produced any new novels or short stories in the next five years, then Jeremy had his blessing to publish *Infernities*, if only to reward the fans who had waited so long. He packaged the letter with the scorched book and mailed it to his "number one fan." Simply knowing the novel existed would be all the inspiration he really needed.

On the way back from the mailbox, he smiled to himself, convinced it would never be necessary for the other Mitchell Coren's book to be published here. He would take that risk for himself.

Fan Favorites From Kristine Kathryn Rusch
FAMILIARITY
A Winston and Ruby Collection

O'Neil De Noux is one of the best working short story writers of detective fiction. I say that every time, with every one of his stories, because it's true.

And he has published almost fifty novels. His awards include The United Kingdom Short Story Prize, the Shamus Award (for best private eye fiction), the Derringer Award (for excellence in mystery short fiction) and Police Book of the Year. Two of his stories have appeared in the prestigious Best American Mystery Stories *annual anthology.*

In other words, you can't go wrong reading a detective story by O'Neil and here is a great one to prove my point.

A Good Shooting
O'Neil De Noux

THE BODY LAY in the street, next to a beat-up green Ford Escort, a heavy-set man in a gray T-shirt and jeans, a blue-steel semi-automatic pistol lying two feet from his right hand. Detective John Raven Beau, standing in his shirt sleeves on the neutral ground along the center of St. Charles Avenue, loosened his crimson tie with its geometric design which wasn't a geometric design at all. A closer look would reveal the small white circles were human skulls. Went with the territory, working Homicide.

Beau waited for a streetcar to pass, tucking his leather-bound notebook under his left arm and watching the curious faces peering out at the crime scene as the green-and-brown electric car clanked by, heading downtown. Beau at six-two, a lean two hundred pounds, was thirty, a square-jawed man with dark brown hair and light brown eyes beneath a hooded brow. His sharp nose gave him a hawk-like appearance. On his right hip sat his nine-millimeter Beretta Model 92F snug in its black canvas holster, his gold star-and-crescent New Orleans Police badge clipped to his belt above the left front pocket of his dark blue suit pants.

The crime scene encompassed the uptown-riverside intersection of St. Charles and Burdette Street, including the corner drug store and the body in the street. Beau's sergeant, Jodie Kintyre, stood alongside the drug store with a young patrol officer. Jodie: five-seven, a sleek one-twenty, wore her yellow blond hair in a long page-boy cut. Her dark green skirt-suit brought out the color in her cat-like hazel eyes, which she blinked at Beau as he stepped up.

"This is Frank Willard," she said, nodding to the patrol officer whose dark brown face shimmered with perspiration on this typically humid summer afternoon. Willard: twenty-two, stood five-nine with a thick-bodied wrestler's build.

She gave Beau the rundown in quick sentences. Willard responded to a Signal 64, an armed robbery, at the drug store and caught the robber on the way out. There was an exchange of gunshots. The robber missed. Willard didn't.

"We have six eye-witnesses inside." Jodie nodded at the drug store. "Snowood's taking statements. Stay with Willard 'til the lab's done with him and take him to the Bureau." She tapped Willard on the shoulder. "Don't talk to anyone but me and Detective Beau here until we take your statement."

"Yes, ma'am."

"Call me sergeant or Det. Kintyre or Jodie, just not ma'am." She hurried off to join the crime scene technician who'd just arrived with his camera and brown evidence case. Beau smiled to himself. At thirty-six, Jodie was getting sensitive when anyone called her ma'am, unless it was a little kid.

Willard looked up at Beau and said, "Hope the old woman's gonna be all right."

"Hope you're not talking about Jodie."

"From inside. Behind the counter. Robber pistol whipped her. Lotta blood."

Jesus!

"What did your sergeant mean, 'til they're done with me?"

"They'll secure your weapon and swab your hands for a neutron activation test to determine if you fired a firearm. Perpetrator too. That's it."

Willard leaned back against the brick wall of the drug store and let out a long breath. He looked so damn young to Beau who tried reassuring him. "I know what you're going through, man. I've been through it. More than once."

Willard turned his dark brown eyes to Beau and said, "I feel sick."

"Don't throw up on me."

"No, not like that." Willard closed his eyes. "I just feel like…jelly inside."

"Not like in the movies, is it? Shoot a man and stand over him making wise cracks. You feel crappy, even when you do it right." Beau watched Willard breathing heavily. "Relax. It looks like a good shooting."

"I don't know how he missed me. Face to face like that." He gasped as if struggling to breathe. "We should teach how to duck and shoot at the range. I was duckin' man."

Beau faced him and said, "Relax. Save it for your statement. Now breathe normally."

Willard nodded and started controlling his breathing. He eyes opened after a minute. "What's your name again?"

"Beau."

"As in John Raven Beau?"

Even rookies heard of me, Beau thought. It wasn't a satisfying thought.

Willard's eyes changed, a recognition maybe, a bonding maybe, standing with John Raven Beau, the half-Sioux, half-Cajun cop who always got his man, one way or the other. Beau was sure Willard thought he'd killed a dozen men at least, when the number was three, exactly. All good shootings. Justifiable Homicides, declared by separate Grand Juries.

A streetcar heading uptown stopped and Beau automatically checked out who came off: a teen girl in a white polo shirt and red shorts, a teen boy in a green T-shirt and khaki pants, and a red-headed woman, late twenties, wearing blue nurse's scrubs and white tennis shoes. Beau watched her stand motionless, staring at the crime scene as the streetcar pulled away.

She remained frozen in place, just staring at the body in the street.

Beau stepped away from the drug store and flagged down a passing patrol car. Must have been a slow day in the Second District with all the cop cars passing, drawn to the scene like moths to a light bulb. The cop leaned over and rolled down the passenger-side window so Beau could lean in and ask, "Could you park your unit over there to block the view of the body from the streetcar?"

"Sure," the eager cop said, pulling into the intersection, hitting his blue lights. His name tag read: Bertucci. Another rookie.

When Beau looked back at the woman in nurse's scrubs, he saw her crossing the street heading straight for him. As she arrived, he could see tears in her eyes. She was about five-five, about a hundred pounds, a very pretty face. Her hair looked strawberry blonde up close.

She pointed a shaky hand toward the body and said, "I think that's my husband."

Beau gently took her elbow and led her away from everyone down to the end of the drug store and had her lean back against the wall. He pulled his portable radio from his back pocket and called Jodie.

"Can you come around the corner?"

Jodie came immediately and Beau moved toward her, keeping a wary eye on the strawberry blonde.

"You have the robber's name yet?"

"We're just going through his wallet now. John Clay."

Beau led the way back to the woman and asked for her husband's name.

"John Clay." She wiped her eyes and Beau could see they were blue, ovaled as she stared at him.

"Talk to her," Jodie said, returning to the body.

Beau took the woman's elbow again and led her to the high curb and sat her down, sitting next to her, feet in the street, but not far enough to worry about passing cars.

"I'm Detective Beau," he began, letting his voice drop. "It is your husband."

She nodded and sucked in a deep breath. She put her head between her knees. Beau waved to Officer Bertucci. Pulling out a buck he said, "Go in the drug store and get me a couple Cokes. Make sure they're cold." He glanced back at Willard who was taking it all in. "You want something to drink?"

Willard shook his head as he watched the strawberry blonde.

"I don't think they're open." Bertucci pointed at the drug store.

"Go inside and steal two Cokes. I won't call the police."

Bertucci gave Beau the look, the I-know-I'm-a-rookie-and-the-butt-of-another-joke-look, until Beau narrowed his eyes and said, "Go!"

As Bertucci entered the store, Jodie came back around and waved Willard to the crime lab technician.

Beau leaned close and asked the robber's wife, "You okay?"

"I'm trying."

"What's your name?"

"Barbara Clay."

He picked up a scent of her perfume now, sweet but not strong. She sat up straight and pulled her hair away from her face, reached into her small purse for a Kleenex to wipe her face.

"I knew something like this was going to happen."

"Something like what?"

She stood and Beau got up as Bertucci came out with two cans of Diet-Coke, saying that was all they had. She waved hers away but Beau took both.

"The Ford Escort around the corner," Barbara said. "It's ours."

She looked back at Beau and said, "You'll want to come home with me. I have the receipts for his guns."

"Where do you live?"

"Two blocks away."

Beau turned to wave at Jodie and bumped into Bertucci standing there with the dollar in his hand.

"Go back inside and put the dollar next to the cash register."

"Yes, sir." Bertucci bounced away.

Beau waved Jodie over and handed her a Coke.

"Thanks." She popped the cap immediately.

He told her about the Ford Escort and the gun receipts.

Jodie nodded. "Get what you can from her." She raised the Coke but stopped at the deadpan look on Beau's face. "You know what I mean." She poked him in the ribs. "I'll get someone to take Willard's statement."

Beau moved back to Barbara Clay and pointed across the street at his unmarked Chevy Caprice. "Why walk when we can ride?"

"I need to walk," Barbara said as she started to cross St. Charles. Beau went with her. They crossed to the neutral ground, pausing for uptown traffic along the far side of the avenue before moving to the sidewalk.

Barbara turned and looked into Beau's eyes. "Did anyone else get hurt?"

"He beat up an elderly woman."

Tears filled her eyes again and she leaned back against the Caprice. Beau waited, notebook under his right arm, Coke in his left hand. He looked around for a passerby who

might be thirsty when Barbara reached for the soft drink, popped it open and took a deep draught. Beau noticed a fresh purplish bruise on her forearm and two older yellowish bruises above her elbow.

She took a moment to catch her breath, wiping the tears away with her fingers. She raised the soft drink without looking up and said, "Thanks. Really." She pushed off the car and Beau settled in next to her as they moved down the avenue, passing beneath the wide branches of the oaks, the air musty smelling like chlorophyll now. The scent was familiar to Beau who was raised on a small bayou just off Vermilion Bay, in swampy, southwest Louisiana.

They turned up Adams Street, crossed to the other side up to Hampson. Barbara dug keys out of her purse and pointed to a two-story apartment house. "In back," she said, guiding him through a Page fence with no gate, around the side of the wooden building, avoiding air conditioners sticking out of the side windows.

"Watch the stairs," Barbara said, leading the way up a steep wooden staircase that was once painted white. "Don't run your hands on the rail or you'll have splinters for years." It was then Beau identified her accent. He knew

HISTORICAL MYSTERY STORIES

O'Neil De Noux's newest short story "Another Body" was published in The Book of Extraordinary Historical Mystery Stories: The Best of the New Original Stories of the Genre *(Mango Publishing, May 2019). The story features New Orleans Police Detective Jacques Dugas who appears in previous novels* The French Detective *and* Howls in the Night.

https://amzn.to/2Y20HzF

she wasn't from New Orleans the first time she spoke. She sounded Midwestern.

As Beau waited for her to unlock the door, he reached down and rubbed his left knee. And for a moment, he thought of the orthoscopic surgery scheduled the following week, to repair the cartilage in his knee.

It was an efficiency apartment, one large room with a double bed in one corner, mismatched dressers on either side, a small entertainment center with a portable TV and two narrow doors beyond, a closet and a bathroom, most likely. The kitchenette stood on the other side of the room.

Barbara put the Coke in the small refrigerator and her purse on a turquoise Formica table. The table had only two chairs, neither matched each other or the table. She moved to the small sink and rinsed out a coffee pot, reached for a bag of coffee-and-chicory. She put a fresh pot on her Mr. Coffee Machine. Beau noticed the place was very clean, smelling of lemon cleaner, curtains fluffed without a hint of dust. The windows sparkled.

Barbara sat in one of the chairs and nodded to the other. Beau sat across from her. She finally looked him in the eye again and said, "He beat up an old woman?"

"Pistol whipped."

Her shoulders sank and tears welled in her eyes again. She put her face in her hands. After a good cry, she got up for a Kleenex, took two matching mugs from the cupboard and asked in a hollow voice, "Cream or sugar?"

"Black."

"It's strong."

"That's the way I like it."

She brought the coffee and sat.

"Earlier you said, 'I knew something like this was going to happen.' What did you mean?"

She took in a deep breath. "I should have said something like this was *bound* to happen." She stared into her coffee and explained. Beau took notes as Barbara Clay laid out her life with John Clay in short weary sentences.

Married two years, Barbara was the sole supporter. John Clay, who had served time in juvenile detention and a ninety-day stint in a parish prison for battery, was supposed to be in welding school. Previously he'd taken auto mechanic classes and air-conditioning classes.

"He could be sweet," Barbara said, taking a sip of coffee. "But he had a mean streak." She lifted her arm and looked at the bruises. "Never hit me, just grabbed and squeezed and shook me sometimes. When he'd been drinking."

Barbara got up and moved to the sink, opened the cabinet below and pointed inside. "I hid his first gun in there. Behind the cans of cleaners. He was drunk. When he woke, I told him he came home without the gun." She came back to the table. "It was a Colt. Nine-millimeter I think. I threw it in the river."

She didn't know what he was doing with a gun. He never seemed to have any money and never came home with anything. "I told him if I ever caught him bringing anything stolen here, I was gone." Her face seemed to tighten and her voice was stronger now.

"I got rid of the gun and he went right out and got a bigger gun. A Smith & Wesson, forty caliber. He said everyone needs a gun in this city. Said he was going to get me a twenty-two."

She looked into her cup again. "I was going to leave him. Started to time and again, but…"

Beau took out a business card and put it on the table. Barbara leaned over and looked at it before stepping back to the kitchen counter and digging two pieces of paper from the silverware drawer. She sat and passed them to Beau. Gun receipts.

"He bought both at gun shows in Kenner. Even waited the five days."

The first receipt, for a Colt nine-millimeter was dated over a year ago. The second, three months later for a Smith & Wesson forty caliber. Willard was lucky one of those rounds hadn't hit him.

"Was it a police officer who shot him?"

Beau nodded. "A rookie. Your husband gave him no choice."

Barbara sighed and picked up Beau's card and said, "It's French? Your name?"

"Cajun."

"I thought you were Mexican. Hispanic."

"I get that a lot." Beau's face remained expressionless. "My mother's Oglala Sioux."

Her eyes lit up. "I'm from South Dakota. Sioux Falls."

"My mother's back up there with my grandparents. Pine Ridge Reservation." Beau knew Sioux Falls was on the other side of the state.

A sad smile came to Barbara Clay's lips. "Fancy meeting a Lakota down here."

At least she had the tribe's name right. *Sioux* was the name given to Beau's people by their enemies, like the Pawnee and the Crow and the white man. Beau liked the word Sioux better. It ran off the tongue with fierceness.

"May I see your driver's license?" Beau asked.

She dug it out of her purse and he copied her pertinent information from it, date of birth, social security number. Her maiden name was Crockett. She looked nice in her DL photo, nicer than most people. She should smile more often. He passed her license back.

"Where do you work?"

"Charity Hospital MRI Unit."

Beau smiled. "I was in one yesterday." His mind immediately flashed back to the MRI Unit at Ochsner Hospital, him inside the hollow center of a space-age machine, lying very still for twenty minutes, with the machine making loud noises. He remembered all the warning signs lining the walls, signs warning about pacemakers, the danger of magnetizing metal objects bought into the room. He had to leave everything outside the unit, gun, badge, belt buckle, even his ballpoint pen.

"Why were you there?" Barbara asked.

He rubbed his knee and explained about the torn meniscus cartilage, went on to explain how he'd torn up the other knee at his spring game at LSU, sophomore year, and had been unconsciously relying on his left leg so much, he'd torn the cartilage cushion between femur and tibia.

"You're getting it repaired, I hope."

"Next week." He reached into his pocket for a small plastic case and took out two pills.

"Naproxen?"

He nodded as he swallowed the pills with the last of his coffee. He tore out a fresh sheet of note paper, jotted down the number of the coroner's office and passed it to her.

"You won't have to physically identify him. Unless you want to. We can match his fingerprints."

She sank back in the chair and looked smaller. He looked down at his notebook as he told her the city would bury him, if she didn't have the money.

"I have a burial policy." She got up and went to one of the dressers next to the bed. She rifled through a large folder and came up with several sets of folded papers. "Yes," she said in a relived voice. "It's right here." She re-stuffed the folder and started back to him but noticed something with the papers in her hand, stepped back and pulled out a different set of papers and brought those to the table.

It was a burial policy for $5,000. Barely enough to bury him. The policy was dated a year ago, shortly after her husband bought his first gun.

"Was your husband home when you left this morning?"

"Sleeping. My shift starts at five-thirty."

"Did he tell you what he'd be doing today?"

"He was supposed to be at welding school." She pulled a business card from her purse. The school was in Metairie. She shook her head. "He never told me what he did. Wasn't much of a talker."

And Beau had to wonder why an attractive, intelligent woman like this would marry such loser? Trying to understand love was an impossibility. Beau's Cajun father told him that long ago, sitting in a pirogue while fishing with his son. "Never even try to figure," his old man said. "De heart go where she wanna to go. Notin' you can do 'bout it. Look at your mama. She too pretty fo' me, too smart and too good."

Beau nodded toward his card, still on the table. "If you think of anything else, call me. Oh, what's your phone number?"

"We don't have one." She asked for his notebook and pen and put down her number at work.

He stood and told her he'd be in touch when they were finished processing the Ford Escort and she could pick it up. "Is there anyone who can come be with you?" he asked as he stepped to the doorway.

She shook her head and said she wanted to be alone for a while. She gave him a long stare and he said she should lock the door behind him. As he moved down the stairs, he heard the latch click. He felt the familiar pain in his knee but his mind was occupied elsewhere.

She has a burial policy. Odd. Maybe not. Maybe she could see the violence in her husband's eyes.

***

JODIE WAS BEHIND her gray-metal government-issue desk in the squad room, Paul Snowood in the chair next to it. The crime lab tech stood on the other side next to Beau's desk, which abutted Jodie's. Over by the coffee pot, Frank Willard stood beneath the unofficial logo of the Homicide Division, a vulture perched atop an NOPD gold star-and-crescent badge. His arms folded, he still looked jittery to Beau.

Snowood was explaining, "...it's what we call here in town an open-and-shut case, 'a justifiable homicide.' Willard jumped the dude comin' out and it was Dodge City for a minute." Snowood: six feet tall, two hundred pounds, over forty (but wouldn't go into it) wore another of his cowboy outfits, gold

shirt with two rows of buttons, dressy brown denim pants, tan cowboy boots. His white Stetson lay atop his desk.

"The dude and Willard drew on each other, like the O.K. Corral. Willard ducked and fired twice and the dude just plain missed. It's what we call back in the badlands, some good shootin' and some bad shootin'."

Jodie looked like she had a migraine.

Snowood, born and raised across the river in the suburb of Belle Chasse, took the fact he was born on the west bank of the Mississippi so seriously, he'd evolved into a turn-of-the-century lawman, straight out of Tombstone. He'd have a handlebar moustache if he could grow a decent one.

Jodie acknowledged Beau with a nod. Snowood turned and grinned his tobacco-laced teeth at Beau and said, "Ah, the plains warrior has arrived." He raised a white Styrofoam cup to his lips and spit into it.

"How's the woman from the drug store?" Beau asked.

Jodie, "She's in stable condition. No fractures. She'll be okay. Eventually."

Atop Beau's cluttered desk lay two semi-automatics, Willard's stainless-steel Beretta nine-millimeter and a blue-steel Smith & Wesson forty caliber. The tech picked up the blue-steel semi-automatic and wiped the white fingerprint powder from it before dropping the magazine out and pulling back the slide. He had trouble with both.

He dusted the magazine and carefully flicked out the rounds and dusted them, finding several good partials, which he lifted with plastic tape.

"Our gunman was arrested four times." Snowood said. "Three juvie arrests for shoplifting and simple battery. One adult arrest for simple battery."

"Damn," the technician said as he struggled to pull back the slide to double-check that no round was in the chamber. Making sure the weapon was empty, he pointed it at the top of the row of windows at the far end of the room and pulled the trigger.

"Well, this confirms it," he told Jodie as he sniffed the barrel of Clay's Smith & Wesson and shook his head. "Got ten rounds here. We only found two casings at the scene. Both from Willard's gun."

Jodie nodded and closed her eyes. John Clay hadn't fired his gun at all. Beau looked over at Willard who was sweating again. Big time.

"Safety's off and it won't fire." The tech shrugged at Jodie. "Gun's malfunctioning."

Willard came over slowly. "Does this mean it's bad for me?"

Jodie shook her head as Snowood said, "Hell no. It's a real gun and we got enough witnesses said he pointed it at you."

Willard didn't seem convinced, probably because it came from a man who looked like a refugee from Mel Brooks' *Blazing Saddles*.

Jodie sat up and told Willard, "We have five eye-witnesses inside the drug store saw him beat up the old woman. Three of them watched him go out the front door and point his gun at you and all swear y'all exchanged gunshots. And our sixth eye-witness, from the street, also saw Clay point his gun at you before you fired and he's a bank president."

Willard wiped the sweat from his face. Jodie opened her hands, palms up and recited the law verbatim. "R.S. 14:20. A homicide is justifiable when committed in self-defense by one who reasonably believes he is in imminent danger of losing his life or receiving great bodily harm and the killing is necessary to save himself from that danger."

"Sounds like a good shootin' to me," Snowood said.

"It's a good shooting," Jodie confirmed.

Willard turned to Beau who nodded and told him, "Relax. I'm serious."

Beau leaned his hands on his desk and looked down at the weapons. He went to brush the silver paper clip away from Clay's Smith & Wesson, but it was stuck. He tried pulling it off and it took a real yank to get it off.

"Glue?" Snowood said.

Beau shook his head and put the paper-clip next to the S&W, which sucked the paper clip to it like a magnet.

Jodie leaned forward. "Maybe the paper clip's magnetized." Beau tried it with Willard's weapon and his stapler but the clip didn't stick. He pulled out his stainless-steel Parker ball point and put it near the S&W and it rolled right to it.

"Damn," Jodie said.

"The gun's a frigging magnet," Snowood declared. "Don't that beat all."

The technician took both weapons, bullets and magazines down to the crime lab as Snowood got up to take Willard home. Jodie reminded the rookie she'd see him in the morning at the Superintendent's Hearing.

"Don't worry," she assured him and started on her paperwork.

As Beau typed up a daily on what he'd learned from Barbara Clay, he told Jodie about the receipts and the burial policy and the short, unhappy marriage. Finishing the daily, he made two copies, one for his records, put one in their lieutenant's In tray and passed the original to Jodie.

Sitting back down, Beau closed his eyes and ran through it all again and came up with the same conclusion he'd come up with

as soon as the word "magnet" came from Snowood's mouth.

Jodie stood and pulled the sheet from her typewriter. "Gotta go," she said. He remembered she had a preliminary hearing in criminal court at four p.m. He opened his mouth to tell her what he was thinking, but said nothing.

After she'd left the squad room, Beau went down to the crime lab. Firearms examiner Peggy Ruffin had the Smith & Wesson completely disassembled and lying on an evidence table. Peggy: five-three, one-fifty, wasn't the friendliest cop, but she was the best firearms examiner in the city.

"The damnedest thing I've ever seen," she told Beau. He'd never seen her so animated. "This weapon is completely magnetized. You could pull the trigger all day and it wouldn't fire." She pointed at the firing pen. "It's stuck to the side of the channel in the slide. Officer Willard is one lucky man."

Beau felt his heart stammering as he turned to leave.

"Hell," Peggy added, "if we could do this to every criminal's gun, I'd be out of a job."

***

BEAU SAT AT the top of the stairs and watched the orange glow of the late-afternoon sunlight fill the small backyard of Barbara Clay's apartment house. A mockingbird bounced from the branch of a camellia bush and scooped an insect from the grass before flying away, a gray and white streak of feathers. He waited and the mockingbird returned to the bush and perched patiently until it spotted another bug and swooped down to get it.

An hour after he'd arrived, just as twilight was claiming the city, Barbara came around the house and stopped at the bottom of the stairs. Even in the dusk he could see her eyes widen as she looked up at him. She was still in her work clothes and came up slowly. By the time she was a few feet away, he could see her eyes were wet.

"We have to talk," Beau said, standing and brushing off his pants.

She fumbled with her keys and he could see her breathing heavily now. She led the way in and flipped on the light.

"Let's sit," Beau suggested, sitting across from her at the Formica table.

Barbara brushed her hair away from her face and said in a jittery voice, "I was at the funeral parlor. You want some coffee?"

"No. But you need to pay attention to what I'm about to say."

She folded her arms in a typical defensive position.

"Whatever you tell me right now is off the record. I'm *not* advising you of your right to remain silent, so I can't use anything you say against you." He paused a moment to see if his words were registering. Barbara blinked twice and wiped her eyes.

"I know what happened," Beau went on. "You couldn't just throw the gun away again, he'd get another, so you brought it to work. To the MRI Unit. Magnetic Resonance Imaging, I remember the signs on the walls."

Barbara took in a deep breath, her blue eyes boring into Beau's eyes. Her lower lip quivered, her voice a scratchy whisper. "I couldn't live with myself if he shot someone."

Beau felt the plains warrior rising inside and he spoke carefully, his voice void of emotion. "You knew he was up to no good. Knew he was using the gun for criminal endeavors. You didn't believe it was for his protection. Otherwise…"

"I wouldn't have incapacitated the gun." Her voice was firmer.

"Exactly. The gun was completely magnetized. Wouldn't fire, but you know that."

The war drums echoed in some racial memory in the back of Beau's mind as he said, "The other insurance policy."

"What other…" Barbara looked away.

"The one you put back when you brought out the burial policy."

She looked at him, got up slowly and went back to the dresser and the folder. She pulled out papers and came back, placing them in front of Beau on the table.

There were two policies. Life insurance on John Clay for $20,000, Barbara Clay beneficiary. The second policy was on Barbara with Cristina Crockett as beneficiary. Beau pointed to the name and Barbara said it was her mother. He checked the dates on the policies. Both were dated shortly after the burial policy was taken out. He noted that John Clay had signed the policy on him, acknowledging the coverage. She didn't take it out behind his back. No need to get John Clay's signature on the burial policy. She'd taken it out directly with the funeral parlor.

Looking back at the blue eyes, he could see her struggling to keep from crying again. Her voice was barely a whisper. "I didn't do it to kill him."

"I know."

"I didn't want him to hurt anyone," she repeated.

"Even you?" He pointed to her bruises and for an instant felt his father's touch inside. His father would have been more than sympathetic with this woman, he would have soothed her with his Cajun compassion, probably joking to make her feel better.

But a moment later the warrior rose again in Beau. "You're a smart woman, Barbara. Don't get too smart. We're pretty smart too."

Beau stood up and stretched.

She looked up and asked, "What happens now?"

"Go back home. You've got a second chance at life. Use it well." He looked around the tiny apartment. "Don't carry this around for the rest of your life." He smiled sadly, letting his Cajun side through. "I'm here to tell you it's all right. You didn't put the gun in his hand. You took it out."

He nodded and turned toward the door.

She said, "What about the officer who shot him? Is he going to be okay?"

"Yeah," Beau said as he reached for the knob. "It was a good shooting."

From Kristine Grayson
COMPLETELY SMITTEN
A Fates Universe Novel

Kristine Grayson

A Fates Universe Novel

Completely Smitten

"Watching the romance play out is plenty of fun."
—*Locus*

www.wmgpublishinginc.com
Also Available at Your Favorite Bookstore.

Teri J. Babcock's first story in these pages is maybe one of the most twisted and fun stories I have read in a long time and, considering I am the editor of this magazine, that is going some.

And I like my share of sweet things from time-to-time and this story almost made me think twice about that. Almost. Enjoy!

Good Fences Make Good Neighbors
Teri J. Babcock

MY HUSBAND AND I were eating the table for dessert when the doorbell rang.

It was Brett and Paige Anderson from three doors down, they of the designer merino running wear and taut abdomens, smiling tightly with their too-white teeth. They were wondering if we knew where their children were.

Funnily enough, because their kids spend more time in our yard then their own, we didn't. Paige Anderson hadn't seen her son and daughter since lunch. Paige looked pale and worried beneath her perfectly applied foundation, and Brett, stoic.

Steve and I watched Brett and Paige cross the street and pick their way up the peanut-brittle driveway to the Dirkson house, and carefully tap the hard-candy knocker, which broke. They didn't get any more help from Laila Dirkson, though she took a long time about it. Maybe she was being passive-aggressive about the door-knocker. That would be just like her.

None the wiser about their children, Brett and Paige walked home, him manly and straight-backed, and her slumped, shoulders shaking soundlessly.

Every house in our neighborhood is made of sugar, as part of a government initiative to reduce dependency on foreign imports. Early last year a government lab made a break-through on matter-transformation, and they decided our neighborhood would be perfect for their pilot project.

Thrilling as it is to be on the breaking wave of progress, I wish they'd asked first. I liked our house the way it was.

Science has made great progress on the mass-conversion front, but no matter how clever the scientists are, they can't make new matter. All matter and energy are conserved; you can't make new mass, just transform what already exists. So, because the government didn't have a lot of extra mass just lying around, they used our homes.

If it's our own property, so the logic goes, we'll be more conservative in our use. But the situation isn't exactly conducive to, shall we say, restraint. It's hard to resist temptation when you're surrounded by it.

Naturally the Andersons, being the paragons of clean living that they are, protested when the information flyer came, saying they didn't actually eat sugar, only stevia and occasionally, organic honey.

I guess the government audit proved they were telling the truth, because they got to keep their house the way it was. Except for the two new beehives in their backyard, and a row of stevia plants in the front. Now they look like even bigger freaks than they did before. Hardly anyone speaks to them; it's too embarrassing.

The husband and I have a bit of a sweet tooth, so most of the exterior of our house and a lot of our furniture got converted. The initial supply was supposed to last us a year, which is now abundantly clear isn't going to happen.

There were a few casualties from the conversion. Like my table. I loved my kitchen table. Mahogany, family heirloom. Had to fight my sister to get it. Literally. I mean we were rolling around on the floor like six-year-olds, pulling each other's hair out. I got a good grip and a hard yank and then she gave in. She says that was when she realized it was beneath her dignity to sink to my level, but I think it was when she knew she was going to lose both the table and half her scalp.

Her kids will get it when I'm dead, anyway. Or they would have done. The government's little white conversion van turned the table into Daniel Belge, dark chocolate with a ganache center, my favorite.

Since chocolate doesn't wear nearly as well as mahogany, I told Steve we might as well just eat it. That's another reason my sister will be pissed, because her district hasn't undergone mass-conversion yet, and if the table had been at her house, it would still be cellulose, instead of cellulite. Ha Ha.

***

FORTUNATELY, IT HASN'T rained since they turned the Sugar-Snap beam on our front porch, so we haven't had to deal with water eating holes in the chocolate tiles of our roof. We had so much chocolate in the house at the time of our assessment, we got an extra allocation. I keep telling Steve we should eat the tiles before summer starts and pick up new ones at Home Depot in the fall, but he hasn't agreed yet.

The day after our roof was miraculously transformed, Paige dropped by to tell me—with a note of envy in her voice that she couldn't quite mask—that she'd trade me some honey for roof tiles, if we decided to replace them.

"You don't want to eat all that high fructose corn syrup," she said, gesturing at the red peppermint spirals (once columnar pines) that lined our driveway. "Honey is so much better for you."

I told her I'd consult Steve and get back to her.

Naturally, the Andersons are planning to move away. They just have to get the permits to move to a Sugar-Free zone, which you think they'd already qualify for, being anti-sugar rebels and everything, but apparently changing zones isn't that easy, even for diet hippies. Paige confided to me that they might have to settle for Low-Carb.

I told her that children are resilient and that, since she and Brett are clearly good parents, no doubt their kids will turn out to be the kind of good, mindful eaters they meant to raise. No matter what subdivision they live in. She was touched by my little speech, which almost made me feel bad, because I didn't really mean it. Her children are a pair of spoiled toads.

Paige made a frowny-smile and waved at the street.

"How can you raise healthy eaters in a place where every home looks like the witch's house in Hansel and Gretel? It's giving my children a complex."

I agreed with her that for sure that would be difficult, and hoped that the paperwork for their transfer wouldn't take too long.

Actually, the kids have been hanging around our house a lot, and Steve says he noticed some of the meringue stucco on the side is missing. Maybe it just broke off. It isn't all that sturdy. But Steve says there should be pieces on the ground, and there aren't.

***

THE LITTLE WHITE government van makes its rounds once a week, measuring and converting. It's a public service, replacing what's missing every week so you don't run out.

Steve and I had a family meeting after the last week's visit left us with no interior walls. Steve ran some numbers, and he figures, at the rate we're going, we're going to be homeless by next year. Not landless—we'll still have our lot—just homeless. The government keeps converting new parts of our house as fast as we eat it.

We're not the only community that's affected by the roll-out of this new plan.

People are protesting now, the family members of people with Type 2 diabetes and people who say they're addicted to sugar.

Now I don't understand how people can claim to be addicted to sugar, as if it were heroin. It sounds to me more like you really, really like sugar and are also addicted to drama, and so need to make your feelings for sugar into a medical problem instead of just something you ought to deal with.

I mean, I like sugar. But I can stop eating it anytime I want.

Anyway, these people want to sue the government for making them live in houses of sugar, because now temptation is constant, so even if they want to, they can't get away from it. Since all of them had so much sugar in their homes when the government people did the assessment, they had nearly everything converted. They were all sad, fat and sweaty-looking. Most of them don't even have furniture. One girl lost all her clothes and had to go shopping for new ones in a smock made of felted candy floss.

The government PR rep, a suspiciously skinny woman, was unrepentant. We're only trying to help, she explained, by making sure your caloric needs are fulfilled, but you have to provide the mass.

I think they ought to go to the landfill and convert garbage instead, but my husband says people would have an aesthetic objection to eating garbage, even if it was totally converted. I think that's silly.

***

STEVE CAUGHT KAYDEN Anderson picking off the stucco red-handed, literally red, his fingers were all stained with dye from the giant lollipops at the end of the driveway where the Chinese lions used to be. How did we get lollipops from lions? The strata brought in all new aesthetic standards when the change happened, that's how. So that we would look like some giant schmaltzy German Christmas craft project. Somebody on the strata board thought it would be charming. That bitch Laila Dirkson, I bet.

The kid was crying and begging Steve not to tell his mother about his criminal behavior, as well he might.

"Is his misdeed theft, or vandalism?" I asked my husband.

"Both," he growled. The kid was shaking in his trainers, and I thought he was going to add to our supply of chocolate, but Steve finally relented.

"I see any more stucco missing, and you're done, kid," he said.

Kayden ran off, and I was sure he'd steer clear of our place for a long while. So of course we hadn't seen him or his sister at all when Paige and Brett came calling.

The next morning there was a story on the radio about the government's mass-conversion unit and how it malfunctioned and turned some retired schoolteacher's little teacup dog into saltwater taffy. The dog was in the neighbor's yard, and because the dog wasn't registered to that location the machine measured the extra mass and converted it.

Of course the government denied this, calling it a hoax. The mass-converter has a safety feature and doesn't alter life-forms,

they insisted, and chided the radio station for making wild claims just because it was ratings week.

Now, I always believe the government. But still, I had a bit of a funny feeling. So I went down into the back yard behind the garden shed. It's quite a steep incline there, so Steve just lets the grass grow long rather than mow it.

Sitting in a depression of flattened grass were the Anderson children. They were perfectly still, and I think almost exactly in the same position they were in when the converter-van surprised them with its beam. Between them was a little pile of meringue stucco. One of Kayden's arms was drooping slightly, because it was such a warm day and caramel doesn't hold up so well when it's hot. Little Melody had strawberry licorice hair and gumball eyes, and her knit sweater had turned into a daisy chain of hundreds of tiny gummy bears. She had a peppermint twist lollipop that she had broken off the fence in one hand, and her mouth was open.

I had a little taste—just a baby finger. Unless you look closely at her hand you wouldn't even notice it was missing. It was the good stuff. Steve had a stash of imported McLaren's under the bed when we were surveyed.

Steve and I brought the kids inside, and talked about what would be best for Mr. and Mrs. Anderson. It's too bad, but the beam isn't reversible. You can use the beam to convert that mass into something else, sure, but not something alive.

Paige Anderson dotes on those children. It would break her heart if she knew they'd been turned into carbohydrates.

Steve and I feel it's better if Paige thinks they ran away. Better if she thinks that one day there'll be a knock on the door, and there are her two kids, a little taller, a lot wiser, looking sheepish and asking to come home.

The next morning I asked Laila Dirkson if she'd noticed Kayden Anderson, wearing an oversized backpack and going up and down the alley. I didn't say I saw him, just asked her if she had.

Her eyes got big.

"Like he was training," she said. Laila ran off and told Paige that it had slipped her mind the other day, but she had seen her son preparing for a long hike. Laila didn't mention me, since she likes to take all credit whenever possible.

It didn't take long for Paige to recall her son's love of nature, and discover that their tent was missing. I did see her children eating some extra large pieces of fruit roll-ups a couple of weeks ago, so the tent probably is really gone, and not just wishful thinking on her part.

The neighbors have all gone off for a search-and-rescue to Pennystone Park, a forty minute drive or two days walk along the highway. I sent a casserole.

In the meantime, Steve and I decided it was time we got into the spirit of the neighborhood and decorate our back fence. We used the giant gumballs from Steve's former vintage bowling ball collection, and the three hundred feet of Twizzlers that used to be old Christmas lights. It looks quite festive, and entirely in keeping with the new bylaws. We put a couple of steps on the alley side of the fence, to make it a little easier to climb over.

It's not till you're in the yard that you can see the extra chain link fencing around the shed. What with the steep incline, it's not so easy to climb back. Especially if you're carrying a gumball that weighs twenty pounds.

Ah, to be young again.

Steve and I had a heart-to-heart, and we agree. Theft and vandalism erode the basis of our society, and if parents can't keep an eye on those juvenile delinquents of theirs, well. It's a public service we're providing. Steve estimates that the additional mass should help us keep a roof over our heads for at least another six months. After that, who knows.

In the meantime, we're checking out other neighborhoods. We might need to move quickly.

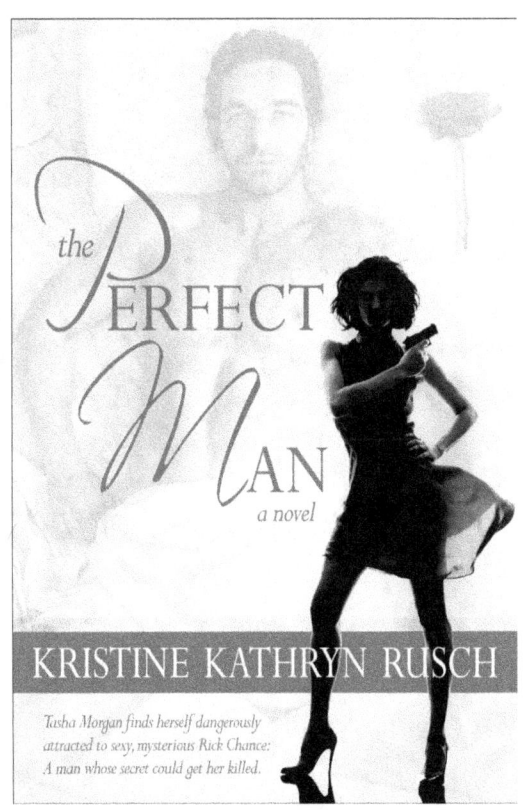

the PERFECT MAN

a novel

KRISTINE KATHRYN RUSCH

Tasha Morgan finds herself dangerously attracted to sexy, mysterious Rick Chance: A man whose secret could get her killed.

www.wmgpublishinginc.com
Also Available at Your Favorite Bookstore.

Ryan M. Williams makes his debut in these pages with a really fun story about a very, very unique library. Head-shaking unique. I mean Pulphouse-*style unique.*

Ryan is not only a well-published writer with over twenty novels and many, many short fiction sales, he is also a librarian, thus he knows this place he writes about, frighteningly enough.

Lost Book
Ryan M. Williams

THE HEAVY LEATHER-BOUND tome dropped onto Alazne's toe. "Ow!"

Alazne hopped on one foot and grabbed her right ankle. She glared at the offending book. The fine embossed leather cover puckered contritely. *Where had it come from?*

Alazne's eyes narrowed. "You did that on purpose, didn't you?"

The book shuffled back until its spine hit the worn wood service desk.

Alazne looked around the cavernous library. Golden light passing through the long windows illuminated languid dust motes. It was quiet right now. The sort of quiet that brought back the memory of days when libraries were always quiet, not that Alazne had witnessed that herself, but it was still part of the popular folklore. For the moment she had the grand sweeping bookcases filled with books in an assortment of muted colors all to herself. Rank on rank climbed tall walls that stretched up to the arched ceiling above.

Alone, unless she counted the gravel of gnomes perched around the computer stations, snorting and salivating over cat videos on YouTube whilst elbowing each other. With no one

151

demanding her time, she returned her attention to the book on the floor.

She lowered her throbbing right foot to the floor and gingerly tried her weight on it. The pain was already ebbing. The pages of the book warped themselves with mournful regret.

Alazne stooped and gently picked up the thick book. It smelled of dust and old leather. It was lighter than it looked. The title inscribed in gold leaf on the cover read *Alder's Compendium of Gastronomic Fungi.* And it bore the subtitle in a smaller typeface, *With Assorted Ways and Means of Preparing the Same.*

The book's covers swelled and collapsed in a fluttery sigh of relief.

"Where did you come from?" Alazne turned the book in her hand and saw nothing except a dirty, gummy patch where the spine label belonged. "I see. You're lost. You don't have your call number."

She ran long fingers across the smooth leather of the cover. Griffin hide, if she wasn't mistaken. Very durable and mold resistant, it was the sort of binding job one didn't often see anymore. She set the book down on the counter. "No problem. I'll get you set up in a wink."

Not literally, of course. But then you knew that winks were not implicated in creating spine labels.

Alazne turned to the computer and typed the book's title into the search engine. *Search returned no hits. Would you like another book on fungi?*

No. Was it possible that it wasn't in the system? Alazne glanced at the book and forced a smile. "No worries, won't take long."

When she turned back, a rabbit peeked over the top of the counter. The rabbit's nose twitched. "Hello?"

"Hello," Alazne said. "What brings you to the library today?"

The rabbit bit its bottom lip. "I'm afraid that I might be late."

"Is that a joke?"

The rabbit straightened. Their ears turned stiffly. "A joke? What do you mean? What do you mean by that?"

Alazne realized her mistake. "My apologies. Could you tell me more? You're late? How could I help you?"

The rabbit's nose wiggled, apparently mollified. On the counter, the book's cover opened a bit and dropped, signaling its impatience. The rabbit twitched. "I mean to say, that is, I am looking, for materials on—" the rabbit's voice fell "—child-rearing?"

Alazne nodded. "Let me show you the materials in question. You can look and then ask for any specific assistance you might need."

Alazne gestured for the rabbit to precede her. The rabbit hopped a few steps away from the desk. They wore the loose pantaloons preferred by so many rabbits, theirs in bright orange. Alazne cast a quick look at the compendium. "You stay put. I'll be back for you in a moment."

***

IT TOOK A LITTLE longer than a moment. The rabbit needed more assistance in browsing through the appropriate section of books as they had become dismayed at the wide selection. It took Alazne climbing up the ladders twice before she managed to settle the rabbit at the nearby tables with three volumes. When she returned to the service desk, she found the compendium standing upright beside the computer. The pages fluttered with irritation, casting glimpses of fine ink and watercolor illustrations.

"It does no good to become agitated." Alazne perched on the stool before the computer. "Let's just see what we can do."

Neither proximity operators or Boolean operators helped in producing a result matching the compendium. Neither did searching by author. Alazne reached for the book. It shuffled back from her fingers.

"I need to look at your copyright page."

She reached again for the book. This time it stayed put, allowing her to pick it up. She flipped open the cover and gently turned the vellum pages until she came upon the copyright page.

The page contained very little information. A rudimentary copyright notice listing the author as Harold Walston Alder. The series of dates indicated an initial copyright in 1854 with a renewal in 1878, making this the later edition. The page had none of the other pieces of information generally found nowadays on the copyright page. No subject headings. No Library of Congress entries.

Alazne shook her head. "I just don't know."

She closed the book and caressed the cover. "Is it possible you were discarded?"

The book shivered in her hands. She ran a soothing hand across the cover. "Shush. I didn't mean that. I'm sure that wasn't the case. Your spine label came off, and once you were lost the record was removed from the system. All we need to do is speak to the head cataloger, who may be able to retrieve the record or create a brand-new record for you. In either case, you'll get a new spine label and get back to your place on the shelves."

The book slipped from her fingers and thudded on her left big toe.

"Ow!" Alazne jerked her injured digit back from the book. "Stop doing that!"

The book shuffled and scooted a little further from her. As it continued to scoot and shuffle, giving every impression of trying to race away from her, Alazne chuckled.

"Now, none of that! You have nothing to be afraid of. Besides, it's not as if you're going to get very far." Even animated books generally did not travel quickly. Unless they were of the flying variety, but in the case of the heavy compendium, that was unlikely.

Alazne stood, wincing a bit about her sore toes, then scooped the book up into her arms and hugged it tight to her chest. The book shuddered once or twice then settled down. She closed her eyes and concentrated.

Oro, I need the desk covered. Can you pop out here?

Affirmative. A brief gust of wind blew through Alazne's hair as Oro popped into view in front of her. Oro's long blonde locks flew out behind her before settling back into place. Oro's gaze dropped from Alazne's face to the compendium she held against her chest.

"Is there a problem?"

Alazne shook her head. "No, not really. Just a lost book. I was going to pop up to cataloging and see if Kit can help locate a record, then see about a new spine label."

"Okay." Oro looked around the reading room. "Anything I should know about?"

"It's been pretty quiet. There's a rabbit back at a table with some child-rearing books. It might need help later."

Oro nodded. "Okay."

Alazne rose slightly on her toes and tapped her heels together three times while focusing on the cataloging department. Her ears popped as she appeared on the 120th floor of the Library. Aggressively cheerful pop music played throughout the open space.

Sunlight streamed through the floor-to-ceiling windows. Catalogers, receivers, acquisitors, and processors went about their business in the space. Some of them reclined in comfortable chairs in front of the windows, while others talked in groups or bent over shared workstations. There was never a dull day in the cataloging department. In recent years the department had tripled in size, remodeled, and continued to expand as publishing continued to change and the number of titles produced each year increased. That didn't even count the printing department's own fantastic growth over the same time as they struggled to produce printed copies of materials previously only published in electronic formats. The wizarding Library had a simple mission: collect everything.

Alazne squeezed the book. Which was why it didn't make any sense that *Alder's* compendium would have been discarded. At least, not unless it had been replaced by another copy. Given the high quality of the compendium's materials, that seemed fairly unlikely.

Alazne walked through the space, nodding friendly greetings to those she passed. Whether you wanted to work in the cataloging department or not, it was prudent to stay on their good side. Ordinarily, she wouldn't bring a simple issue like this to Kit. In this case, however, she thought that Kit would be interested. Kit had been something of a mentor to her over the years since Alazne had taken Kit's introduction to cataloging course while getting her degree.

As usual, Kit sat in her high-backed chair in front of the windows on the south side of the building. At 92 years old, Kit had lost none of her energy, but she complained of being cold. She wore her usual sort of outfit. Today was a thick, rainbow-colored wrap over a blue sweater on top of a bright yellow dress. Black leather gloves disappeared beneath the sweater sleeves. A book floated in front of her, next to the screen which displayed the record. Several other books stood beside her chair in a patient line. These were the chosen few, referred to Kit for original cataloging.

Kit turned, her lined face already smiling, as Alazne approached. "Alazne, how lovely to see you! What have you been getting up to down there in the reading room?"

The tone of the question conveyed Kit's meaning. She didn't approve of Alazne's decision to remain in public services, working in the reading room. She still wanted Alazne to transfer to cataloging, said that she had a knack for it. It was tempting, especially the idea of working for Kit. Of course, cataloging was a gigantic department. She wouldn't be working directly under Kit if she transferred. There was a long training process and apprenticeship to move through the department. They didn't just turn new hires lose.

Without warning the *Alder's Compendium* began to swell in her arms. At first Alazne thought that it was trying to slip away again. Why, she couldn't say. She held it tighter.

"It's a bit skittish. I found it when it landed on my foot. It seems to have lost its spine label, and I couldn't find it in the system."

Kit twirled her index finger and crooked it. "Why don't we just take a look at you?"

As Alazne started lowering the book it continued to swell even more in her hands. It

slipped. The cover flew open, pages flapping as they turned, stopping on an elaborate pen and ink drawing of an arm sprawled across two pages. Bulbous renderings of fungi sprouted from the flesh in the grotesque image.

Alazne gasped as the book supported itself, floating in the air between her and Kit. Kit's cold blue eyes narrowed. She stood. Her pale lips thinned.

"So." Kit lifted her black-gloved hands, holding them out in front of her with her palms facing the book. Her fingers moved in careful signs. "A Trojan horse, clever."

A Trojan horse? Alazne's gut sank. The compendium was a trap. Watercolors spread across the pen and ink drawing, bringing life and dimension to the image. The flesh of the arm became a pale grayish brown, swollen and glistening with moisture, and dotted with tiny fungi around the larger forms. The bulbous shapes erupted in sickening yellow and red flesh, moist and shining. The light shifted, moving across the arm and the fungi until the light aligned with the light shining through the windows. The colors took on a vibrant life. Dew on the arm and fungi caught the light in bright sparkles. The picture still looked flat, but Alazne didn't believe it would remain so.

Something was coming through the book.

And she had brought it to Kit. With a sharp gesture, Kit dismissed the books waiting for cataloging. They flew away in an orderly line. Lights flashed from the ceiling. An alarm sounded. Kit's voice echoed through the floor.

Evacuate. Mandatory evacuation. All personnel must evacuate immediately.

Kit's attention remained on the floating compendium as the people on the floor began popping out of view. The image took on more dimensions, swelling beneath the page as if it was nothing more than a thin film stretched across the image now.

Kit turned her hands palms up and slowly brought them up toward one another as if closing a book. The compendium shook, and the page swelled even more, threatening to burst through the film. The arm rolled slightly, showing more fungi as it rotated the inner surface of the arm down into the rich leaf-strewn ground beneath it. Alazne caught a whiff of corruption and decay. Muscles and tendons moved beneath the fungi.

Kit looked across the book at Alazne. Despite the noise of the alarms, she heard Kit clearly. "You must go."

"No! I'm not leaving you!"

"I should've realized immediately that Alder was an anagram. This book is a manifestation of Redlar the Corrupt. The consumer. It was his way past our wards. If successful in infecting the library—"

The page swelled further, stretching against the membrane separating it from reality.

"Can we contain it somehow?"

Kit shook her head. "There isn't time and we couldn't do it alone. Our only chance is to seal this floor and prevent it from getting out until the others have time to evacuate as much of the collection as possible."

"No!" Alazne couldn't accept it. The thought of Redlar the Corrupt sent a chill through her, but she couldn't let that stop her. There had to be a way to get the book out of the library. She looked at the windows. The compendium was bound in griffin hide. And they were on the 120th floor.

"Hang on." She sent the thought at Kit. Before Kit could question her meaning, Alazne reached out and grabbed the compendium. She rose on her toes and tapped her heels together three times as she concentrated on the space outside the window.

Alazne popped back into existence hanging onto the book 120 stories above the ground. Wind tore at her clothes. The griffin hide-bound volume recognized its freedom. The cover flexed and flapped. She lost her grip and fell backward, plummeting toward the ground.

Above her, the compendium flapped off toward the horizon. A cry of rage faintly reached her ears past the buffeting wind. Redlar the Corrupt wasn't happy. But the memory of flight in the griffin hide couldn't be denied when faced with the open sky. The book dwindled to a speck as Alazne dropped.

Heart racing, she tried very hard not to panic. She brought her heels together, tapping three times as her mind scrambled for a safe destination—

—she smashed into the floor behind the desk in the reading room. The impact knocked the wind from her chest. Tears stung her eyes. Her fingers clawed at the worn hardwood flooring, seeking reassurance that she was once again safe on solid ground. Everything ached.

Oro looked down at her. "Are you back then? It's just that, I have a lot of work."

Alazne attempted a nod as she struggled to suck in a shuddering breath. She reached up a hand. Oro took her hand and helped her to her feet. Her lungs burned as she sucked in gulps of air.

"What was all that ruckus?"

Alazne tried to find her voice, but she still couldn't speak. There was a pop of air and Kit appeared beside Oro. She seized Alazne and pulled her into an embrace.

"There you are! I was so worried." Kit stepped back. Her hands gripped Alazne's shoulders. "Brave, foolish librarian! That was well done."

"Nothing," Alazne wheezed.

Kit shook her head. "You're destined for much more than this room."

Long ears and a twitching nose popped up over the corner of the desk. "Excuse me. I'd like to borrow these."

Oro disappeared in a small gust of air filling the space she had occupied. Alazne shook her head. "I belong here."

She turned to face the rabbit. "I'll be happy to help you with those."

Kit sniffed disapprovingly and then said, "We'll see. I won't forget what you did today."

With a tiny puff of wind, Kit popped away. No doubt going back to restore order to the disrupted cataloging department. There were a lot of scared people to bring back. The evacuation hadn't even reached this level yet.

Alazne took the rabbit's card and books, checking them out with practiced ease.

"Good luck! Have a great day! Thanks for coming in!" Alazne waved to the rabbit as it hopped out of the reading room.

Her back throbbed. She rubbed it with both hands and looked around the quiet library. This was her corner of the library, helping those who came in.

Even the gnomes still chuckling over kitten videos.

⟡

A Dangerous Road

A Smokey Dalton Novel

New edition with reader's guide
and discussion questions

KRIS
NELSCOTT

Edgar Award Finalist

A DANGEROUS ROAD

A SMOKEY DALTON NOVEL

WITH READER'S GUIDE AND DISCUSSION QUESTIONS

www.wmgpublishinginc.com
Also Available at Your Favorite Bookstore.

Dayle A. Dermatis is the author or coauthor of many novels (including snarky urban fantasies Ghosted, Shaded, *and the forthcoming* Spectered*) and more than a hundred short stories in multiple genres appearing in such venues as* Fiction River, Alfred Hitchcock's Mystery Magazine, *and DAW Books.*

She is the mastermind behind the Uncollected Anthology project, and her short fiction has been lauded in year's best anthologies in erotica, mystery, and horror. She also appears as a guest editor in the Fiction River *series of anthologies.*

I am glad to say that this is her second appearance in these pages and I hope for many more.

Acceptable Losses
Dayle A. Dermatis

HER ANSWER TO THE interview question would haunt Juana to the end of her days.

"Dr. Salazar," the reporter had said, "how did you come up with the idea?"

"My partner was vegan and trying to convert me," she'd said. She'd even laughed a little as she said it. "She made miso soup and sushi with brown rice and vegetables, and over dinner kept telling me about all the health benefits of seaweed. And it got me thinking…"

If she hadn't *thought*, none of this would ever have happened. If she hadn't fucking *thought*, she wouldn't be in this terrible position, with this agonizing decision to make.

***

SEAWEED. NORI, WITH its amazing amount of protein. Wakame, with ten times more calcium than milk. Kelp, chock full of iron. All of it low in calories and high in minerals and many vitamins.

Easy to harvest, to soak, to dry, to transport.

"Why don't more people eat seaweed?" Juana wondered aloud to her partner.

They'd rented a condo on the beach in Channel Islands, California, for the week, cheap at this time of year because the marine layer blanketed the coast in lowering grey clouds, keeping the area a good ten-plus degrees cooler than Los Angeles until mid-afternoon. The fog had finally burned away, and they'd settled on the deck to enjoy the sun and growing warmth.

Because of the weather the beach was almost empty, and a stiff breeze still blew in off the ocean, snapping the nylon flag hanging over their heads and bringing the sharp scent of the sea.

Juana had had seaweed on the brain ever since that dinner, and now, watching their adopted son, Nathan, drag a piece of bull kelp five times longer than himself along the beach like a pet on a leash, she was obsessing.

Susan shrugged, closed whatever she'd been reading on her tablet, and took off her glasses. Juana sometimes wondered if Susan really needed reading glasses, or if she wore them to get people to take her seriously. Her delicate Asian features and tiny stature made her look more like a manga character than a director of award-winning documentaries about food, nutrition, and farming practices.

"Some people think it sounds weird or disgusting," Susan said. "Part of the problem there is the name; it would be more correct to call it sea vegetables. Anyway, in some areas, like Great Britain, it's actually considered a delicacy, so it's expensive. And then there's the problem of availability."

"The oceans are vast," Juana said.

"Seaweed is as photosynthetic as any other plant," Susan said. "So it can grow only in the strip between the shore and where the ocean floor gets too deep. Japan has a lot of coastline for its size, which is why their diet is primarily fish, and seaweed's a big part of that. Populations of larger continents where it was easy to develop farming—both growing crops and herding animals—had less need of the ocean."

Juana nodded slowly. "Plus, not enough coastline to feed the bulk of the people, who live inland."

"Exactly," Susan said. "Nathan Njau Salazar!" she bellowed suddenly in a commanding voice she'd practiced to project across soundstages, again something unexpected given her stature. "Not so far!"

Nathan turned and headed back their way across the hard-packed sand near the gentle waves, his body language belying his birth name, Njau, which was African for *bull*. His shoulders hunched and he stomped his toddler displeasure at being reined in.

Juana closed her eyes for a moment, remembering the circumstances of adopting him as an infant. The drought and subsequent famine had nearly destroyed everyone in his village in Kenya, and his family had offered him for adoption to save him from starvation.

That had been three years ago. She and Susan had tried to keep in contact with his family, but they'd failed. She didn't know if they were still alive.

She couldn't get the memories of his parents, his older brother, the villagers, out of her head. Their sticklike arms and legs, their gaunt faces making their eyes look huge, the children's bellies distended. She and Susan had donated food, money, whatever they could, but it hadn't been enough.

It was never enough.

She opened her eyes, blinking in the bright sun. Nathan had moved a few yards in from the surf and was digging with intense focus. She wondered if he were trying to dig to China. At some point, she and Susan would have to try and explain to him the geographical fallacy of that.

"It's easy to grow, right?" she asked. "I mean, you just need the right salinity of the water and something for it to attach to."

"Most of it's free-floating, but yes, I don't think there's very much to it." Susan shook her head. "But you've got a PhD in Biology;

you know all this. What do you—?" Her eyes widened. "*What* are you thinking?"

Juana looked at Susan, into those beautiful brown eyes, feeling a swell of emotion, and then she looked out at their son, and felt the connection between the three of them, sizzling like lightning. "I'm thinking it's time to change the world."

***

FIRST IT WAS research, and then it was getting a grant to take a sabbatical from UCSB and do more research. Norway had patented a floating cultivation platform, but she was interested in the viability of building on-land tanks as well. The Food and Agriculture Organization of the United Nations had done a paper on the prospects for seaweed production in developing countries, concluding that none of the studies in Africa had been promising.

Juana intended to prove them wrong.

When Susan came into her study, wearing a pair of cotton pajamas with green snowflakes on the pants, she remembered to look at the time on her laptop.

"Is it really that late? Sorry," she said, stretching, and then covering Susan's arms with her own as Susan reached over the back of her chair to hug her.

"It's not about me," Susan said. "You need sleep, honey. Burning the candle at both ends, yadda yadda."

She rose, took Susan's soft hand in hers, and led her to Nathan's room. They stood side by side just inside the doorway, watching his sleeping form. The base of his spaceship lamp glowed, a faint nightlight of stars sprinkled across him. She wanted to run her hand over his rough dark hair, but knew if she did, she'd wake him.

"It's about him," she whispered. "It's about his family. We can't save them, but…"

"*We're* his family," Susan reminded her, sotto voce.

"You know what I mean," Juana said. "I'm looking at Africa right now, but the rest of the world… There's poverty everywhere. Hunger. We can change that."

"I know," Susan said, and leaned her head against Juana's arm. "I know. But come to bed?"

"Soon," Juana promised.

She made it just before dawn.

***

SHE WROTE HER own papers, arguing her plan, backing it up with facts and figures. She argued the additional benefits of using seaweed as fuel. She studied the African coastline—concluding that the west, and along the coasts of Namibia and Angola, where there was the least amount of population and thus the greatest amount of available land, would make the most sense for factories and warehouses full of giant tanks. She posited road patterns and traffic routes.

First Africa, then the rest of the world. In places where drought wasn't an issue, the growing tanks could be inland, with seawater made locally. She thought this only privately, wanting Africa to prove its success first.

She sought funding: grants, donations, partnering with corporations. Found people who agreed with her ideas, and enlisted their aid in convincing other people it would work.

She mortgaged their own home to the hilt, with Susan's grudging acceptance, because really, did they need it when they were moving to Africa for the foreseeable future?

"It makes sense," she argued, more than once, a bottle (or two) of Trader Joe's two-buck-chuck Chardonnay empty between them. "I'll supervise the building of the test tanks. You can get footage of everything, just like you've been doing all along: not just for a possible documentary, but for PSAs, advertisements…"

And to capture what they both believed was history in the making. Juana was sure of that.

"What about Nathan?" Susan asked.

"We've always talked about him experiencing other cultures," Juana said. "And home schooling him. You don't have any other projects lined up yet, right?"

"Would you know if I had?" Susan muttered.

"What?" Juana reared back. "Of course! I..."

"You've been busy," Susan said. "I know. It's just that you haven't been really *present*."

Juana didn't want to admit if that were true. She chose silence, questioning herself. Had she missed something important Susan had said? Had she been neglecting Susan in her mad focus on the project?

"No, you're right." Susan released a long breath, tipped her head back to slide the last dregs of pale golden liquid in her wineglass down her throat. "It does make sense, for Nathan, for your project, for the world."

It wasn't until it was too late that Juana remembered the conversation and realized just how much she'd sacrificed.

***

WESTERN AFRICA WAS hot and dry in a way that Southern California simply wasn't. They were in an area Wikipedia referred to as "the most inhospitable on the planet," arid even by the ocean.

The buildings were squat, mud structures that did have some similarities to the Spanish adobe style. The sky was almost always a pale blue uninterrupted by clouds. At night, the stars were breathtaking.... Nathan was learning the constellations, taking an interest in astronomy beyond the average five-year-old.

But then, given who his parents were, Juana expected nothing less. She did notice that he adapted to the climate better than either of them, and they (well, Susan, really) educated him on his Kenyan heritage, as best they knew it. They planned a trip there, once things settled out with the building of the test tanks.

Juana had never really succeeded at veganism, so they all lapsed into pescetarianism, eating local fish, accepting eggs and goat's milk and cheese from area farmers. Susan could still make a mean sushi, though, and seaweed, first from the ocean and then from the tanks, was a staple vegetable for them.

Juana had to admit she'd never felt better, and Susan said the same.

The main facility had been built by the time they arrived: a cavernous main space in

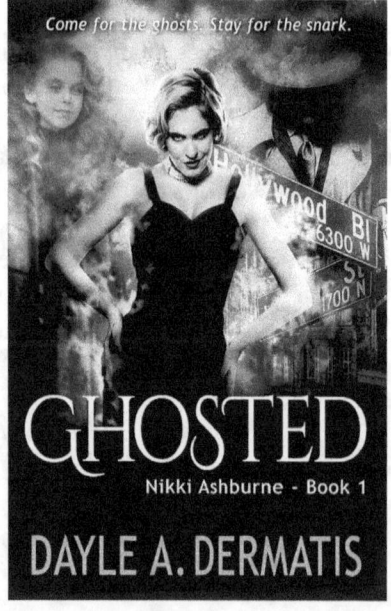

which the first test tanks would be erected, an infrastructure that included generators and massive fans (air conditioning was useless in a building whose roof would be retracted for most, if not all of the time) and a few small offices and labs for Juana, the scientists, and the engineers who'd done the main tank design based on her ideas. She was there every day (not rain or shine, for there was no rain), supervising the building work, poring over designs and specs and test results, doing more research, reviewing more grant applications.

This evening she stood on the industrial metal balcony that ringed the upper level; catwalks extended out over each tank. The workers had gone home; she was left with the hum of the generators and the clank of metal as she walked out over the kelp tank. The sultry, saline-laden air wrapped her in a moist shroud.

Kneeling, she opened the hatch in the grated floor and dipped a test tube in, filling it with water. Capping off the tube, she slid it into the rack next to her, then closed the hatch and stood, carefully.

She had never been one for heights, and despite the fact that the waist-high railing didn't have an opening large enough for her to fall through (unless, perhaps, she squeezed herself—no, she doubted even petite Susan could fit), she always felt a level of vertigo.

Nathan loved climbing the railing and peering over; like most children, he had no fear, took joy in the giddy exhilaration of being high, of viewing the vastness of the tanks. He wanted to swim in them; was disappointed when she told him there were no fish to play with.

Each tank housed a different type of seaweed, so they could more easily adjust conditions as necessary as well as harvest more efficiently.

She and her team of experts had thought of everything...or so she hoped.

She backtracked along the catwalk to the balcony, repeated the process with the final tank, then with relief descended the metal stairs to the first floor.

The lab was quieter, and one of the few rooms that was air conditioned, which was important for the equipment. Juana shivered; she'd been acclimating to the heat, and this room felt uncomfortably frigid.

She set the rack of test tubes in the refrigerator for testing in the morning. It would be better if she did it now, but she grudgingly admitted it was late. Susan and Nathan would be done with dinner, but she'd be able to kiss Nathan goodnight and tuck him in, and have a glass of wine with Susan, curl up with her on the patio and look at the stars. She missed that.

She sat down with her tablet to do a final review of the day and sketch out her schedule for tomorrow, and when she saw the calendar, she cursed in several different languages.

Tomorrow a governmental agency was coming to do a walkthrough of the facility and inspect the progress and the tanks. She'd tasked her staff with the details, but she had to be prepared, too.

And if she was going to spend the day dealing with bureaucrats, she wouldn't have time to test those water samples.

With a sigh, she texted Susan, and went to the refrigerator to retrieve the samples.

***

TWO YEARS LATER, the tanks were in full production. Local and far-flung villages benefitted from the new food source, and regular truckloads were being distributed into neighboring countries along with the seaweed being harvested directly from the ocean.

It was a working woman's vacation, but a vacation nonetheless, as they loaded up three jeeps—one for Juana, Susan, Nathan, and their driver; the other two for four researchers, two interpreters, and a mountain of gear and equipment—and headed out to test, document, and film. They'd already had researchers in the field, but this was the first time Juana and Susan had gone.

The first night, they camped on the scrubby desert plain, a guide with a gun keeping watch. Nathan had declared himself old enough to have his own tent, and Juana had had a vague hope of reading over some reports before she slept, but alone with Susan (as alone as one can be in a tent surrounded by other tents), she could be persuaded to set her reviews aside that night.

And the next, and even the next. Juana finally had time to step back and admire the stars.

But at the villages, they both kicked into professional mode, Juana with her questions and statistics, Susan with her questions and cameras.

They were both aliens to the villagers, curiosities, but Nathan won them over. Soon, laden with information and film, they moved on to the next.

The bottom line was clear and positive: the villagers were thriving, thanks to the new food source.

And, for a brief while, they thrived as well.

***

JUANA WAS PULLING all-nighters working to obtain funding for new facilities. She was more annoyed than surprised when she came down with the flu, and guilty when Susan and Nathan got sick as well.

She felt wretched enough to take a few days off. Since she'd fallen ill first, Susan was well enough to care for her, feeding her broth and crackers until her appetite returned, and keeping Nathan from being too enthusiastic that his other mom was home and available.

"It's kind of nice, having you home," Susan said, sitting on the edge of the bed with a bowl of water and dabbing a cool cloth on Juana's face. Her fever had broken, but it was just hot and dusty as usual.

Juana nibbled on a cracker. "Even like this?"

Susan smiled. "Even like this."

But Juana saw the sadness behind the smile, and vowed to cut back her hours. Which she succeeded in doing when she started to feel better and Susan and Nathan succumbed. Their roles reversed; now she was the caregiver, and if she caught up on email while Susan slept, well, that was just being efficient.

Juana and Nathan recovered, although Susan's coughing never fully seemed to subside, and she still had bouts of diarrhea.

At first they didn't think much of it, but then fatigue set in, and Susan was always cold. They traveled to a hospital in Nouakchott, where she was diagnosed with another strain of flu and sent home with fluids and medication.

Juana and Susan had bonded over, and joked about, the fact that they'd both come from driven families where they were taught not to complain. "I'd have to be bleeding out my eyeballs to get my mother to take me to the ER," Susan once said, and Juana had countered with "My father finally learned that 'I'm not feeling well,' meant 'get me to the ER *right now!*'"

The memory of those conversations would come back to haunt Juana, reminding her again and again that neither of them took Susan's symptoms as seriously as they should have.

When Susan collapsed, she was airlifted to Spain. Juana went with her, leaving Nathan with her assistant, who was like an aunt to him already.

"It's mimicking all the signs of iodine poisoning," the doctor said. He and Juana were in a waiting room; he'd wanted to talk to her away from Susan, who was heavily sedated anyway. There were flowers painted on the walls, cheerful yellows and bright oranges and soothing blues and greens, but they didn't change the fact that this was a hospital, and that things weren't cheerful or able to be soothed away.

"Has she been exposed to large amounts of iodine?" the doctor went on. He was sturdy, blond, a Swede who'd married a Spanish woman, his accent a mixture of both languages.

Juana told him about the seaweed. It was common knowledge that some seaweed was high in iodine, but the soaking process leached most of it out, and Susan hadn't really changed the amount of seaweed she was eating. Plus, Juana ate roughly the same amount (more, probably, given that at 8 inches taller, she outweighed Susan by 50 pounds), and Nathan's diet had included seaweed practically since he'd been eating solid food.

"That seems highly unlikely," the doctor said. "Eating too much iodine-rich food doesn't cause toxic effects. Iodine poisoning comes from direct ingestion, as from an overdose."

The doctor went back, did more tests, decided that Susan's body wasn't processing iodine properly. He couldn't, however, say how, or why, or why it would be happening now. He reviewed her medical records and couldn't find any other change that would explain it.

The fact that Susan wasn't eating any seaweed now didn't help. They'd waited too long.

***

JUANA ARRANGED TWO memorial services, one in California and one in Africa. But she sent Susan's body to be autopsied to the nth degree, hired a nanny for Nathan, and called in every resource she could think of, every contact she'd ever made. She was a biologist, not a medical doctor, but she was going to figure this out.

She knew damn well that her tenacity was rooted in guilt and loss. All those late nights, all that time away from Susan.

Finding the answer wouldn't bring Susan back.

But maybe it would help Juana look Nathan in the eye again.

She ordered reports of all the studies they'd done on people whose diet now regularly included the seaweed: all the field studies, all the data, every scrap of information that had been collected over the years.

She put two of her top people—Ember, who'd spearheaded most of the studies and conducted extensive interviews in the field, and William, whose analytical skills were off the charts—on the project.

If she thought she hadn't been sleeping before, well…

It couldn't, she thought, be related to the seaweed they grew in the tanks versus the seaweed grown offshore. Because seaweed didn't grow in soil, it couldn't be officially certified "organic." But Juana and her team had done everything they could to avoid contamination; the last thing she wanted was to bring more GMO food into the world. The guidelines she placed on everything—tanks, growing process, water quality—were more stringent than any governmental laws or policies she'd encountered.

There could be *nothing* in the tank-grown seaweed that could have caused this.

And yet…and yet…

She and Ember and William sat around her computer station in her lab, each with laptops. There were no windows here, and she had no idea if it were day or night outside. Even in here, she could hear the hum of the generators.

She was always cold now, it seemed. Susan had been her hearthstone.

"It seemed so random, none of the field researchers put it together," Ember said, pointing at the information she'd pulled up on her screen.

"There's no rhyme or reason to it," William insisted. "The only thing we can prove is that there don't seem to be any deaths of the same nature involving people who didn't eat the seaweed—at least, not the seaweed we've grown."

Which still narrowed it down to thousands of people.

"Of the people who did?"

"Different ages, genders, ethnicities, amount of seaweed eaten, length of time they'd been eating the seaweed—although it doesn't seem to happen quickly, which is one reason why nobody related the two. There's no correlation to where the people lived, their family status, their jobs, their incomes, or their genetic backgrounds…"

"Although," Ember said, "a few people recovered, and those were ones who had access to good medical care and were treated early."

"It doesn't seem to affect across families, which is another reason it didn't flag," William added.

They had doctors studying all the patients' medical histories, and thus far they'd come up blank. No pre-existing conditions, no allergies or intolerances, no genetic issues in common among any of those who had died.

There was no way to predict who would be affected. No way to test, not even a way to make an educated guess.

And the statistics, black-and-white, cold and unfeeling, said approximately one in a thousand people would die.

Juana went home. It was, in fact, night, very late. Away from the facility, the night sky blazed with stars that looked close enough to touch.

Nathan was asleep in her bed. He was too old for that, really, but she didn't have the heart to wake him, move him. He curled on his side, peaceful in the pale light that filtered in from the open doorway.

She shut the door, and by feel in the dark, slipped out of her shoes and crawled under the covers, still clothed. Susan's absence was still a gaping void; despite far too many nights when Juana had worked late, she and Susan had still slept twined together, even for a scant few hours. Juana would slip into bed as quietly as she could, and Susan, not really waking, would roll toward her, reach for her….

Juana had never slept well alone again after they'd met.

But that wasn't what kept her awake tonight.

Millions of people in Africa alone were affected by drought and famine. Millions of people around the world would have the chance to live, to thrive, if they had access to decent food—a food she could provide.

At what point did the chance of death weigh in? What percentage was acceptable? And was that even her choice to make? Should it be the choice of the people who were far more likely to die of starvation instead?

Dawn barely pinked the sky before she was up again, eyes burning from lack of sleep. She made coffee, gulped it down, drove back to the facility.

She walked the balcony, the catwalks, checking the readings. Everything in working order.

They couldn't find anything that made this seaweed different from the seaweed that grew in the ocean less than a mile away. And yet, it randomly sickened one-tenth of a percent of the population.

Another facility had been built, a third was in progress, and a fourth in the early developmental stage—and that was just in Africa alone. There were discussions, plans, fundraising happening all over the world.

She went back to her lab.

On a personal level, if she pulled the plug, she would be ruined. She had no money, and finding a job would be a challenge. How would that affect Nathan?

There was so much invested by so many people: money, time, hope, dreams.

People would starve, villages would die.

Was it true that the needs of the many outweigh the needs of the one?

What about when the one is someone you love beyond all reason?

Her phone buzzed; one of the major investors, a philanthropic organization.

She had to answer.

She looked at Nathan's picture on her desk, remembered his family, his village.

She looked at Susan's picture on her desk, remembered….

She made her decision, and answered the phone.

~

Robert Jeschonek's stories just shout Pulphouse *in so many ways. I have been very lucky to have a story of his in every issue so far. Actually, readers have been lucky.*

Robert's stories have appeared in dozens of magazines and he has published dozens of novels as well. He has even worked for DC Comics and early in his career sold me a couple stories when I was editing for Star Trek *at Pocket Books. He seems to be able to do it all.*

In this original story, he proves just that. He can write in any form and in any style and about any topic. Enjoy.

A Choose Your Own Fangle Adventure
Robert Jeschonek

"BUT YOU DON'T *look* like Peter Pinnacle." The ten-year-old girl frowned behind her bright red horn-rimmed glasses as if someone had just told her the biggest lie of all time. "You're *older*…and *fatter.*"

"Because my friend Wes Carmichael wrote the first book in the series a long time ago." Jake Bartholomew smiled patiently, all too aware of his graying hair and overweight appearance. How many times had he had to explain this already today? Readers expected him to be forever thirty, like Peter in the books, not 47 and gone to seed. "So would you like an autographed photo?" He patted the stack of 8 x 10 glossies spread out on the table before him.

The little girl tipped her head to one side. "But how do I *know* you're *him?"*

Jake tapped the framed certificate propped up near the edge of the table. "See this? It's a notarized affidavit, signed by the author. It proves he based Peter on me."

"It proves nothing," said the girl's surly father, a tall executive type with glossy black shoe-polish hair and a look of perpetual disgust on his puffy red face. His sole concession to it being the weekend was not wearing a tie with his slick gray business suit. "*None* of these people are *remotely* convincing."

Jake looked up and down the line of tables crossing the floor of the community center gymnasium. The two dozen men and women seated there, he knew, were *exactly* as advertised—the real-life people on whom certain well-known characters in modern literature were based.

Getting all of them together and going on tour had been *his* idea in the first place...though it was clear by this, the seventh stop, that the Celebrity Based-On Experience wasn't exactly the cash cow he'd imagined it might be.

And it seemed it was about to get a little less cash-rich still.

"We want our money back," snarled the guy. "You're no more the *Man of Means* than that woman over there's Raven Silhouette from the *Jet Set* books."

Looking at the table next-door, Jake caught the eye of the woman sitting there—a middle-aged redhead named Colleen Halloran who looked a lot more like Raven in *Jet Set* than *he* resembled Peter Pinnacle.

Not that Surly Dad cared. "Money back *now*, and count yourself lucky we don't *sue*."

Jake stared at the guy for a moment, wishing for the umpteenth time that he could be the actual character who'd been based on him. Unlike Peter Pinnacle in the *Man of Means* books, dealing with conflict was not often his strong suit. Though many of Peter's mannerisms were based on Jake's, the character's conflict expertise had *definitely* come from other sources.

If only Jake could have been cut from the same cloth in that regard. Maybe then, he would have felt as if he deserved to be there. Maybe then, he wouldn't have spent his whole life trying to measure up to a fictional character.

And fiction wouldn't have had such a dramatic impact on his reality.

***

EVERY MOMENT IN life is a chance to choose your own ending.

Like that night, seven years ago, when Jake and his newly-proposed fiancée, Gina Lafferty, strolled a few blocks away from the crowded Inner Harbor in downtown Baltimore, Maryland.

Jake was feeling pretty good—more like his fictional counterpart, heroic Peter Pinnacle, than ever. Finally, he'd resolved some of the guilt he'd felt over the way he'd gotten his connection to the character. He'd known from the start he'd done wrong, that Peter (if real) wouldn't have approved of such an underhanded deal...and eventually, he'd done better in life to make up for it. He'd taken some classes, gotten an honest job, given a few bucks to charity, and upgraded his conscience. Good things had come to him since, not the least of which was beautiful, blonde Gina.

She loved the hell out of him, put his ring on her finger, held his arm like a trophy when they walked. When he was with her, the past seemed far away; reality reshaped itself around them, making it seem like his mistakes had never happened.

Then, the two of them went down the wrong side street, and a guy with a gun approached them, demanding their valuables. The street was dark and quiet, and no one else was around.

Adrenaline blazed through Jake as he faced that choose-your-own-ending moment. A flurry of mental math rushed through his brain as he considered the following choices:

1. He and Gina could run for their lives, hoping the attacker couldn't keep up.

2. He and Gina could hand over their valuables, including the engagement ring.

3. He could try to negotiate with the attacker, to at least get him to let them keep the ring.

4. Feeling more like Peter Pinnacle than usual, because life was good and his girl had said "yes," he could try to rush the gunman and seize his weapon before he got off a shot.

Which option did Jake pick? What outcome resulted from his choice?

The wrong *option. And the* worst possible *outcome.*

***

"ARE YOU GOING to fork it over?" Surly Dad snapped his fingers and pointed at his palm. "Or am I going to have to get *nasty?*"

"Suit yourself." Jake gestured at the admission table near the door at the far end of the gym. "Go tell them I said you're authorized for a refund."

"Damn right I am." Surly Dad sneered at him. "So I guess now I can tell everyone I kicked Peter Pinnacle's ass, huh?"

"Will you tell them you kicked *Geiger Hellsacre*'s ass, too?" Suddenly, a dark-skinned giant of a man was looming over the troublemaker—gray-haired but sufficiently beefy to stomp him hard without working up a sweat.

Surly Dad changed his tune. "That's, uh…no." He shrank and shivered as he stared up at the giant…then held up a pen and folded piece of paper. "Autograph?"

"*Outta' here!*" roared the giant—Sherman Ostrander by name. Unlike some of the based-ons, it was *instantly* easy to see his resemblance to the character he'd inspired.

The crowd in the gym—fifty paying customers and half that number of special guests—watched and laughed as Sherman swatted Surly Dad's ass, sending him scurrying out the door without his cherished refund. Jake laughed, too, glad there'd been a little show to lighten things up.

"And *keep* running!" Sherman was in total Geiger Hellsacre mode, playing the role of the massive sidekick from the *Blow by Blow* books to the hilt. "Or Fee Fi Fo *Punch*, I'll tear you a *new* one and feed you to my *dinosaurs* for *lunch!*"

Suddenly, the screech of a referee's whistle sounded from across the gym, followed by hip-hop music blasting from a sound-boosted speakerphone.

Looking toward the noise, Jake saw a tall, gangly figure unfolding from the main doors, dressed in the wildest outfit ever. A psychedelic top hat towered over glittering, giant sunglasses studded with white feathers. A tuxedo jacket made of what looked like bubble wrap had strings of jingling bells and flashing, multicolored LED lights strewn around it. The bubble wrap bulged at his abdomen, pushed out and down in the shape of a woman's pregnant belly.

Further down was a big paisley diaper and bare, hairy legs. His shoes were totally mismatched—a bright red sneaker with a light-up sole on his left foot, and a black rubber galosh over a white go-go boot on his right.

Then there was the bullhorn with actual *horns* attached, into which he howled his first words to the crowd in the gym.

"Elcome-way oo-tay e-thay ow-shay, ids-kay!" His voice was like that of a minister in a fire-and-brimstone church, except for the Pig Latin. "Eet-may Addy-day O-nay *Ants-pay!*"

"Who the *hell*?" Sherman was half-laughing when he said it.

"And *no!*" The newcomer crowed like a rooster, flapping his bubble-wrapped arms. "*I don't believe my shit, either!*"

***

THE AIR IN the gym was electric with weird possibilities. All eyes were on the freaky new arrival as he launched into what looked like a cross between a Native American rain dance and an Irish jig.

"Did you hire this guy?" Sherman asked the question in Jake's general direction. "To spice things up or somethin'?"

"You think I'm *that* good a promoter?" Jake was just as mesmerized as everyone else, gaping at the crazy performance.

"Want me to run him out?" Sherman cracked his knuckles.

"Don't you dare." Colleen giggled. "He just turned this event into a surprise party."

Just as she said it, the freak stopped dancing and sagged like a marionette with his strings cut. Then, without lifting his head, he spoke. "Did somebody say…"

Suddenly, he charged across the gym toward Jake, Sherman, and Colleen, wailing at the top of his lungs in a ululating cry like the classic jungle yell from the old *Tarzan* movies.

He blew right past Sherman and flung the top half of his body on the table, coming to rest inches away from Jake.

"Did you see a *mountain gorilla* in a pink tutu and combat boots lumber through here?" he asked in a high-pitched, childlike voice. "Don't answer that!" His voice dropped to a whisper, and he looked suspiciously from side to side. "They're *listening.*"

Jake noticed his breath smelled like strong black licorice. "What can I do for you, pal? We're kind of in the middle of something here."

"Exactamente!" The guy thrust out a banana painted blue and shook it like a hand. "*Daddy No-Pants,* at your service-ice-ice!"

Jake scowled. "You call yourself Daddy…"

"But *you* can call me Incog-*neato!* 'Neato' spelled en-ee-ay-tee-oh." Springing back from the table, he made an elaborate bow. "Can you *dig* it?"

Jake looked at Colleen and Sherman with eyes wide in disbelief. "So what do you *want*, Incogneato? Why are you here?"

"I came for the *ice cream*! But I *stayed* for the *flibbertigibbets!*" Incogneato flung

  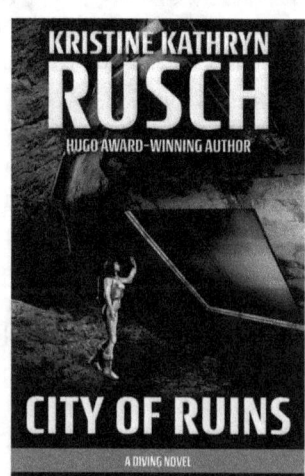

up his arms and shouted the words, though he didn't need to. Everyone in the room had gathered around to get a closer look at his madcap performance. "Nothing I like better than a *flibbertigibbet* dipped in *gazpacho* with a little *sassafras whiskey* and *armadillo gelato* on the side!"

People laughed at the clownish freestyling. All around, Jake saw phones going up as guests and paying customers alike snapped photos. Once they hit social media, maybe there'd be more late arrivals at the gate.

"So this is the *kook* show?" Incogneato jumped up and down, making his bells jingle.

"You mean *book* show?" said a little boy with a stack of autographed glossies in his hands.

"*Good show!*" said Incogneato in a British accent.

"It's more a show for folks who're *part* of books," said Sherman. "Well-known characters were *based* on us."

Incogneato straightened, looking serious all of a sudden. "*Fiction* books? With *fictional* characters?"

"Correct," said Sherman. "We're all about the make-believe here."

"Well, *poo!*" Incogneato snorted and stomped his sneaker-clad left foot. "*I'm* only interested in *fangle* these days!"

"Fangle?" said Colleen. "What's that?"

Incogneato yanked up the bullhorn again and barked into it. "What's *fangle?* You might as well ask what *grabbatuba* has to do with *quinkydink.*"

"Well *everybody* knows *that,*" Colleen said with a twinkle, playing along. "But *fangle's* a different story."

Incogneato rolled his eyes and lowered the bullhorn. "Think *fake news…true lies… post-fact world.* Where do we draw *the line?*" Incogneato did a kind of soft-shoe and stopped by pinching the brim of his psychedelic top hat. "Think *fact* meets *fiction* and goes on a *shooting spree.*"

"What's *that* supposed to mean?" Sherman was sounding tenser by the minute.

Again, Incogneato straightened and grew serious. "The real world has become more and more like *fiction, sahib.* We've got reality TV, virtual reality, augmented reality, you name it. The games and commercials and news cycles bury us in *stories* so *deep,* with so many possible *angles* and *opinions* and *outcomes,* that actual *reality* not only doesn't *matter,* it effectively doesn't *exist.* It's a tangled mess of fact and fiction—which *some* of us call *fangle,* thank you veddy much." The serious mode ended in a flurry of jingling jumping jacks as Incogneato sang "Mairzy Doats" in a booming falsetto.

"'Fangle,' huh?" said Sherman.

The jumping jacks and singing ended suddenly. "I'm surprised you've never *heard* of it, *kemosabe! You* people are what fangle's all about! *Fictional* works are based on your *factual* selves! *You* bridge reality and *un*reality, fiction and *un*-fiction. You're the perfect subjects for my next *work of art.*"

Jake got a chill up his spine that pretty much lifted him right up from his chair. "*What* work of art?"

At that moment, three men in camouflage fatigues with assault rifles hurried in and slammed shut the doors to the parking lot. The crowd gasped as one at the sight of the weaponry. A woman screamed.

"*This* one!" Incogneato pulled a fistful of gold and silver confetti from a pocket under the bubble wrap and tossed it overhead. "Now *tell* me, who wants to be *really famous?*"

***

JAKE'S BLOOD FROZE in his veins as he got the picture. Incogneato wasn't a harmless buffoon after all. The stakes in the gym had gone from how much money the show would bring in to how many guests and customers would walk out of the place alive.

If only the real Peter Pinnacle, Man of Means, could have been there.

Giggling, Incogneato scurried over and used Jake's chair to climb up on the tabletop.

"Sing Hallelujah!" He belted the words ecstatically into the bullhorn. "Get happy! There's *plenty* of famous to go around!"

As Incogneato disco-danced on the table, his three armed helpers closed in on the crowd with rifles raised. There were five kids in the gym, including the boy with the autographed glossies, and they all started crying at once. The adults did the opposite, most of them falling silent, though their worried expressions revealed deep concern. They were all too familiar with what usually happened when guns appeared at a public function.

Watching the panicked faces of friends and strangers alike, Jake couldn't help thinking how unlucky they all were, being caught in such a situation with a man like him who sucked at conflict.

Playing the theme from the movie *Fame* on the boosted speaker-phone and singing along through the bullhorn, Incogneato proceeded to dance from table to table, working his way down the line in a head-whipping frenzy. As soon as he got a few tables away, Jake huddled with Colleen and Sherman. Others in the crowd were whispering, too, seizing the opportunity to confer while the freak was distracted.

"We are so fucked." Sherman's eyes kept darting from one gunman to the next.

"There must be *something* we can do," hissed Colleen.

"Have you *seen* all the ammo clips strapped to those assholes?" Sherman shook his head angrily.

"What if we all rush one of them, take his gun, and use it against the other two?" asked Colleen.

"You do realize those Bushmasters are modified for *full automatic*, don't you?"

Colleen scowled as Incogneato started working his way back to them. "We can't just let this *happen*."

"It's the end of the road," Sherman said matter-of-factly. "The good news is, we won't have to do this shitty based-on road show anymore."

Just then, a black rubber galosh flew over and bounced off Jake's head.

"Hey, Pea-Brain!" Three tables away, Incogneato lifted off his psychedelic top hat, turned it upside-down, and reached inside. His hand emerged with a .357 Magnum revolver, gleaming silver under the gym's fluorescent lights. "Yeah, you. C'mere a minute."

Jake hadn't taken three steps before the ref's whistle blew.

"Ot-nay own-day ere-they!" Incogneato gestured with the pistol, wagging the barrel upward. "Take the *high road*, buckaroo bonsai!"

Nervously, Jake clambered up onto a table, then worked his way over to join Incogneato.

Meanwhile, a middle-aged woman in the crowd spoke up, her voice quivering. "P-please may I take my son home, sir?" The autograph-hound little boy stood in front of her, and she kept her hands clamped on his shoulders. "He's a g-good boy, I swear it."

"I wouldn't *dream* of stopping him..." said Incogneato...but when the woman turned to go, he amended his statement. "... *stopping* him from becoming *famous* with his *Mommy dearest* thanks to capital-M *me*!"

The woman slumped, holding on to the boy tighter than ever.

"Grasshopper!" Incogneato fiddled with the front of his diaper as Jake crossed the table to stand beside him. "Now where did I put that *sword?*" He reached all the way in, let out a high yodel, and jerked his hand back out again. "Never mind. We'll just have to make do." With that, he tapped Jake solemnly on each shoulder with the barrel of the .357. "I now pronounce you Sir Tallywacker of the Fangle Faithful."

Jake stood stock-still, remembering that long-ago night in Baltimore, afraid to make a move with the gun in play.

"I couldn't have asked for a better *special helper*." Incogneato threw an arm around his shoulders and gave him a big squeeze, pretending to wipe away a tear. "After all, it's not like you're one of *them*, are you?"

Jake stared, shell-shocked. "What—?"

Incogneato lowered his voice. "Don't they know you don't *belong* here? Don't they know what a *liar, liar, pants on fire,* you are?"

Jake couldn't believe his ears.

"Don't sweat it, Langostino. Your secret's safe with me…as long as you help Daddy No-Pants like your invisible friend, Corky Porker, tells you to." When he said it, Incogneato oinked like a pig and popped a bubble on his bubble-wrapped chest.

***

JAKE BARTHOLOMEW LOOKED *patient as he stood in line at the bookstore in Altoona, Pennsylvania, but inside, he was hypercharged. His heart was pounding, the hairs on his neck, arms, and legs were standing up, and the blood in his veins and arteries was sizzling with adrenaline.*

It was twenty years ago, and Jake was 27 years old. He'd never done anything like what he was about to do before, and it showed. But most of the other people in line were nervous, too, so he blended in. If he could just keep it together a little longer, he'd be fine.

He was ten people back, then five, then three—then next. The book in his hands was only moments away from being signed by the author at the table.

As the woman ahead of him walked away, Jake gulped and stepped up to the table. The author smiled up at him and extended a sun-tanned hand, reaching for the hardcover book.

"Hello." The author, a brown-haired man in his late 20s or early 30s, had a welcoming smile. He held Jake's gaze for a moment before reeling in the book. "What's your name?"

"Jake."

"Thanks for buying my book, Jake," said the author. "And for coming to the signing."

"Thank you, Mr. Carmichael."

"Wes. Call me Wes. So have you read it yet?"

"Not yet, but I loved the first three in the series," said Jake. "I hope you write lots more Alley Commando *books."*

Wes chuckled. "Even better, Jake. I'm working on a new series right now called Man of Means.*" He opened the book to the dedication page and reached for his pen. "So how would you like me to inscribe this? 'To Jake?'"*

"Actually." Jake leaned down and lowered his voice. He was so nervous, he was afraid he might stutter, but he didn't. "Make it out to 'The Witness.'"

Wes looked baffled. "'The Witness?'"

Jake swallowed hard and nodded. "To your hit-and-run accident that landed that woman in the hospital the other night."

Wes's composure flickered. "Excuse me?"

Jake felt the impulse to end it right then, but he'd come too far. And he was desperate, in debt to some bad people. They didn't want to hear about how his deal had gone south; they just wanted their money.

"I have photos, if you'd like to see them." Jake reached inside his jacket.

Suddenly, Wes got his smile back. "'To Jake' it is." Hastily, he scribbled the inscription in the book, then closed it decisively and pushed it across the table.

"I'll see you later, then." Jake took the book. "At the coffee shop next door."

"Thanks for coming!" Wes fidgeted with his pen. "Next!"

And Jake wondered, as he walked away to wait in the coffee shop, if Wes would even meet him. But he did. He only kept him waiting long enough for Jake to think of what else he might want to sweeten the blackmail deal.

***

"I NEVER BREAK a promise, bunkies!" Incogneato shouted from atop the table. "And when I'm double-Dutch *done* with you people, ain't *none* of you *not* gonna be *famous!*" Blowing on the ref's whistle, he spun on his heel and stopped with a stomp. "*Depending!*"

The crowd, hemmed in by the three gunmen, listened restlessly, looking terrified. Based-ons and visitors alike were burning with tension but mostly afraid to speak up.

"Somebody ask me 'depending on what?'" Incogneato shook Jake by his arm. "I won't bite! I won't even tickle!"

Jake had been distracted, thinking about his secret. To him, being found out after all this time was almost as distressing as whatever impending danger Incogneato had dreamed up. "Depending on what?"

For no clear reason, Incogneato slapped him in the face so hard it stung. "Who here has read those pick-your-own-adventure books?" He threw his hand up and looked around as a few other hands rose reluctantly in the group. "Well *congratulations,* fangle wranglers! You're about to *live* one of those! One of *three* endings will happen in this very *place* to you very *people!*"

With that, he pulled out his boosted phone and cranked the opening measures of "Thus Spake Zarathustra" from the movie *2001: A Space Odyssey. Dah…dah…dah…dah-dah!*

"Hold onto your sphincters, my Frito banditos!" Incogneato pumped an index finger in the air. "Ending one! *Everybody lives! Yaaayy!*"

Again, he blasted "Thus Spake Zarathustra."

"Ending *dos! Deux! Zwei! Half* of you live, and *half* of you die! Yay! Boo! Yay! Boo!"

"Zarathustra" blared a third time.

"Ending *three! Allll* of you *die! Awww!*" He made an exaggerated sad face and shook his head—then broke into a broad grin and grabbed hold of Jake's earlobe. "Except *this* phony!" He pulled Jake over and gave him a rough noogie. "*Oops!* Did I just give away your *secwet?* I guess that makes *me* a *wiar,* too!*"

Jake caught dirty looks from Colleen and Sherman. The self-hatred that usually ticked away at the heart of him surged to the surface.

He saw the direct line connecting this moment to the past, and he realized yet again that nothing good had come from that meeting in the Altoona coffee shop two decades ago.

***

"YOU'RE KIDDING ME." Wes the author, unhappy after hearing out Jake, looked like he might be ready to laugh out loud.

"You're blackmailing me, and this is what you want?"

"The money, too." Anxiously, Jake looked around the coffee shop, but no one was paying any attention to him and Wes in the back-corner booth. No one seemed to recognize the author, though he'd been signing books next door just over an hour ago.

"You want me to Tuckerize you? Mention you by name in a book? I do that shit for free all the time."

Jake had never heard the word "Tuckerize" before, but it didn't matter. "You've got it wrong. I want you to base the main character of your new series on me. And I want everyone to know it."

Wes leaned forward and folded his arms on the table. "Like fuck, I'll do that."

"And you can't kill him off," said Jake.

"You can't tell me what to write."

"And I need a signed and notarized certificate that proves the character's based on me."

Suddenly, Wes's eyes widened, and he slammed a fist on the table, jarring coffee from his untouched cup. "Fuck that noise, you little shit!" His voice was low but fierce, oozing with rage. "I'll destroy you, you fucking nothing!"

Though Jake's instinct was to back down, he forced himself not to waver. He'd already shown Wes the pictures in his pocket, which he'd taken late the night before from his bedroom window with his digital camera. He was nervous as hell, but he knew Wes's threats were empty, his pushback a joke.

The thought of it made him feel a little bolder. "You know what else I want? Dedicate the first book in the series to me for inspiring the main character."

"Did you hear a word I just said, you piss-ant?" snarled Wes.

"By the way, the dedication is a dealbreaker." Jake smiled. "Pretty sure the cops and the woman in intensive care will agree with me."

Wes glared for a long moment, then slumped back in his seat. "Maybe I'll just turn myself in. Save myself the trouble of this bullshit."

"Suit yourself," said Jake, though he hoped he wouldn't. He had no idea where he'd get the money he needed if he lost this golden goose.

For a long moment, he and Wes locked eyes in the booth. The road forked before them, its dual choices equally possible, equally choosable. Neither choice favored the author...and neither took the female victim into account. If Wes gave a damn about her, he didn't let on. As for Jake, his concern was only for himself and his future.

Maybe that was where it started to go wrong for him. Maybe that was when, unknowingly, he bought a one-way ticket to the back street in Baltimore, the years of regret that followed, and Incogneato's shit-show.

Pick your own adventure, and the ones that come after pick you.

***

"IN ANSWER TO the number one question on everyone's minds, *yes, I am* a little teapot, short and stout!" Incogneato belched into his bullhorn, then whistled a few bars of the teapot song. "Regarding the *number two* question, your lives or deaths will be decided by a naked mole rat wearing a mini-merkin and a tiny bowler hat."

Incogneato laughed himself silly, but no one else in the gym joined the hilarity. Someone *did* speak up, though, in the midst of the gales of laughter.

"This is all for some kind of *work of art*, you said?" Colleen asked it twice before she got through to him.

"Well, yes." Incogneato had to stifle another laugh fighting to get out. "In a *big picture* sort of way."

"What's that supposed to mean?" asked Sherman.

"The whole *world* is becoming *fangle*," explained Incogneato. "Not only in the sense that truth and fiction are becoming indistinguishable from each other...but *reality* is taking on the *rhythms* of fiction. We see more and more cosplay, Ingress, Pokémon Go, Fakebook, and Netflix bingeing. Cathartic eruptions of violence are becoming *expected* and *routine,* as our society becomes more like a thriller novel or action movie. And that's a *good* thing."

"Is that so?" said Sherman.

"Because *that* is the way of the *future."* Incogneato hopped across the tables and crouched next to Sherman and Colleen. "When the boundaries between fact and fiction evaporate, we will be truly *free* and *unconstrained.* Mores and power structures will *fade away. Everything* will have *meaning,* yet *nothing* will have *consequence.* And *this*, according to my calculations, will be the *start* of it. Killing or sparing so many *basedons* in such a fictionally contrived way will *light* this candle and power up fangle manifestations all over the planet!"

"Uh-huh." Sherman nodded, not sounding convinced. "Makes perfect sense."

"And here's the *primo* part!" Incogneato leaped to his feet and scattered confetti while howling like a wolf. *"You* guys will finally get to be *main characters*—not just *basedons.* When the video goes *viral*, you'll be *world-famous*, and *everyone* will know what *fangle* is."

"You make it sound so *rewarding,"* Sherman said sarcastically. "And *rational."*

"But who gets to choose?" asked Colleen. "You said there are three choices, so who gets to pick?"

Incogneato waggled his phone overhead. "Can you say, 'randomized prize drawing app?' *Soooo* stinkin' cool, huh? And guess who gets to run it?" Snapping around, he tossed the phone to Jake, who dropped it. "And now, without further ado—Sir Tallywacker, *spin...that...wheel!"*

***

HOW LONG DOES it take to get over something in a work of fiction? Pages? Chapters? What does it take to make redemption possible in a book? A cathartic event? A miracle? Someone in greater need than the hero?

In real life, the timeframes and triggers can be much different. After that night in Baltimore, Jake had struggled for years. Sometimes, he had blamed his obsession with Peter Pinnacle and vowed to stop trying to be something he wasn't. He had even contacted Wes and begged him to stop writing the Man of Means *books, which of course Wes refused to do. They were just selling too damn well by then.*

Sometimes, the pendulum had swung the other way, and Jake had tried to be more like Peter than ever. He had blamed his inability to measure up to the character for what had happened to Gina Lafferty—for every bad thing that had happened in his life, in fact.

Sometimes, Jake had even convinced himself that what had happened in Baltimore hadn't been real, that it had all played out on the written page with no impact on non-fictional life. He had even composed actual rewrites *on paper with less difficult endings, hoping one of them would supersede the ending he abhorred.*

But the one thing lacking in all those rewrites and what-ifs and blame games was a transformational incident, a true second chance that could let him make up for his mistakes by proving himself again.

Though who could say (even him) what choice he might make if such an incident ever came his way.

***

WHEN JAKE CROUCHED on the table to retrieve the phone he'd dropped, Sherman rushed over and grabbed it first. "Don't do it." His voice was a rough whisper. "Don't play along with this nut."

"No choice." Jake reached for the phone. "He'll just do it himself or get somebody else to do it."

"Time for you to *step up* and fill your character's shoes," snapped Sherman. "Time

for *all* of us. The based-ons are *with* you. Just give us the *signal.*"

"Oh, Sir Tallywacker!" called Incogneato. "Time's a-wasting! My *contractions* are starting!" He thumped his baby bump with the grip of the .357.

"We're ready!" whispered Sherman. "Let's give this weirdo a *true* taste of reality." Nodding firmly, he handed over the phone and backed away.

All eyes were on Jake as he stood, the fates of everyone in his hands. Heart pounding, he looked around at them, friends and strangers alike, looking to him for mercy.

"Come on, Gunga Dim!" Incogneato let off a long blast on his ref's whistle. "If you make *me* pick, I'm gonna pour some sugar all *over* these hanging-by-a-threaders!"

It was all coming down to the wire. The three gunmen had their rifles up, pointed into the crowd. The kids were crying, the adults were freaking, the clock was ticking, and the shit was about to go down.

How many similar scenes had Jake read in books or seen in movies? There was always a gauntlet like this in the third act or reel, a battle for the hero to test his or her skills and overcome his or her inner conflicts. At the end of the gauntlet, the hero always found victory.

But people like Jake didn't often become heroes in real life, did they?

"Tallywacker! It-quay issing-pay around-yay!" With a wild whoop, Incogneato yanked the bubble wrap away from his baby bump, exposing a zippered gold plastic shell. When he jerked the zipper down, candy poured out, showering the people closest to his table. "*Arriba! Arriba!* Consider your *last rites* performed, you candy lovers, you!"

Jake's hands shook as he raised Incogneato's phone. The prize drawing app was still on the screen—a round gold "GO" button surrounded by three squares, each labeled with an outcome: ALL DIE, HALF DIE, NONE DIE.

Gut and jaws clenched, Jake stared at the screen, then looked at Sherman, Colleen, and the others, then the gunmen. People would die if he gave the signal to fight back; no question. But people might also die if he played along and ran the app. Or they might be spared.

What would Peter Pinnacle do? What would Gina want him to do? Better yet, what would Jake—the old Jake, back before the blackmail and Baltimore—want him to do?

"Don't be a *don't-bee!*" howled Incogneato. "*Do* be a *do-bee*. Don't make us wait *forever* to bring the fangle."

Suddenly, a wave of calm washed over Jake. What if Incogneato, in all his insanity, was on to something? If fact and fiction were coming together, would it even *matter* what he did? Or would it matter more than *ever?*

"Bitch, please!" Incogneato bounded over to the table and snatched the phone from Jake's hands. "The suspense is *killing* me."

With that, he hit the "GO" button, and lights flickered on the screen as the app spun through its options.

That was when, as Jake watched, other options spun through his own mind. See if you can guess which of the following four he chose:

1. He lunged at Incogneato, wrestling for his gun. The other based-ons took that as a signal and charged the gunmen, who promptly mowed them down. Meanwhile, the .357 went off in Jake's gut and passed through to take out the only other survivor of the shooters' assault, a young woman who was trying to run away.

2. Jake shoved Incogneato into the crowd, leaped off the table, and ran for his life. The Bushmaster rifles chattered away behind him, leaving him the only survivor of the massacre aside from the gunmen and Incogneato. Later, after the killers were rounded up by the authorities, Jake's testimony sent them to prison and made him a celebrity.

3. Paralyzed with fear, Jake did nothing. The prize-drawing app selected "NONE DIE," and Incogneato and his people slipped away, leaving everyone alive.

4. Channeling the action-hero spirit of Peter Pinnacle and determined to finally redeem himself for past mistakes, Jake kneed Incogneato in the groin and pistol-whipped him with the .357. Miraculously, he then got off a lucky shot that took out one of the gunmen. The other two hesitated just long enough for Sherman to grab their dead ally's rifle and cut them down even as the rest of the crowd scattered. Everyone except the gunmen survived—but Incogneato, in defeat, still succeeded. The blurring of fact and fiction into fangle accelerated, with him recognized as the movement's founding father. Jake, in turn, had characters based on him in numerous books, TV shows, and movies, bringing the cross-pollination of factual and fictional figures full circle in his life.

***

NOW THAT YOU'VE seen the four choices, which one did you pick? Did it match Jake's choice?

If your answer was any of the above, *congratulations*, you've chosen correctly. And welcome, one and all, to the fangle, fangle, fangle that we've come to know and love.

www.wmgpublishinginc.com
Also Available at Your Favorite Bookstore.

New York Times bestseller Kristine Kathryn Rusch has won more awards in science fiction and mystery than just about anyone and she is the only person to win the Hugo Award for her writing as well as her editing. She writes under three major names, Kristine Kathryn Rusch, Kris Nelscott, and Kristine Grayson. Plus a few minor names.

She has a new Diving Universe novel coming out later this year as well as a new Kristine Grayson book that just came out.

Say Hello to my Little Friend
Kristine Kathryn Rusch

HE WAS STRANGE from the start, yet oddly compelling.

I can explain the strange. The compelling is harder.

He'd come into my bar about 3:30 Friday afternoons, thirty minutes before the official start of Happy Hour. He'd take a seat as far from the door as he could get. He'd order two drinks—one, a piña colada, the other, light beer on tap.

Then he'd wait.

He was stunningly handsome. That's the thing you'd see first off. The square jaw, the black-black hair, the laughing blue eyes all accented his broad shoulders and perfect male model physique. Only he dressed like a regular guy: nice suit with a jacket he'd remove when he sat down, white shirt, and shoes that could use some attention. Before the drinks arrived, he'd loosen his tie and roll up his sleeves, revealing muscular arms.

And then he'd nurse the beer.

Any red-blooded woman would look at him, as well as a handful of red-blooded males. So of course I looked at him. I'm as red-blooded as the next woman—even if it is my bar.

I'm red-blooded, but not pretty. I'm perfectly cast in my role as bar owner. I'm muscular and broad-shouldered too. My father used to say I looked like Bette Davis—and he didn't mean the young beauty of her early roles. He meant the battle-axe from "Whatever Happened to Baby Jane?" with the crumpled skin and the bugged-out eyes and the voice that sounded like she'd smoked a thousand cigarettes too many.

A few men like this look. They figure I'm easy (I'm not) because I'm lonely (I'm not that either), and they try to woo me with lies. The occasional guy who enjoys my friendship takes it a stage farther, but we usually agree to go back to platonic after a few months.

Men who look like this guy never give me a second glance. And if one of them had slept with me by accident (and none of them had), it would have been an invitation that came at last call, and the night would end with him chewing his arm off in the morning.

I know that. So when I started talking to Mr. Weird But Beautiful, I did it not because I wanted him (even though I did). I did it because he looked like he needed some advice.

To understand why he needed some advice, you need to know what my bar looks like. It's not a fern bar or a sports bar. There are no big screens scattered around, all turned to ESPN. There are no giant booths with huge backs because I don't want couples making out in my place and getting us slapped with violating the decency laws.

There are round tables of various sizes scattered across the floor, and they get pushed aside on Saturdays, when my favorite DJ comes in to spin the tunes—usually oldies, because I don't tolerate that hip-hop crap in my bar.

The rest of the time, it's the juke that's been here since I bought the place. A pool table against the back wall gives the regulars a reason to return besides my lovely presence.

The bar's the first thing you see when you come in the door. The backbar is large and mirrored, so it looks like we have even more booze than we do. I put the expensive stuff back there because the business travelers who've just had a meeting in the big conglomerate across the street make it worth my while.

The bar is a classic U and made of expensive wood with a polyurethane top, so that I can wipe the thing off every night. Everyone vies for the twenty bar stools that surround the outside of the U, and during Friday Happy Hour, the line for those stools can be five deep.

Although it's not fair to call them stools. They're actually tall chairs with rounded backs that hug the backside of whoever's sitting there. I bought the things from a bar going out of business about five years ago, and they're the best purchase I ever made. They keep the hard drinkers—the guys who pass out with predictable regularity—in their chairs. These guys don't fall four feet to the floor, hitting their head on the bar rails on the way down and thinking lawsuit when they finally wake up.

Guys who drink like that—and every neighborhood bar has them—keep our local taxi service in business, especially weekend nights. I don't even have to call any more. At closing, half a dozen cabs show up here like they've been summoned. I confiscate keys, pour the hard drinkers into the cabs, and sign the tab. Then when the drinkers come back for their cars, I won't hand over the keys until I get reimbursed.

It works for all of us, and rarely does the hard drinker get mad.

I take care of my people. That's what I'm known for.

Which is why no one was surprised when I started talking to Mr. Weird But Beautiful.

He started coming in long about February, with that uncomfortable look most first-timers in a bar often have. He wore a shiny silk suit and a matching silver tie, and he looked good enough to eat.

When he sat at the bar, I was surprised. When he ordered his light beer and piña colada, I waited for the pretty business associate to show up for their meeting.

Only she never came. The beer got nursed and the piña colada disappeared, although I never saw him take a sip.

And as the bar filled up, a bottle blonde stopped beside the empty chair, leaned against the bar, and displayed her assets prettily for him. After she ordered, she turned to him, and he smiled one of those Tom Cruise mighty megawatt smiles, the kind that makes you hot just thinking about it.

She smiled back and I could tell she was feeling like I was feeling—the right word and she was his.

He had one of those deep Barry White voices which carried even though he probably didn't intend it to.

Her eyes danced and she leaned in, just a bit, as he said, "Please say hello to my little friend."

Then he looked down.

She flushed, grabbed her drink, and left the bar.

And he leaned back, looking very confused.

Now most guys, when they have a pickup line that fails, try another one. And any guy who looks like him doesn't need a line at all.

It was a testament to his attractiveness that no woman ever dumped a drink on his lap or slapped him or called him names. Every woman he approached—and by April, he was approaching the desperate ones as well as the pretty ones—gave him that what-the-hell-did-you-just-say? look and fled.

But he never varied his line, he never altered his routine, and he never ever got anyone to say hello to his little friend.

Until, of course, me.

***

IT WAS JUST after Easter when I finally had enough. When you have regulars in your place, you develop an emotional attachment to them. Sometimes that attachment is loathing, sometimes it's friendship, and sometimes it's pity.

With Mr. Weird But Beautiful, I found myself feeling oddly responsible. I wanted to sit next to him and say, "What? Your mother never taught you manners?"

But I knew that wasn't the way to approach him.

Instead, I pulled a bar stool over to his other side, the side away from the empty stool he hogged every Friday, and said, "Your little friend routine doesn't work."

He looked at me like he didn't know I could speak English. Maybe he thought the only sentences in my repertoire were "Light on tap and piña colada, right?" and "That'll be six-sixty-five."

It seemed to take him a minute to process this new sentence, and then he said, "It's gotta work."

"Nonsense," I said. "You need a new line, that's all. Half the women in this place would go home with you if you asked them right."

"I don't want them to go home with me. I want them to go home with Marty."

That's when I sighed. I couldn't help it. "Look," I said, "to get them home with Marty, you need to charm them first."

"No," he said. "That's not fair. *Marty* needs to charm them."

"Marty can work his magic in the privacy of your own bedroom," I said. "You—."

But by that time, Mr. Weird But Beautiful was giving me the what-the-hell-did-you-just-say? look. He flushed and he was starting to get out of his chair when I grabbed his wrist.

His muscular oh-so-strong wrist.

"I'm trying to help you here," I said. "It's been nearly three months, and you can't get a girl to spend thirty seconds with you. You're going about it wrong."

He pulled his wrist from my grasp. "First, I don't want her to spend time with me. I'm trying to fix up Marty. Second, Marty and I do not share a bed or even a house. Third, what the hell even makes this your business?"

183

"Nothing, I guess," I started, but by the time I finished the third word, he was gone.

Without paying for his beer or his piña. And, as usual, the beer was barely touched, but the piña was gone.

It really bugged me that I never saw him drink it.

Especially this time. When I was sitting beside him from the moment I set the drinks down.

***

I FIGURED THAT was the last I'd see of Mr. Weird But Beautiful, so I wrote off the drinks and went back to my routine. No one asked after him, even though a few of the regulars noticed he was missing.

These were the closeted guys, one of whom got very drunk on a Friday in March, sidled up to Mr. Weird But Beautiful, and said, "I'll say hello to your little friend" in a suggestive voice, and nearly got tossed across the room.

Mr. Weird But Beautiful left after that too, although that time he paid, hands shaking. He did come back, though, the following week, and when his closeted stalker came up to him a second time, Mr. Weird But Beautiful held up his hand.

"Look," he said in a polite voice, the same voice he used for his pickup line. "I vote Democrat. I believe in equal rights. I know we should be flattered because you're probably a very nice man. But believe me when I say that my friend and I are not your type."

The closeted stalker nodded once, then went back to his chair, probably trying to maintain some dignity. He never approached Mr. Weird But Beautiful again, but he did watch from time to time, maybe hoping Mr. WBB might change his mind.

Although I could have told him that he wouldn't. A guy who doesn't change his pickup line is not going to change his orientation, no matter how much the other party hopes he will.

Believe me, I know. Because most guys are oriented toward beautiful—or at least pretty—and no matter how friendly they are, no matter how much they talk to me or flirt with me, they're not going home with me, and they're certainly not going to invite me to spend time with their little friend.

At least, not when they're sober. And I've been a bartender long enough to know,

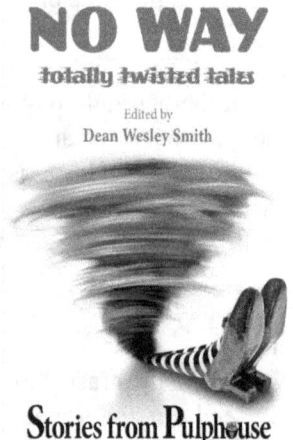

they're not worth a damn when they're drunk. After a while, you look for meaning, you know? Just a kind word, a phrase, a bit of understanding.

I try a little kindness once a night, just to keep my hand in the game, which was why I talked to Mr. Weird But Beautiful in the first place.

Sometimes kindness pans out. Sometimes it doesn't.

And sometimes it leads you places you never thought you'd go.

***

HE CAME BACK the next afternoon. Mr. Weird But Beautiful, who never darkened my door on any day but Friday, had shown up on Saturday wearing a blue chambray shirt, faded jeans, shit-kickers with no added heel. If anything, he looked even more delectable. The blue shirt stretched just enough to show the muscles on his chest. The jeans hugged his ass the way…well, the way I wanted to.

He didn't sit at the bar. Instead, he took a table in the middle of the room.

And since none of the cocktail waitresses would go near him, I had to wait on him. From the bar, I said tiredly, "Beer and piña, right?"

He looked at me, those blue eyes flat, his expression reserved, his tone one you'd use with a six-year-old. "Just the beer."

So I brought him the light, still foaming over the stein, and onto the tray. Man, was I out of practice.

I set down the napkin, then the beer, and started to leave, when he said, "I've been thinking about our conversation."

"Good," I said, and returned the tray, wiping it down before I set it near the server's station.

"And I'd like to ask you a few questions," he said just a little louder.

Jodi, the cocktail waitress, raised a single eyebrow. It was her who-does-this-asshole-think-he-is? look.

But there was no one else in the place. So I told her to man the bar, and I walked back to him.

He kicked out the chair beside him. I sat. This wasn't going to be an easy conversation.

"So why doesn't it work?" he asked. "That line, as you call it."

My turn to give him the incredulous look, and I almost hauled out one of the sentences I'd been thinking since he first came in—"What? You were raised by wolves?"—but if I did, he'd bolt, and spend the rest of his life trying this stupid gambit at bars all over town, until he finally gave up and stayed home—alone—for the rest of his life.

I couldn't decide if that outcome was a crime against nature or just the way things should be.

For a minute, I toyed with answering the question delicately. But I'd tiptoed around delicate the day before, and it hadn't worked. This guy had spent *all night* wondering why "Say hello to my little friend," repelled women. He wasn't going to get delicate.

He might not even get blunt.

"Look," I said in my best I've-been-around-the-block voice, "we all know that most men name their penis, okay? We know you have a close relationship—a friendship—with that part. We just don't need to know it from the moment—"

"You think Marty is my penis? Are you nuts?" He stood up, bumped the table, and knocked over the stein. I slid my chair back so I wouldn't get doused in light beer.

Jodi tossed me the bar rag, but she wasn't getting anywhere near good ole WBB.

"Who else would he be?" I asked as I set the rag on the table and went for some bar napkins.

"My friend," WBB said. "You know, the guy who comes in here with me. The guy who drinks the piña coladas."

"I hate to tell you this, pal," I said as I tossed half the napkins on the table and the other half on the stain spreading across the floor. "But you come in here alone."

I expected an argument. I expected him to tell me all about this Marty, who accompanied him. I expected to hear every detail about the delusion.

Instead, WBB said, "That fucking son of a bitch," handed me a twenty, and walked out of the bar.

***

HE WALKED BACK in an hour later, dragging an ugly little man who had blood dripping from his nose. WBB picked up the little man—who couldn't have been more than three feet tall—and said,

"This. This is my little friend. Marty the fucking bastard. Say hello, Marty."

"Hello," the little man said in a nasal tone. He was dripping blood over the floors I had just cleaned the beer off of.

"Hello," I said. "Do you want to press charges? I can call the police."

The little man shook his head. Blood dripped everywhere.

"Show the nice lady what you can do, Marty," WBB said. "She's been kind to me. She deserves to know."

I flushed at the word "kind." No one had noticed before.

Marty closed his eyes. His nose was still dripping.

WBB shook him. "*Show* her."

And Marty disappeared. But the blood kept dripping on my floor. Ping, ping, ping.

Jodi and I exchanged glances. I'd seen a lot of strange things in my bar, but that was the first legitimate disappearing man.

"Now," WBB said. "Explain what was going on."

He shook his fists. Only Jodi and I knew that there was a little guy between them.

Either that or WBB was David Fucking Copperfield.

"*Tell* them," WBB said.

"We had a bet," the little guy said, and reappeared as he spoke. He was dangling between WBB's hands and looking as forlorn as a human being could. "We bet that no matter how good-looking he is, he couldn't get me a date."

"The rest of it," WBB said.

The little guy sighed.

WBB shook him again.

"We handicapped him," the little guy said, "by making him say, 'Say hello to my little friend.' You know, like in golf. Figuring the good player needed a level playing field with the ugly player. Me."

"Ugly." WBB said. "Damn straight."

I didn't say anything. I'd seen bar bets before. But judging from WBB's face the day he first came in—all stunned at the way the bar looked and smelled—he didn't. He had no idea that cheating was part of the process.

"How much was the bet for?" I asked.

"The year-end bonus," WBB said. "Five grand."

"He doesn't need his," the little guy said. "People give him stuff because he's so pretty."

I stared at WBB. His beautiful blue eyes flashed. He was furious.

He shook the little guy one more time for good measure. "Tell her the rest of it. I'd say, 'Say hello to my little friend.' And then you *what*?"

The little guy cleared his throat. "I disappeared."

He vanished then quickly reappeared.

"To everyone except me," WBB said. "I could see the little bastard."

"I hate to tell you this," I said, "but he disappeared long before you came into the bar. If he really was with you."

"He was," WBB said. "*Tell* her."

The little guy shrugged one imprisoned shoulder. The movement looked like it hurt. "It's my only talent. It's all I can do. I trained it. Because people always looked at me with pity. I'm short and I'm ugly and you wouldn't believe the jokes."

"So you turned the table on your friend?" I asked. "A man who was going to help you? You played a trick on him?"

"He promised he wouldn't," WBB said. "He promised he'd stay visible."

"I did!" The little guy said.

"To me," WBB said. "And only me. The man who believed in him. I figured once someone talked to him, she'd want to go out with him. I used to think he was clever."

The little guy tried to wipe his nose but WBB held him fast.

"I *believed* in him," WBB said, and dropped him.

The little guy bounced in the pool of his own blood.

"Fucking bastard," WBB said, and left.

And of course, I never saw him again.

***

HIS LITTLE FRIEND, on the other hand, haunts my bar like an out-of-work Rumpelstiltskin. I think he makes his living by winning bar bets.

Like "betcha I can't appear and reappear." Like "I can make a piña colada vanish without even touching it." Like "I bet a handsome man like you can't get a woman to give me a second glance."

I let him stay. He's a curiosity. Now that they're used to him, the regulars place bets right alongside his. The entire place is getting rich.

Except me.

Because there's a part of me that still wants the fairy tale. You know, you help the gorgeous guy, and even though you're a plain Cinder Ella, he sees through the grime and makes you his princess.

But WBB hasn't come back. I haven't even gotten enough courage to ask his little friend for WBB's real name.

I know real life is not a fairy tale.

But I also know that tiny men who look like Rumpelstiltskin can't disappear at will.

And yet this one does.

Somehow that's not quite enough to overcome my belief in the way the world really works.

You see, I own a bar. I know that people never change their orientation. And WBB, for all his willingness to help his little friend, was oriented toward beautiful—or at least pretty.

And no matter how nice I was, and how much I was willing to help him, and how much his pride made him come back to talk to me, to explain he really wasn't crazy, I knew he wasn't going home with me.

I knew he was never going to invite me to spend time with his little friend.

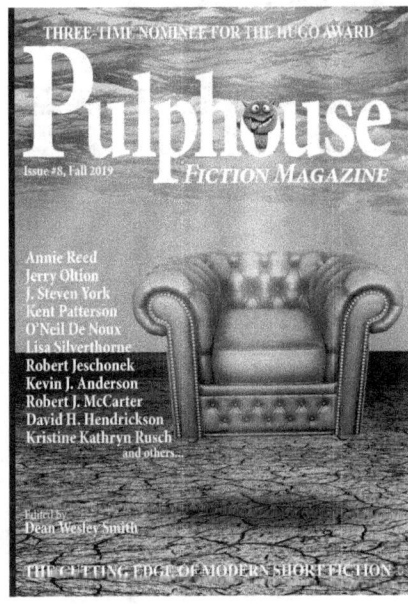

Minions at Work - "White Space"
J. Steven York